How had she [...] rodeo man?

Melanie knew how hard the life was; she'd lived it herself, following her dad around the country.

"Guilt..." Dusty murmured. "I understand that. I feel so bad that I left home after the funeral. I kept calling to check in on the boys, but it wasn't the same as being here for them like you were. It's no wonder that Miller is so attached to you."

"I'm attached to him, too," Melanie said. "I know I shouldn't have gotten so involved, but I think I fell for him before I even realized he was your nephew. And then when I met the others..."

"Those kids are pretty special," Dusty agreed.

"Your whole family is," Melanie said.

His handsome face contorted. "Except for me..." he murmured.

"Don't," she whispered. She reached across the console now and gripped his forearm. He affected her so much—even when he wasn't trying.

He was the most special of them all to her...

Dear Reader,

Welcome to Willow Creek, Wyoming. If you haven't read the first two books in my Bachelor Cowboys series with Harlequin Heartwarming, you'll have no problem figuring out what's going on. And if you've read the first two and are returning to Ranch Haven, you're not the only one. Black sheep of the family Dusty Haven is finally coming home! And he might be more confused by what's going on at his family ranch than new readers will be. His scheming grandmother Sadie Haven has been up to her old matchmaking tricks. But that's not the only way she's blindsided poor Dusty, who's still reeling from the loss of his twin and somebody even closer to him.

I come from a big family, so I love writing about family dynamics and sibling relationships. I'm the youngest of seven with three older sisters and three older brothers. I'm a little like Sadie in that I might have meddled a time or two in my siblings' lives. But like Sadie, I've always had their best interests at heart. Also like Sadie, things might not have always gone according to plan. Maybe that's why I enjoy writing so much. My characters have to do what I want them to...usually. Sometimes they seem to have minds of their own and that's been the case with this series, Sadie and her family.

I hope you enjoy *The Bronc Rider's Twin Surprise*!

Happy reading!

Lisa Childs

HEARTWARMING

The Bronc Rider's Twin Surprise

—

Lisa Childs

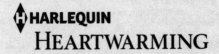

HARLEQUIN
HEARTWARMING

If you purchased this book without a cover you should be aware that this book is stolen property. It was reported as "unsold and destroyed" to the publisher, and neither the author nor the publisher has received any payment for this "stripped book."

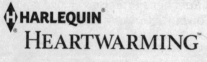

HARLEQUIN®
HEARTWARMING™

ISBN-13: 978-1-335-42678-9

The Bronc Rider's Twin Surprise

Copyright © 2022 by Lisa Childs

Recycling programs for this product may not exist in your area.

All rights reserved. No part of this book may be used or reproduced in any manner whatsoever without written permission except in the case of brief quotations embodied in critical articles and reviews.

This is a work of fiction. Names, characters, places and incidents are either the product of the author's imagination or are used fictitiously. Any resemblance to actual persons, living or dead, businesses, companies, events or locales is entirely coincidental.

For questions and comments about the quality of this book, please contact us at CustomerService@Harlequin.com.

Harlequin Enterprises ULC
22 Adelaide St. West, 41st Floor
Toronto, Ontario M5H 4E3, Canada
www.Harlequin.com

Printed in U.S.A.

Ever since **Lisa Childs** read her first romance novel (a Harlequin story, of course) at age eleven, all she wanted was to be a romance writer. With over seventy novels published with Harlequin, Lisa is living her dream. She is an award-winning, bestselling romance author. She loves to hear from readers, who can contact her on Facebook or through her website, lisachilds.com.

Books by Lisa Childs

Harlequin Heartwarming

Bachelor Cowboys

A Rancher's Promise
The Cowboy's Unlikely Match

Harlequin Romantic Suspense

Bachelor Bodyguards

His Christmas Assignment
Bodyguard Daddy
Bodyguard's Baby Surprise
Beauty and the Bodyguard
Nanny Bodyguard
Single Mom's Bodyguard
In the Bodyguard's Arms
Soldier Bodyguard
Guarding His Witness
Evidence of Attraction
Boyfriend Bodyguard
Close Quarters with the Bodyguard
Bodyguard Under Siege

Visit the Author Profile page at Harlequin.com for more titles.

With great appreciation for my hardworking, insightful editor, Katie Gowrie!

CHAPTER ONE

"WELCOME HOME!"

"Welcome back!"

The shouts startled Dusty Haven so much that he dropped his duffel bag onto the brick floor of the kitchen. Bits of confetti rained to the ground and onto his hat and shoulders. "What the…"

How had they known he was coming home at all, let alone this early on a Sunday morning? And why would they have thrown him a party?

The shouting stopped and a shocked silence gripped the room, like it gripped him. He couldn't say anything as he peered around the enormous kitchen at the faces of his family. At least, most of his family…

His oldest brother Jake and Jake's new wife, Katie, weren't here. They must still be on their honeymoon. He felt a quick jab of guilt over not making it back in time for the wedding, but they'd only given him a couple days' notice.

They weren't the only ones missing. Dale and Jenny...

Dusty's twin and his wife were gone forever since the car accident that had claimed both their lives ten weeks ago.

How can they be gone that long already?

The wound felt fresh to Dusty, his heart hollow from having them ripped out of his life. But their loss hadn't affected his life as much as it had everyone else's.

His young nephews were here, confetti stuck to their hands as they gathered around him. Seven-year-old Miller's cast was off now, but he didn't look much steadier than he had when Dusty had seen him last in the hospital over two months ago. And five-year-old Ian's mouth was open, his hazel eyes blank. Had he forgotten already who Dusty was? Or had Ian confused Dusty with his dad, like he had during those first couple of weeks that Dusty had stayed after the accident?

And Little Jake...

If the two-year-old would have said anything before, he was silent now, staring up at him with big, dark eyes. The other little boy, standing with his nephews, was a stranger to Dusty. He had light blond hair and bright blue eyes that were narrowed with speculation as he studied Dusty's face. He was the first to break the silence.

"Who are you?" he asked, like this was his house, like Dusty was the stranger.

And maybe he was. He certainly felt strange coming back now, knowing what he'd recently discovered. Ignoring the boy's question, he looked for his other brothers.

With Jake gone, they'd had to step up to help out on the ranch and with Dale's orphaned sons. The youngest of his brothers, Baker, stood near the French doors to the patio, as if tempted to slip out of them and run away. While Ben, not surprisingly, had his arm around a beautiful woman. Women had always been drawn to Ben. This one was petite and blond. Was the little blond boy hers?

Grandma was here, with Old Man Lemmon of all people. She towered over the short, white-haired deputy mayor of Willow Creek. Mr. Lemmon offered Dusty a slight wave, and Dusty nodded back in acknowledgment. He couldn't even look at his grandmother, not right now. Not after everything he'd learned. So he just skimmed his gaze over her where she stood near the hearth of the mammoth fireplace.

His eye caught a long sign dangling from the old barn beam that served as the mantel.

"Welcome back fromyourhoneymoon."

They must have run out of room on the sign. This party wasn't for him; it was for Jake and Katie. Trays of cookies and glasses of punch covered the stainless-steel countertop of the long kitchen island.

A young woman, with her dark golden hair bound in a braid, stood at the counter; she was nearly as tall as his grandmother. Another woman with wavy brown hair stood beside the taller woman, or rather, almost behind her, as if she was trying to hide from him.

His heart stopped beating for a moment as shock gripped him. *What the*...

When his gaze met hers, she gasped and dropped the glass of punch she held. Fortunately, the glass was paper and just bounced off the bricks, splashing red punch across the floor. He'd spent the last eight weeks searching everywhere for her. And she was here.

Seeing her was so jarring, he felt his whole body go stiff. But he didn't have to ask the question burning in his mind. Because he knew… and he finally met his grandmother's gaze. Her eyes were as dark as the toddler's eyes, but so full of knowledge and secrets. Somehow she'd known, somehow she'd done this...

He'd already felt so betrayed and now *this* compounded that feeling even more, overwhelming him. Before he could say or do anything, a door creaked open then slammed shut and Feisty, the little Chihuahua his grandmother had rescued years ago from a hot car, started barking and raced past him to the man striding into the kitchen, carrying a giggling red-haired woman in his arms.

Feisty tugged at the bottoms of Jake's jeans, growling deep in her throat. Jake chuckled, and the woman in his arms said, "Feisty, you'll have to wait your turn. I get to kiss him first!" And she looped her arm around his neck and pulled his head down for a kiss.

Applause broke the silence as the others clapped and cheered. And the greetings were shouted again. "Welcome home!"

"Welcome back from your honeymoon!"

"We missed you!" the little blond boy said.

Katie wriggled down from her new husband's arms and embraced the kid. Though he didn't look anything like the petite redheaded, green-eyed woman, this was clearly her son. Dusty should have realized that; he knew her boy was living here now. "We missed you too, Caleb," Katie said, "so very much!"

The little boy pulled back from his mother's arms and said, his tone almost accusatory, "We used all our confetti on *him*."

Jake laughed, either from his new stepson's comments or from Feisty licking his face. He put down the long-haired Chihuahua and replaced her with the boy, lifting him into his arms. The little kid slung his arms around Jake's neck and nuzzled close before pulling back to focus on Dusty again.

"He must be a ghost, or some kind of apparition," Jake mused. "Because it can't be who I think it is…"

Dusty grinned then, even as his heart pounded hard in his chest and he forced himself to not look at *her*. He couldn't see her now anyway as she and the other woman were crouched over on the other side of the island, cleaning up the punch. He'd spent all these weeks looking for her, and she was here. How long had she been here?

"Funny, Jake," Dusty murmured.

And, really, the entire situation was funny, in that kick-you-in-the-gut ironic way that made Dusty feel as if the wind had been knocked completely from his lungs. It hurt to breathe, hurt for his heart to beat…almost with the same intensity as when he'd gotten the call about Dale's accident.

Jake's call…his deep voice vibrating with emotion…

Dusty had known, the minute Jake had uttered his name in that tone, that something was terribly wrong. Tragically wrong…

And then it had gotten worse.

"Is he a ghost?" Caleb asked. Apparently, he'd interpreted his stepfather's remark as being literal. Maybe that was why he'd been staring at Dusty with such confusion.

That was probably what Dale's sons also thought as they continued to silently stare up at Dusty. He was identical to his late twin; with his dark golden hair and hazel eyes, he was the only one of the Haven brothers who looked like Dale. Miller and Ian looked like him too, whereas Little Jake, with his dark hair and eyes, was the spitting image of his namesake, his uncle Big Jake. None of the boys had answered their new cousin's question. They just stared at Dusty as if they couldn't believe what they were seeing.

But maybe that wasn't strange since the rest of Dusty's family was looking at him the same way, and maybe they couldn't believe what they were seeing either. They couldn't believe that he was back.

Of course, none of them knew the real reason he'd been gone, except for Grandma, who'd obviously outmaneuvered him. She'd brought *her* here...

How? How had Grandma known? Had Dale, before he'd died, broken his promise not to tell anyone?

He tried to peer around Jake toward the kitchen island where the brunette had been hiding behind the other woman, but Jake stepped closer to Dusty, blocking his line of vision. He set the little boy back on his feet.

"Caleb, this is your uncle Dusty," Jake said as introduction.

The little boy gasped and stared up at Dusty, his blue eyes wide with awe. "You're the famous rodeo rider? You look bigger on TV."

Dusty usually heard that comment the other way around, that he looked bigger in person. But here, at Ranch Haven, among his brothers, he was the shortest...now that Dale was gone.

The kid continued, his voice nearly shaking with excitement. "Me and Mommy watched you on TV riding bulls and bucking broncos. Is it true you won Midnight in a bet because you were the only one who was ever able to ride him?"

Dusty's lips twitched with a smile. *This* never got old—a kid's excitement over the rodeo. He'd once been that kid himself, in awe the first time his mom and dad had taken him and his brothers to the rodeo. Then every year it had come to town after that, he'd begged his parents to take them back. That had only happened for a few years; then his dad had died and his mom had taken off.

Grandpa had taken him to the rodeo again, unbeknownst to Grandma. He'd done some other things Grandma hadn't known about either, like sneaking his cigars.

"Did you?" Caleb prodded when Dusty had yet to answer. "Did you ride Midnight?"

He grinned. "I did, but I think it was only because Midnight let me ride him." The bronco was sensitive, so sensitive that he must have picked up on Dusty's distress and let him have the win that last time. During their first encounter, Midnight had definitely been the victor, leaving Dusty with a hamstring injury requiring physical therapy.

Jake groaned and shook his head.

"What?" Dusty asked. What had he done wrong now?

"See, Daddy Jake!" Caleb exclaimed. "I knew if I made him my friend that Midnight will let me ride him too!" He turned his attention on Dusty again. "Did you give him lots of carrots? Is that why he let you ride him?"

"Your horse has the best eyesight in the entire state of Wyoming," Jake said with a chuckle. "Thanks to Caleb here trying to make friends with him."

"Midnight is friends with Daddy Jake too," Caleb said. "And with Uncle Ben."

Dusty snorted. "The mayor's been playing cowboy?" he scoffed.

Ben stepped forward. "Somebody had to." He released the blonde to reach out and pat Dusty's back so hard that Dusty stumbled forward a foot. "I didn't think you were ever coming back."

"None of us did," Baker said as he finally left his position next to the patio doors and joined them.

"Not *none* of us," Grandma's deep voice carried across the kitchen to Dusty. She sounded smug.

Of course, she would have known he was coming back because she was probably the one person who'd known why he'd really left after the funeral. Somehow, she'd known what he'd been missing, and the manipulative old woman had brought *her* here. But she'd never bothered to mention that to him when Dusty had called the ranch to check on his nephews. She'd never said a word.

But then, he hadn't either. He hadn't told anyone except Dale that he was married. Dale was the only one Dusty had told about needing physical therapy for his injury. Dale was the one who'd pointed out to him that Dusty was obviously falling for his physical therapist, Melanie Shepard. So Dusty had been happy to share the news of his elopement with his twin, knowing that, unlike the rest of their family, Dale wouldn't judge him. But Dusty had sworn him to secrecy. And it had been obvious at the hospital, after the accident, that Dale hadn't shared his secret with their brothers, just like when they were kids.

After he'd buried his twin, he'd come home to find his wife gone. He'd been searching for her for weeks.

Somehow, undoubtedly thanks to Grandma's meddling, she'd wound up here. But when Dusty leaned around Jake and peered at the kitchen island, only the tall blond woman stood there now. The other woman was gone.

Had he once again lost his runaway bride?

DIDN'T THINK YOU were ever coming back...

The words reverberated inside Melanie's head as she leaned back against her closed bedroom door, her right hand pressed against her chest. Her heart pounded fast and furiously. Felt like it was knocking against her ribs. And not just from how fast she'd run up the back stairwell to the second story of the enormous house. It had been beating this hard since Dusty had first stepped into the kitchen and everyone had yelled welcome home and thrown confetti at him.

Everyone but her.

She hadn't mistaken the sound of boots against the hardwood floor for Jake's footsteps. It was almost as if she'd known...and maybe she had from the slightly uneven rhythm. Maybe that was how she'd known it was him. *Her husband.*

Her hand moved from her chest over her swelling belly.

Their father.

Didn't think you were ever coming back...

Baker had voiced aloud Melanie's thoughts— and one of her reasons for staying at Ranch Haven once she'd realized it was where Dusty had grown up. She'd stayed because all of Dusty's family had thought he wouldn't ever come back, that he'd fled from a family tragedy just like his mom had after his dad's death. His mother had never returned.

Why had Dusty?

Melanie had overheard some calls his brothers had made to him over the past several weeks, during which they'd alternated between begging and badgering him to return. But he hadn't. He'd stayed away for two months.

Why was he back now?

A knock rattled the door at her back and she jumped away from it. Had he come for her?

Her heart beat harder at the thought, but then she shook her head. No. If he'd cared anything at all about her, he would have been honest with her from the beginning.

"Miss Melanie…" a soft voice, cracking with emotion, called out.

Her hand shaking, she grabbed the knob and opened the door to her seven-year-old patient. She'd been hired on at the ranch to help heal his broken leg after the car accident that had killed his parents. Tears streaked down his face from hazel eyes the same combination of green and gold as his uncle's.

"Miller, what's wrong?" she asked. "Are you okay?"

He nodded, but clearly he was not. She held

out her arms and he rushed into them, burrowing close to her. His small body trembled against her as sobs racked him.

Her heart ached. Miller tried to act so much older and tougher than his seven years. He always denied how much he was hurting, no matter how apparent the hurt was, both physically and emotionally. No matter how strong he pretended to be, he was still just a little boy.

Her arms tightened around him, holding him as close as she could, wishing she could absorb his pain. Since Melanie didn't usually work with her patients for very long, she tried not to become too attached to any of them. But that had proved impossible with Miller.

Unfortunately, he wasn't the first patient to whom she'd gotten too attached.

"Uncle Dusty just…" he hesitated "…he looks so much like Dad. I know Uncle Jake was joking, but seeing him *is* like seeing a ghost…" A shudder passed through him, making his small frame tremble again.

Melanie understood exactly what he meant. When Miller's uncle had walked into the room, it was like she'd seen a ghost too. But not the ghost of Dale Haven.

The ghost of Dusty Chaps, the man she'd thought she'd known. The man she had married…without realizing that he didn't actually exist. That he'd never been real…that *nothing* had been real.

CHAPTER TWO

Fourteen weeks earlier...
The beginning...

FOR THE PAST six weeks, Dusty had been struggling to remain professional. The last thing he wanted to do was make his physical therapist uncomfortable or to have her feel threatened. So he'd fought really hard to ignore how beautiful she was, with her thick brown hair and eyes the color and warmth of melted chocolate.

He'd tried to ignore how her touch felt when she worked with him, how her hand against the back of his thigh had his skin tingling and his pulse racing...despite the pain. He hadn't been hurting just from his hamstring injury but from how badly he ached to touch her, and to kiss her.

"You are officially released from therapy," she told him, her full lips curving into a slight smile as she stepped back from the massage table where she'd rubbed down his thigh after he'd completed what was apparently his last session of exercises.

The sports clinic where she worked was in Las Vegas, close to the apartment that Dusty used as his home base. The building was all polished concrete and exposed ductwork with state-of-the-art exercise equipment in the main area. Tall doors opened onto rooms off that main area. Some were offices and some were massage rooms like this one. There was a long leather table in the middle of the space, which had dark paneled walls with dim lighting and faint music humming from hidden speakers.

"You are healed well enough to ride again," she told him.

He sighed. "There's no place to ride right now." The rodeo finals had been in November; it was March now and, while there were some events, Dusty usually waited until the season was in full swing in June or July before he started competing. He didn't want to get hurt before the stakes got high.

Twenty-nine was old for a rodeo rider, and even though Melanie Shepard had healed his hamstring, he still had more aches and pains than he cared to acknowledge. He wasn't ready to give up the sport he loved—not yet and probably not ever.

"You said you were riding when you got hurt six weeks ago," she said. "Where was that? Do you own a ranch?"

"No," he was quick to reply. While his brother Jake claimed they were all equal partners in Ranch Haven, it really belonged to Jake and Dale. Just as Dusty had ignored his attraction to Melanie, he ignored the twinge of resentment over his twin's love of the ranch.

What had happened to the dreams they'd had since their parents had taken them to their first rodeo when they were five years old? As little kids riding hay bales in the barn, they'd plotted their future of joining the rodeo right out of high school and touring around the country.

Dusty had followed through on their plan... while Dale had bailed on him, choosing the ranch and Jenny Miller over their dreams. Now his twin had a bunch of kids and no hope of ever living the life they'd dreamt of, the life Dusty had been living alone. And suddenly he felt more alone than he ever had. And he didn't want to leave Melanie.

"You're no longer working for me...with me...whatever then, right?" he asked.

She narrowed her eyes and studied his face

before nodding. "Not unless you get hurt again."

"So go out with me," he urged her. "I'll take you to dinner. Or a movie."

She shook her head.

"Why not?" he asked. "We don't have to act professional anymore."

"I wasn't acting," she said, her usually warm voice suddenly cold.

"Of course not, I know," he said. How was he bungling this so badly? Because she'd started to mean something to him…like, *everything*.

They hadn't just worked on his hamstring during his frequent visits to the clinic. They'd talked. A lot.

They'd shared stories about the rodeo. During the season, she traveled the circuit too. He'd met her before, when she'd been with her dad and when she'd been working with other riders. And a strange flutter had always passed through his heart over how beautiful she was.

But she'd acted so professionally even then, even when she hadn't been working with him. She'd always seemed so guarded, but over time he'd gotten her to open up. He knew she'd grown up on the circuit, that her dad had been a professional bull rider before becoming an announcer, and her mom had once been a barrel racer, like his.

He ignored the twinge of resentment he felt whenever he thought of his mom. He should have been over it by now; he hadn't seen her in years.

"And I told you before that I don't date rodeo riders," Melanie reminded him.

He suspected it was because of her dad, because of his cheating. Shep Shepard was an infamous womanizer, even now that he was much older and unfortunately still married to her mother. For some reason, Dusty, too, had a reputation for being a heartbreaker.

He wasn't sure why. He had never cheated on anyone. He'd just never dated anyone for very long.

Maintaining a relationship was too hard on the road, and traveling to rodeos was something he never had any intention of giving up, not even when he got old. He planned to eventually do what Melanie's dad had done when injuries had forced him to quit riding and become a rodeo announcer. Like Shep, Dusty had the moniker for it—the name he'd legally taken because he hadn't wanted any connection to his mother. When she'd returned to the circuit, she'd used the Haven name. He'd wanted no association with her, no connection to her…maybe because he was afraid he was too much like her.

But he wasn't.

And he could prove it.

"So don't date me," Dusty said.

A slight smile curved her lips and she said, "That was kind of my plan."

"Marry me," he said.

She laughed. But he didn't.

He was serious, and his heart pounded hard in anticipation of her answer.

She just stared at him like he'd hurt his head instead of his hamstring.

So he repeated his question—his proposal. "Marry me, Melanie."

Now...

SHE COULDN'T LEAVE MILLER. Her intention when she'd fled up the back stairwell moments ago had been to pack up her stuff and run away, like she'd run away from that apartment she and Dusty had shared for such a brief time. *For our honeymoon...*

She didn't have time to think about that now, to think about how little she'd known the man she'd married, or at least whom she'd thought she'd married. She had to think about that wonderful couple who'd just returned from their own honeymoon; this celebration was for them and she wasn't about to let anything ruin it for Jake and Katie.

She squeezed Miller one more time before easing him away from her with her hands on his thin shoulders. She stared down into his tear-stained face and asked, "Are you feeling better now?"

He drew in a shaky breath and nodded. "Yeah, I know Uncle Dusty isn't my dad."

From what she'd learned since living at the ranch, Dusty could not have been more different than his twin in personality even though they'd been identical in appearance.

"My dad isn't ever coming back," Miller continued in such a tone of finality that Melanie's heart ached for him all over again. He and his brothers were too young to have lost their parents, but she suspected that such a tragic loss was devastating at any age. Miller released that breath he'd drawn in a ragged sigh. "Nobody thought Uncle Dusty would come back either."

Melanie certainly hadn't. But now that he had…

She had to figure out what to do, how to

handle this when everything inside her urged her to run. Yet how could she leave Miller? The other boys? The ranch? The friends she'd made here?

And why should *she* leave when Dusty wasn't likely to stay long anyway?

"We should get back to the party," she said. "Before Caleb and Ian eat all the goodies Miss Taye baked for the party."

Miller snorted. "It's probably already too late for that."

"I'm sure Taye saved us some," she assured him, and a rumble of hunger emanated from her swelling belly.

Miller giggled. "You've been eating almost as many cookies as Caleb does."

She had been eating a lot more lately, but then, she wasn't just eating for one anymore. She was eating for three. She drew in her own shaky breath now and tried to slow her racing pulse. "Okay, let's go back to the party."

She hesitated a moment before opening the door, worried that she might find Dusty waiting for her. But when she opened it, she found the hallway was empty and silent but for the murmur of voices coming up from the stairwell leading down to the kitchen. She cocked her head and listened for a moment, but she didn't hear his voice, which was a bit distinctive from his brothers' because it had a slight twang to it that he must have picked up from traveling with the rodeo or from other rodeo riders.

Was Dusty just not talking at the moment or had he left already? She wasn't sure why he'd returned to the ranch; nobody had been expecting him. Was he back just to pick up that bronco everybody else had grown tired of taking care of for him?

Or had he returned for another reason...

For her?

No. When he'd noticed her standing next to Taye, he'd looked even more shocked than she'd been when she'd heard his footsteps in the hall. He obviously hadn't been expecting to find her in his home. So he hadn't come back to the ranch because he'd known she'd been living on it.

She should have been relieved but instead a pang of regret struck her heart, making her gasp with surprise.

Miller's small hand slipped into hers and he squeezed, as if the little boy had sensed she needed comforting almost as much as he did. "Let's walk down there together," he suggested.

His cast had just come off a couple of weeks ago, and his leg was still weak. He often struggled on the stairs. She needed to stay for him, for so many reasons, but the most important was his physical therapy.

While she could not give the little boy back everything he'd lost, she could help him regain his mobility and his strength. She squeezed his hand in hers and smiled down at him. "You've got this," she assured as she had so many times over the past several weeks.

Like that day two months ago when she'd brought him home from the hospital and they'd discovered a party that had been thrown in his honor. And Melanie had discovered so many things she hadn't known about the man she'd married.

But despite all she'd learned, she still didn't know so much about him. Like why he'd come home. Like if they were even legally married because she hadn't married Dusty Haven. She'd married an alias, a man who didn't even really exist.

CHAPTER THREE

"YOU'RE A LITTLE LATE," Ben chided him, "if you came back to help out while Jake was gone on his honeymoon." He gestured to where their oldest brother stood a few feet away from them, with his arm wrapped tightly around his bride while his stepson leaned against his legs. The little blond boy kept peeking at Dusty through the fringe of bangs that fell into his eyes.

Dusty was a lot late, and it had nothing to do with Jake's absence from the ranch but with his own. If he'd come back sooner…

He would have found what he'd been looking for. He turned again to his grandmother, and this time, instead of looking away from him like she had before, she met his gaze with a pointed look and a slight smirk.

Anger surged through him again. He'd already been mad at her before discovering Melanie—because of what else he'd recently discovered. Sadie had more secrets than he'd ever suspected, but then, he had never suspected she would keep anything from him or his brothers. He'd always trusted her.

That had been his first mistake.

His second had been not trusting Melanie with the truth about his family and about himself. Was she going to give him a chance to explain now?

Or was she going to take off like she had from their apartment? Was she packing her bags right now to run away from him again? She must have slipped up the back stairwell to the second story where the majority of the bedrooms were.

"I can't talk right now," Dusty said as he tried stepping around his brother.

Ben moved with him, blocking his escape. "You say that a lot, like every time we've called and asked you to come home to help out."

"I've been busy…" Searching for somebody who might have been here the whole time.

"Doing what?" Baker asked as he stepped closer to Ben, so that the two of them blocked his escape. Ben's eyes, the same brown as his perfectly styled hair, were assessing; and Baker, with his dark hair and topaz eyes, towered over both of them.

Dusty wished now that his younger brother had slipped out the patio doors he'd been standing by when Dusty had first walked into the kitchen.

"I can't do this now, guys…" he murmured. Not when she could be packing or even on her way out the front door while they trapped him in the kitchen.

Ben emitted a low growl. "I'm so sick of you saying that," he said. "You need to stop running away now!"

"I'm not running," Dusty said. Not unless he had to chase Melanie.

"Sure looks like you want to," Baker remarked. "You look about as wild-eyed as that bronco of yours when he rears up in his stall."

Ben snorted. "He only does that for you now. He's fine with the rest of us."

Dusty wasn't interested in his horse—not now. He could think only of one thing—one person. His wife. And he needed to make sure she hadn't left him again.

Instead of physically shoving aside his brothers, like he was tempted to, Dusty narrowed his eyes and stared at them with that same stern look Sadie had turned on them every time she'd caught one of them trying to pull something and had called them on their nonsense. "So you two have been here the entire time that I've been gone?" he asked. "You've been helping out with the ranch and with the boys?"

Baker's face flushed and he ducked his head down. Ben let out a sigh, which he followed with an admission. "No. Not like I should have been. It all fell on Jake, the same as it always has."

"Are you guys huddled together over here trash-talking me?" Jake asked, and he looped one arm around Dusty's shoulders and his other around Baker's.

"Yup," Ben replied. "We're all talking about how we can't understand why smart, beautiful Katie O'Brien would marry such a slacker."

Jake grinned with such happiness that warmth flooded Dusty's heart. He couldn't remember the last time he'd seen his oldest brother this happy. No, he remembered. Twelve years ago, Jake had been this happy when he'd been dating Katie O'Brien. Then Grandpa Jake had died, and Jake had quit college to come home and manage the ranch. He'd given her up then, probably because he hadn't wanted her to make the sacrifices he'd chosen to make for the ranch and for their family.

Jake chuckled. "I'm not the only one who got lucky," he said.

Dusty's brow furrowed at what sounded like

arrogance from his usually humble brother. He would have expected a comment like that to come from Ben, not Jake. "Are you talking about Katie?" he asked. "Because I'm not convinced she's all that lucky."

"Me neither," Jake admitted. "But I was actually talking about Ben. He got lucky, too, that a beautiful, smart woman chose to take him on."

"What?" Dusty repeated. Maybe he was so shocked from seeing Melanie that he'd gone a bit dense. Or was Ben more serious with that blond woman than Dusty had realized?

Despite Ben's vow to stay single and focus only on the city he'd been elected to serve, he'd involved himself with a woman?

Dusty shouldn't have been surprised that his brother had changed his mind. *Nothing* should have surprised him anymore...

"Oh, he doesn't know?" Jake said.

"He wasn't taking my calls," Ben said, continuing their conversation about Dusty without actually including him.

"You should make an announcement," Jake urged Ben.

But Ben shook his head. "No need. The only one here who doesn't know is Dusty, and this is your day, Jake. It's your party, big brother."

"But this is big news," Jake insisted. "Ben Haven giving up his bachelor status…"

Dusty's mouth fell open as shock gripped him. "You're getting married?"

Ben grinned and nodded. "Sure am."

Baker laughed. "I'm not sure what's bigger news—that he's getting married or that he fell into Grandma's manipulations despite all his claims that he was too smart for that to happen to *him*."

Ben shrugged. "I can't help it. When Sadie's right, she's right, and I would have been a fool to let Emily Trent get away without making her my bride."

"Marrying them doesn't mean you can't still lose 'em…" Dusty mumbled as nerves twisted his stomach. Where had Melanie gone? Had she left already?

Dusty tried to tug free of his big brother's grasp, but Jake's arm tightened around his shoulders and he turned him toward him. "What are you talking about?" he asked. "What's going on with you? Why are you home?"

Dusty's mind started racing then with the thoughts and memories running through it. At no time during any of his many phone conversations with his brothers had any one of them mentioned Melanie to him. And nobody had noticed his reaction to seeing her except maybe the woman who'd been standing next to her. Clearly, nobody but his grandmother, of course, knew that Melanie was his wife.

But was she his wife? Or had she filed for divorce when she'd fled from their marriage? He hadn't been anywhere long enough for her lawyer to serve him with a divorce petition because he'd spent the past two months searching for her everywhere but here.

Had she been here that entire time?

Before he answered any of his brothers' questions, he wanted to talk to Melanie first and then his grandmother. He needed to know what the heck was going on with his bride, and then he needed Grandma to explain all the secrets she'd kept from him and from the rest of their family.

"GLAD YOU REJOINED the family," Katie said as Miller and Melanie descended the last step into the kitchen.

Before greeting the new bride, Melanie peered around her to the other people in the enormous room. *He* was here. He hadn't left. He stood with his brothers near the fireplace; Big Jake had his arm around him, as if he was holding him in place, as if he alone was keeping him from running. Emily was doing the same thing with the smaller boys, corralling them at the table where they drank punch and ate cookies.

"Melanie?" Katie said, drawing her attention back to her.

She'd thought the new bride was referring to Miller when she'd mentioned rejoining the family, since Katie didn't know they were sisters-in-law. Nobody knew that she was family, except maybe for Sadie. If she *was* family, legally.

She'd wed Dusty Chaps at a little chapel on their first date; his alias was the name on their marriage certificate, not Dusty Haven.

Katie hugged Miller and then Melanie. "Everything okay?" she asked, her brow wrinkling slightly with concern. Then she glanced down at Melanie's stomach. It was straining the buttons on the blouse she wore over a pair of knit pants with an elastic waistband that was probably stretched nearly to the breaking point.

If she'd intended to run off when she'd seen Dusty, she wouldn't have even needed to go upstairs to pack any of her stuff since hardly any of it fit anymore.

"She's hungry," Miller answered for her when she remained silent, too overwhelmed yet with the shock of seeing her husband that she wasn't able to reply to her friend's question. She glanced at the fireplace again, where Dusty was still talking to his brothers. "Her stomach's growling super loud. Did Caleb and Ian leave any cookies?"

"There are a lot of cookies left," Taye assured him. "And punch too."

"Thanks for cleaning up my spill," Melanie said. She'd tried to wipe up the mess she'd made when she'd dropped her cup of punch, but Taye, as intuitive as ever, had shooed her off, recognizing that she'd needed to get away.

"Are you all right now?" Taye repeated Katie's question, her voice lowered to a whisper, as if she didn't want to worry Miller.

He'd stepped farther down the counter in search of his favorite cookies. But in case he was still listening, Melanie lied. "Yes, I'm fine."

"Really?" Taye asked skeptically. "You looked like you saw a ghost when you dropped that cup."

"What happened?" Katie asked. She hadn't been there when Dusty had come into the kitchen, when his gaze had locked onto Melanie and startled her even though she'd suspected he was the Haven coming down the hall. Something about the uneven rhythm of his walk…from all his old injuries…and maybe a new one…

Where had he been all these weeks?

"When Melanie saw Dusty, she dropped her cup of punch," Taye noted, "like she thought she saw…" She trailed off, with a nervous glance at the seven-year-old who'd returned to Melanie's side with a handful of cookies.

"Miss Melanie looked like she saw my dad's ghost," Miller finished for her. "That's what I thought he was at first…" A little shiver had his body trembling, and Melanie reached out for him, sliding her arm around his shoulders to comfort him. "But Miss Melanie never met my dad," he continued, and he leaned his head back to peer up at her, "so why would Uncle Dusty look like anybody to you? You never saw him before either."

Taye's brow furrowed as she studied Melanie's face. "That's right. Dusty was gone before we moved into the ranch."

Following the death of her grandson and granddaughter-in-law, Sadie had hired Taye to cook, Emily to teach, Katie to do the accounting, and Melanie to work with Miller, but they hadn't started their positions at the ranch until after the funeral. And according to everyone who'd attended the service, Dusty had left immediately after it. He hadn't even stayed for the memorial luncheon in the church community room.

"And you're not from Willow Creek," Taye continued, "so how could you have seen him before…unless…"

Melanie should have told them. She knew that now, but she hadn't wanted to admit how stupid she'd been, especially to these strong, smart women who she respected so much. But before she could say anything, a sharp whistle rent the air.

Katie giggled before chiding her husband. "That better not have been meant for me to come running to you like Feisty, Mr. Haven."

Jake laughed. "No way, Mrs. Haven, I was trying to get everyone's attention for a moment. This family of ours is kind of noisy."

"Noisy or nosy?" Dusty remarked.

Melanie tensed, trying to not react the way she always had to the sound of his husky voice with that slight Southern drawl. Every time she'd run into him at the rodeo over the years, she'd been struck dumb in his presence, inwardly giddy over his good looks and his charm and the way he'd looked at her, with such intensity. Despite her efforts not to react now, her pulse quickened and her skin heated. He could he affect her with just his voice. Even now…

He hadn't seen her yet. She should have run.

But Miller leaned heavily against her, and she couldn't move without him falling. And if she left the ranch, he would be so hurt. He had come to rely on her physically and emotionally.

Jake chuckled. "Maybe we haven't missed you as much as we thought we had."

Melanie's heart ached with how much she'd missed him, but she'd been missing the man she'd thought he was, not the man she'd found out he was. Sure, he wasn't married to someone else, like she'd been led to believe. He hadn't abandoned a wife and kids like she'd originally thought when she'd shut off her phone, packed up her stuff and fled the apartment they'd shared. But he'd abandoned his family all the same, even when they'd needed him the most these past couple of months.

"But…" Jake continued, and he turned toward Katie. "My darling wife, will you join me?"

The whistle might not have brought her to his side, but his endearment and smile had Katie rushing to him now. Melanie couldn't blame her; Jake was a good man. The minute

Katie joined him, Jake released Dusty and embraced her instead.

Dusty didn't bolt for the door like Melanie, and probably Jake, had suspected he might. Her pulse quickened even more when he turned toward her, and she was worried that he might approach her now in front of all of them. But he stayed beside Jake, his new sister-in-law and his other two brothers.

Sadie and Lemar "Lem" Lemmon had taken seats at the table near Emily and the smaller boys. The elderly woman was smiling wider than Melanie had ever seen Sadie Haven smile, but then Dusty turned toward his grandmother. And Sadie tensed like Melanie had, and her smile slid away, her mouth turning down as her brow lined with confusion.

Had she expected Dusty to be happy with her? Obviously, he wasn't thrilled that Sadie had brought Melanie here. Melanie hadn't been thrilled either when she'd realized Dusty's connection to Ranch Haven, but she hadn't ever been completely certain that Sadie had known who she was. So she hadn't risked bringing it up in case her being hired to help Miller had just been some cosmically crazy coincidence.

Clearly, Dusty didn't think that. And Melanie had been naïve to ever entertain the thought that it had just been a coincidence. She'd been even more foolish when she'd married a man she'd hardly known and believed that they were both committed to their relationship.

The little boys were chattering around the teacher they adored, so Jake cleared his throat to draw everyone's attention again. "Emily, you need to come up here too," he told her.

The teacher shook her head. "No, this party is for you and Katie."

"Help me out, guys, get her up here," he told his stepson and nephew.

Ian and Caleb tugged her up from the bench and toward the hearth where the majority of the group had gathered. Ben wrapped his arms around her and Little Jake, whom she still carried, and she leaned back against him.

Taye emitted a soft sigh. "Wow, they're all so happy…" There was no envy in her voice, just affection and a wistful longing.

Tears stung Melanie's eyes as those same emotions rushed over her. Affection for the people who'd become such good friends, and longing for that kind of real relationship for herself. She'd thought she'd had it for a while, during those four blissful weeks after her impulsive elopement, but then her world had come crashing down around her. Starting with the mysterious phone call her husband had received one day, which had had him rushing back to a home and a family he'd never told her about. She wouldn't realize until after arriving at the ranch that her world hadn't crashed nearly as hard as Miller's and his brothers' world had. If only Dusty had been honest with her...

"Katie and I want to thank all of you for helping out these past couple of weeks, so that we could enjoy our honeymoon," Jake said.

"Uncle Dusty wasn't here..." Caleb muttered with a kid's blunt honesty and confusion over Jake being so inclusive.

Ben chuckled and squeezed the little boy's shoulder. They'd grown especially close the past couple of weeks that Ben had moved into the house while Jake and Katie had been gone.

Jake smiled but continued as if his stepson hadn't interrupted. "We missed you all and we're thrilled to be home again with our family." He reached out then and squeezed Dusty's shoulder. "All our family..."

That was why Jake was such a good man; he could forgive his brother even though Dusty hadn't been there for them after the funeral like he should have been. Jake was a better person than Melanie was, because she wasn't sure she could ever forgive Dusty, and she knew for certain that she would never trust him again. Trusting him was a mistake she would not make twice.

"And now our family is about to expand even more—"

Katie gasped and lovingly admonished, "Jake, I thought we were going to wait before we make any announcement."

Taye laughed and whispered conspiratorially to Melanie, "I thought she was glowing…"

Melanie had been so preoccupied with Dusty's reappearance that she hadn't noticed. But Taye was right; Katie was radiant. While that might have just been marital bliss, Melanie wondered if she was no longer the only pregnant woman at the ranch.

Jake grinned. "I was talking about Ben and Emily's engagement," he told her. "We have so much to celebrate…" He beamed at his bride.

"Yes," she said, and she turned toward Ben and Emily. "Congratulations, you two! I'm so happy that Emily finally gave you a chance, Ben."

"Hey, she was the one who chased me," he said then grunted when Emily elbowed him. "She chased me until I caught her," he added with one of his wicked grins. He and Emily were truly perfect for each other.

Taye emitted that wistful little sigh again.

"Yes, congratulations, you two," Jake added to his bride's sentiment. Then he literally tipped his hat to his grandmother. "And to you, Sadie March Haven, for your recent success from all your scheming."

She didn't deny his claims, just smiled. But it wasn't as wide as she'd smiled earlier, because Dusty was staring at her again. Melanie couldn't see his expression, just the tension in his long, lean body.

Then Jake warned, "Baker and Dusty, you better watch yourselves, or you're going to be following Ben to the altar like he and Emily are following me and Katie."

All the color fled from Baker's face and he shook his head as if horrified. And Jake grinned widely. "I expected that reaction from Dusty more than you, Baker," he said. "But he's just standing there. What cat got your tongue, Dusty?" he prodded the rodeo rider.

Dusty shook his head. "I can't get married."

"There's the reaction I expected," Jake said with a laugh. "See, Grandma, it's not going to be as easy as you think to carry out your matchmaking plans."

"I can't get married *again*," Dusty said. Then he raised his voice and added, "I'm already married."

Panic pressed on Melanie's chest, stealing away her breath, so she couldn't speak, couldn't shout the protest she wanted to shout at him.

Ben shook his head in disbelief. "What?" he asked. "You're married? When? Who? Where is she?"

"Yes. Months ago." Dusty turned toward Melanie and pointed. "To her. To Melanie."

Everybody's head swiveled in her direction, their faces revealing either shock at the news or confirmation of the suspicions they must have had.

Miller was clearly stunned as he tugged free of Melanie's arm around his shoulders and stared up at her. "You're my aunt?" he asked.

She wanted to deny it. She wanted to continue pretending like she'd been doing all these weeks that she wasn't really married to Dusty, that she hadn't really made the biggest mistake of her life. But she couldn't lie to this little boy. She loved him too much. So she nodded and replied, "Yes, I'm your aunt."

"But I've been calling you Miss Melanie, and I should have been calling you Aunt Melanie, like Aunt Katie," he said. "Why didn't you tell me?"

"Yes," Taye added softly. "Why didn't you tell us?"

She was one of the ones who'd looked as if she'd suspected, but she'd never asked. The young cook, with her blond hair and blue eyes a startling shade of pale blue, seemed to possess a wisdom beyond her years. She must have been waiting for Melanie to open up, but Melanie had done that once, with Dusty, and had her trust shattered. She hadn't been willing to do that again.

Melanie's pulse had already been racing so much, ever since she'd heard Dusty's footsteps, that it was a wonder her heart hadn't exploded with all the blood pumping in and out of it. Now all that blood left her head, making her so dizzy and unsteady that her legs folded beneath her and she dropped to the kitchen floor, just as she'd dropped that glass of punch earlier.

Unlike the paper cup, she didn't bounce and spill over; she just collapsed. Unfortunately, she didn't lose consciousness. She was completely aware of everyone fussing around her with concern. Taye and Miller were on their knees next to her while the others rushed to gather closer, until someone moved them all aside and strong arms wrapped around her, lifting her. It had been more than two months, but she immediately recognized her husband's touch, his smell.

She dragged in a deep breath of air, scented with the spicy aroma of the aftershave he used and hay and horses. He always smelled like this, always so good…

But, unlike other times, she didn't burrow into his neck; she didn't clutch him close. Instead, she finally, blissfully, passed out.

CHAPTER FOUR

THE MINUTE SHE'D fallen to the floor, panic pressed down hard on Dusty's chest, like the weight of his vest with a thousand-pound bull standing on it. And when she went limp in his arms, her head lolling back, that panic intensified to terror.

"Baker!" he shouted. "What's wrong? What happened?"

"I don't know," Baker said. "Carry her into the living room and I'll grab my EMT bag from my truck."

"I'll get it!" Ben said, already running from the room with the little blond boy and Ian following close behind.

The kids were scared too, like Dusty was. They all cared about his wife. It appeared she'd been living with them longer than she had with him. His arms trembled, not with her weight, but with fear as he carried her into the living room. He hesitated a long moment before lowering her onto the couch and stepping back so that his brother, a firefighter and paramedic, could treat her.

"She's breathing," Baker assured him. "Her pulse is strong too."

"She was hungry," Miller said, his voice tremulous as tears streaked down his face. "I didn't give her the cookies. I should have given her the cookies."

"This isn't your fault," Dusty assured the little boy. It was his. The way he'd showed up, the announcement he'd made…

It must have been too much for her. But why?

"What's wrong with her?" Dusty asked his brother.

Baker shook his head. "I'm not sure why she would have passed out like that."

Katie cleared her throat. "I… I don't know if I should say this, but…"

Before she could finish, Emily blurted out, "She's pregnant, Baker, with twins."

Shock staggered Dusty, and his head got so light that he felt as if he might pass out too.

Pregnant.

Twins…

He forced those thoughts from his mind; he'd have to deal with that revelation later. Right now he had to make sure that his wife was all right. Baker was dressed like a cowboy now rather than an EMT—not like he'd been the last time Dusty had seen him in his official capacity at the hospital, his clothes stained with blood. He'd been first on the scene of the accident that had taken Dale and Jenny, and probably would have taken the boys, too, if Baker hadn't been there. If he hadn't saved them.

Dusty needed his younger brother to promise that Melanie and his unborn babies would be all right now. "What's wrong with her?" he asked again. "Do you know?"

Baker nodded. "If her blood sugar got low enough because she hadn't eaten, that could have caused her to pass out." He glanced at Dusty now, accusatorily. "What's going on with you two? Where have you been?"

"She needed the cookies," Miller said with self-recrimination. "It *is* my fault…"

Dusty reached for the kid, but before he could close an arm around him, the little boy ran from the room. A combination of regret and relief rushed through Dusty. Right after the accident, everybody had been worried that Miller might lose his leg. They'd also been concerned that even if he didn't, he might never be the same again. While the seven-year-old's gait hadn't been even or fast, he was running again. Because of her...

He turned back to the couch where his wife lay, her face so pale that the only color was from the shadows of her thick black lashes and of the lock of hair that curled against her cheek. He reached out to push it back, as he had so many times before, and her lashes fluttered. Then her eyes opened and she stared up at him.

For a moment, her gaze softened and her brown eyes warmed, but then she blinked and tensed. "What—what are you doing here?" she asked.

"I could ask you the same thing," he replied. He looked up at his grandmother, who now hovered behind Katie and Emily. "But I think I know."

He would deal with his grandmother later. First, he had to make sure that his wife—his *pregnant* wife—was all right. "Should we take her to the hospital?" he asked his younger brother.

"How do you feel?" Baker asked Melanie. "Steadier?"

"Here're the cookies!" Miller exclaimed, running back into the room just as he'd run from it. "Here they are!"

Melanie's brow furrowed with confusion as Miller pressed the cookie into her hand. "What—"

"Eat it," Dusty advised her.

Baker nodded. "You probably have low blood sugar from not eating and from the pregnancy."

Melanie gasped, and color flooded her face now as she looked up at everybody standing around staring at her. But she didn't glance at Dusty, as if she couldn't bear to even look at him right now. She took a bite of the cookie, but maybe she did just so she didn't have to say anything.

Ben and the five-year-old boys, Ian and Caleb, rushed through the front door they'd left wide open. Ben, a duffel bag dangling from his hand, panted as if they'd run the entire way.

Caleb took the big bag, which had Willow Creek Emergency Services screen-printed on the side of it, from Ben's fingers and carried it over to the couch. His little arms strained from the weight of it. "Here it is, Uncle Baker! Here's your medical stuff."

"What happened?" Ian asked.

And Dusty wasn't sure if the question was because the little boy hadn't remembered Melanie had passed out or if it was because of how awkwardly and silently everyone was standing around her.

"She just needed to eat," Miller replied, watching as she chewed and swallowed the chocolate-chip cookie he'd brought her.

Caleb nodded as if he completely understood. "Cookies make everything better."

Melanie smiled at the little blond boy. "Yes, they do," she said. "I'm fine now. I'm sorry if I scared you." She focused on Miller then, holding out her free hand.

His small fingers shook as he reached and clasped hers. "I'm sorry I didn't get you food right away."

"It's not your fault that I forgot to eat," she told Miller. "Taking care of me isn't your responsibility."

"No, it's mine," Dusty said.

Baker glanced from him to her and back. "Were you serious? You two are married?"

"I'm not your responsibility either," Melanie told him, her usually warm voice icy-cold instead.

"Melanie…" He wasn't entirely sure what to say to her, but he knew that he didn't want an audience for this reunion with his runaway bride. "We need to talk," he said, and he gazed around at his family. "Privately…"

THE LAST THING Melanie wanted was to be alone with Dusty again. But her collapse had already alarmed the little boys too much. She didn't want to frighten them any more by getting emotional in front of them. Darn pregnancy hormones...

That had to be what had caused her to faint, combined with the low blood sugar Baker had diagnosed her with. And just a few bites of cookie had not been quite enough to steady her. When she rose from the couch, her legs threatened to fold beneath her again.

This time, before she could fall, Dusty swung her up in his strong arms. Her pulse quickened and she wriggled, trying to free herself from his hold. "I can walk," she insisted.

"You're still shaky," he said. "It'll be safer for you if I carry you upstairs."

She didn't feel safer. She felt threatened and afraid, and not just of Dusty's reaction to the news of her pregnancy, but of the feelings spiraling through her, making her pulse quicken and her skin tingle from his closeness. "It's not necessary," she murmured.

But Dusty ignored her, kind of like he had that day he'd left for home without telling her anything about it, anything about the family she'd married into. Clasping her even closer, he headed for the front stairwell, which was rarely used.

Miller started after them, but Baker reached out to hold him back. "Uncle Dusty will take care of her," he told the little boy. "She'll be okay."

"I don't believe you! You're a liar!" Miller lashed out before tugging free of his uncle's grasp and running out again, this time through the front door that, again, had been left wide open.

Alarmed at how upset Miller was, Melanie struggled to free herself from Dusty. "Let me go," she said, pushing against his broad shoulders. "Miller needs me. I need to go after him."

But Dusty didn't loosen his grasp a bit. "You can't go running after him. You need to take it easy until you're feeling stronger."

"He's right," Baker added. "You're not strong enough to go chasing after him. You need more than a couple bites of cookie to raise your blood sugar back up, and you need your rest."

"I'll go make sure Miller is all right," Jake assured her. "You need to lay down for a while, Melanie."

She needed to run, just like Miller had, but instead she was carried up the stairs. Almost effortlessly. Dusty was strong, incredibly so; he wouldn't have won all the championships he had if he wasn't as physically fit as he was.

At the top of the stairs, Dusty paused in the wide hallway. "Which room is yours?"

She could have resisted revealing that information, but she pointed to a closed door. Better that they have the discussion they needed to have here, in private. Or as relatively private as Ranch Haven ever was, with all the people living in the main house.

Dusty shifted her weight against his right hip as he opened the door with one hand.

She gasped with concern that he might aggravate his old injury, any of his old injuries. "You shouldn't be carrying me," she said. "I'm fine now. Really I am."

Dusty shook his head in rejection of her claim. "No, you're not all right. You just passed out." And he shuddered, as if reliving that moment with horror.

Had it affected him? Did he care about her at all?

Or was Dusty like his mother who'd taken off right after their dad died, abandoning her five sons? Did he care only about himself?

He pushed open the door and carried her

through it, then closed it with his back. He leaned against it for a moment.

During the weeks Melanie had been living at the ranch, she had learned far more about her husband than when she'd lived with him. So she knew how Dusty had shut out his family years ago, even before his twin had died, how he'd left right after high school and had returned only for short visits.

If only she'd known who he really was before she'd married him...if they were even really married. He hadn't married Melanie using his real name. But he also hadn't been already married, as she was led to believe before she'd left him. When Traci, the wife of Dusty's friend, had showed her a portrait of Dale and his family, she'd believed it was Dusty. It was what the woman had told her.

She hadn't known anything about Dale to believe otherwise. And she hadn't known anything real about Dusty, except that he was a rodeo rider. While she would like to blame him for everything that had happened between them, she really couldn't.

She was the one who'd broken her own rule. She hadn't just dated a rodeo rider; she'd married one. She'd married a stranger.

She was the one who'd made a terrible mistake.

I'VE MADE A terrible mistake...

"What's wrong, Sadie?" Lem asked as he joined her in her suite. For years he'd been Old Man Lemmon to her, just like he was to everyone else in town. But in spending time with him recently, she'd begun to think of him as just Lem like she had when they'd been kids in school together. Rivals, really. They weren't rivals anymore; they were actually becoming friends.

"Are you okay?" he asked with concern.

Once she'd seen that Melanie had regained consciousness and been assured that she was all right, Sadie had rushed to her private rooms to regroup and to reconsider the wisdom of some of the decisions she'd made.

Baker had said that Melanie would be all right despite passing out like she had. Was the young woman really okay? Was it just low blood sugar brought on by her pregnancy? Or by the shock of her husband showing up without warning?

"Dusty's back," she replied, a little shocked herself even though *she*, unlike Dusty's brothers, had never doubted that he would return. Eventually...

But now that he was back, she would have to deal with what she'd done. And Dusty, if the angry looks he'd been giving her were any indication, was not happy with her surprise for him. In anticipation of an ugly confrontation with her grandson, she paced her suite while Lem stood next to the open door.

His brow was creased, and his blue eyes narrowed with concern as he studied her. "You should be thrilled," Lem remarked. "Just like Jake said in the kitchen, all of your matchmaking is proving quite successful. Jake and Katie are married. Ben and Emily are engaged."

And they were happy. That was all Sadie wanted for her family, for all of them to be happy again after the devastating losses they'd suffered.

Lem continued, "And now Dusty's back, and apparently his wife has been here this entire time. Did you know?" He chuckled at his own question. And for a short man, he had quite the deep belly laugh. "Of course you knew. That's why she's here."

Sadie nodded. "I knew. And I thought…"

She'd thought she'd done the right thing then, bringing Melanie here even though Dusty hadn't brought her. He'd left her behind in Nevada when he'd come here after the accident.

The terrible, tragic accident…

Sadie drew in a shaky breath and suddenly

felt a bit light-headed herself. Feisty, as if sensing her discomfort, started yapping and jumping at Sadie's legs.

"Sit down, old woman," Lem advised as he guided her to a chair. "If you fall down, I won't be able to lift you up like Dusty did Melanie."

"You're an old fool, Lem Lemmon," Sadie said as she dropped into her favorite chair. Feisty immediately leaped onto her lap and started licking her chin. "A gentleman is not supposed to remark on a woman's age or her weight."

"I think you're perfect," Lem said, and his face suddenly flushed as if he'd just realized what he'd admitted. Then he blustered and added, "Perfectly stubborn."

"You were right the first time," she said, but she was just teasing. She knew she wasn't perfect, far from it, and from Dusty's coldness to her since his arrival, he was well aware of how imperfect she was.

Not that her grandson didn't have every right to be furious with her. But if he'd just told them about his marriage, if he'd admitted why he'd left after the funeral or whom he was looking for, she would have immediately come clean with him about what she'd done.

Instead he'd been stubborn…nearly as stubborn as she'd been.

She sighed. "You're right," she said. "I am perfectly stubborn."

That was her terrible mistake. Instead of waiting for her grandson to share his news, she should have just told Dusty that she knew he was married. Of course, he would have been annoyed to learn that she kept tabs on him through his manager, the man who signed up his sponsorships, who got Dusty money for wearing corporate brands on his vest. The man who'd helped him legally change his name. But Dusty wasn't the only one Sadie hadn't been forthcoming with…

She should have told Melanie that she was well aware of their relationship as well. But the poor young woman had been so skittish when she'd first arrived at the ranch. Sadie had worried that if she'd revealed she knew the physical therapist was her granddaughter-in-law, Melanie would have taken off. And Miller had needed her—not just as a physical therapist, but *Melanie*, with her sweet compassion. The two of them had bonded at the hospital even before they'd come to the ranch. So Sadie had been reluctant to do anything that might make her new granddaughter-in-law leave Ranch Haven.

She'd wanted Melanie to stay here for Miller and for Dusty. Because Sadie had known he'd come back, and she'd thought that they would both stay here at the ranch then.

Now she was afraid that instead of bringing them back together, she'd pushed them even further apart.

What if they both left...

Like Lem was leaving now, walking through the open door to the hall. Was he so disgusted with what she'd done, with her manipulations, that he didn't want to be around her anymore?

A twinge of pain struck her heart for some odd reason. It wasn't as if she actually gave a hoot what Old Man Lemmon thought of her. They'd been rivals in childhood and enemies for years.

But then Ben had tried turning the matchmaking tables on her a few weeks ago and invited Lem to dinner one night; he'd been around the ranch entirely too often ever since. Sadie should have been relieved that he was leaving.

But she found herself asking him, "Where are you going?"

"To get Baker," he said. "I think he should check you out too."

"I'm fine," she assured him. And physically she was. Emotionally…

She hadn't been fine for a long time. But she'd had her moments of happiness, in those moments when her grandsons and great-grandsons had been happy. She wanted them all as happy as Jake and Ben were now.

"No, you're not, woman." Lem argued with her, just as he always had since they were little kids. He was one of the few who'd had the guts to take her on, to challenge her. Her husband had been another, but the original Big Jake Haven was gone now. "You're not fine because you just told me that I was right." He shook his head. "So something must be terribly wrong."

It was. Instead of a joyous reunion between husband and wife, Melanie had passed out and Dusty was angry. Just with Sadie or with Melanie too?

Since she'd never admitted to either of them that she'd known about their marriage, she hadn't been able to ask either of them what had gone wrong between them. Dusty's manager hadn't even been aware that they were separated. Why? What had caused Melanie to leave him? Was it because he hadn't told her about his family, about the ranch?

And why hadn't he? Was he ashamed of them? Or of himself?

Sadie wasn't sure she could come up with a scheme to fix this…to fix her grandson's marriage or her own relationship with him…

CHAPTER FIVE

IS IT TRUE?

Is any of it true?

The thoughts flitted through Dusty's head, making him as dizzy as he'd felt earlier when Ben's blond-haired, blue-eyed fiancée, Emily, had blurted out that Dusty's wife was pregnant.

With twins…

Melanie had squirmed out of his arms right after he'd closed the door to her bedroom. And Dusty, still shocked over all the recent revelations, had let her go. She hadn't gone far, though. She sat on the edge of her bed while Dusty, not certain how steady his own legs were now, continued to lean against that closed door. The solid hickory was probably all that was holding him up.

"Is it true?" He asked the thought that looped through his mind. "Are you pregnant?"

She looked thinner to him—or at least her face did, her cheekbones sharper, her eyes bigger—but her skin was luminescent, as if she were lit from within.

And her body...

Her blouse did appear tight, the buttons straining across her breasts and across her stomach, which had always been flat until now. His mouth dried out, making his tongue stick to the roof of it so he could barely speak. His voice was just a gruff murmur when he added, "With twins?"

She didn't speak, probably couldn't with the way her teeth were biting into her bottom lip, but she nodded.

And his heart stopped beating for a moment, or at least that was the way it felt to him when he pressed his hand against his chest.

Twins...

He couldn't think about that now, couldn't think about how he was going to be a father... like Dale had been. No. He would never be the kind of father that Dale had been. During Dusty's visits home to the ranch, which hadn't been as frequent as they should have been, Dusty had watched his twin with his young sons. Dale had been so solid and steady and patient with the rambunctious boys.

Dusty had teased his twin that Dusty's job, riding broncos and bulls, was a lot easier than what Dale did, helping Jake with the ranch, raising a family with Jenny…

But Dale hadn't regretted not joining the rodeo with Dusty. It was clear that he'd reveled in the life he'd built, in the family he'd made. Tears stung Dusty's eyes as they did every time he thought of his twin, but he quickly blinked them away and focused on his wife.

He had another question for her, one that was nearly as important as verifying if she was really pregnant. "Were you going to tell me?" he asked.

And she hesitated so long that he answered for her. "You weren't."

She sighed. "I don't know."

"You could have called me," he said, his stomach plummeting with the realization that she hadn't even planned to tell him that he was going to be a father. "I didn't have the service to *my* cell turned off, and I still have the same number. You *should* have called me."

Her face flushed then. "I figured you'd find out if you ever came back home."

"I went back to our home, right after the funeral," he said, now angry with her as well as his grandmother. "Because you shut off your phone." He'd gone out of his mind worrying about her, wondering what had happened, needing her…so badly. But she'd shut him out. If he was honest, though, he'd shut her out first when he hadn't taken the time to explain to her why he'd had to leave so suddenly after Jake had called him. He'd never forget arriving at the hospital that day…the pain of losing Dale so fresh. And, facing his family in his grief, he hadn't been able to find a way to tell them he'd gotten married, so had kept the news from them.

"You wouldn't talk to me," she reminded him. "You just took off, and I could tell something terrible had happened. So I called Tom, but he didn't know either. And I thought he was your best friend…"

Dusty shook his head. Tom was just a guy Dusty had known since he'd joined the rodeo circuit. Dale had been his best friend…even before they were born. He'd been his best friend in the womb. Tears stung his eyes, but he blinked them back to focus on her. "I talked to Tom, and he warned me that you'd packed up all your stuff and left. And when I got back to our home, I saw that he was right. You'd left me without a word, without even leaving a note to explain why you took off."

She and all her things had been gone. All but one. And if she hadn't left that behind, he might have wondered if it had ever happened, if they'd ever been married. She'd left behind her ring; the gold-and-diamond band he'd bought in the chapel gift shop moments before sliding it onto her finger. He wore it now on a chain around his neck.

Her flush deepened to a darker red. "When I said home, I meant here," she said. "I was waiting to see if you were coming home to the ranch. But you don't really consider it home, do you?"

"It's where I grew up," he said. "So it'll always be home, but I haven't lived here for more than a decade." Since he'd left eleven years ago to fulfill the dream he'd had for so long; the dream that had had everyone comparing him to their absent mother. But now he knew why Darlene had really left.

"But they needed you here," Melanie said. "With Jenny and Dale gone, the boys needed all their remaining family around them. And Jake needed you to help him with the ranch."

Now his face flushed with guilt and regret. If he'd only known…

"How did you wind up here?" he asked, although he was pretty darn sure that he knew: Sadie. "How did you find out about Ranch Haven?"

She emitted a little puff of breath. "Not like I should have. Not from you."

Heat suffused his face again with embarrassment and shame. He should have told her about his family, but he'd had no idea how. And then he'd been afraid she would be angry that he'd misled her into thinking he had no family, and that he'd lose her. He hadn't been wrong; he'd lost her for the past two months, having no idea where she was. That she was here...

She continued. "I was offered a job as physical therapist to a seven-year-old recovering from an auto accident."

Yep, Sadie. "And you didn't think that was suspicious?" he asked.

She shrugged. "No more suspicious than the man I thought was my husband racing off at the crack of dawn after some mysterious phone call."

His skin burned as his embarrassment increased.

"I took the job because I wanted to get away from the rodeo," she said.

Away from him...

"I had no idea he was your nephew. I had no idea you *had* a nephew."

"So you've been here all this time?" he asked.

She nodded. "For the past eight weeks."

Now anger replaced his shame. If he hadn't been so anxious to find her, he would have. If he'd stuck around just a little longer.

"I've been here with your family longer than you were," she declared, her voice thick with recrimination.

"I would have been back already," he said in defense of his long absence. Despite what his family thought of him, he wasn't his mother. Or at least he wasn't what his family and he had once thought their mother was: selfish, self-absorbed…

"Where were you all this time?" she asked. "Were you riding again? Back on the circuit?"

She must not have been talking to her father, or to any of her family either. At least, she hadn't been talking with them about *him*. She must not have been watching rodeos or the news either. Or she would have known that his absence from the circuit had been noted as well. His manager had put out a statement to explain it was due to a loss in his family.

Dusty hadn't just lost his twin and sister-in-law, though. He'd lost his wife as well.

"No, I wasn't riding," he said. "Well, except for that rematch with Midnight, but that was a private thing…" A challenge he hadn't been able to turn down, a much-needed boost to an ego that had suffered from his wife's abandonment, which had felt so much like his mother's. Until he'd found Darlene Haven, until he'd learned…

"Then what were you doing?" she asked. "Where have you been all this time?"

"I was looking for you!"

She jerked back then. "You were?"

"You had to know," he said. "I called your parents every day. Your boss. I checked in with all your friends." Heck, he'd staked out some of their houses and apartments. He was lucky no one had reported him for stalking. But she hadn't been in any of those places.

Her face flushed a deep crimson, and he knew that she knew, but she must not have cared, because she hadn't let any of them tell him where she was. *Here.*

"You were here," he said, still shocked that he'd looked everywhere else, but it had never occurred to him to check back at the ranch. Knowing now what he knew about Sadie, maybe he should have suspected. But how had Grandma known? Had Dale told her? "When did Grandma contact you?" he asked, wondering if she'd called her earlier, like right after the accident.

"She hired me a week and a half after you left that night," she said. "She contacted me through my boss, and I went to the hospital in Sheridan to work out a therapy plan with Miller's surgeon. He was released the day after the funeral, and I drove him here."

He snorted at the irony of that. "So you were on your way to Willow Creek as I was leaving..." And if he hadn't left, he would have known where she was this entire time. Maybe this was some kind of twisted punishment from his grandmother for his taking off like he had.

She nodded. "Yes, I was driving Miller back."

"I don't understand any of this," he admitted. "Why did you leave our apartment? Why did you move out and shut off your phone?" His chest ached with the hollowness he'd had since the accident—since he'd lost his twin, his sister-in-law, and his bride.

She drew in a shaky breath. "I left because I realized I didn't know you...that I didn't know anything about you. I never even knew you had a family..."

"I didn't have time that morning to tell you about them," he said. "When Jake called about the accident, about how serious it was, I just had to get here as fast as I could." He'd already known he was too late to help his twin or Jenny, but his nephews had needed him.

Apparently, they'd needed her more. At least, one of them had: Miller.

"You had a month before that night to tell me about your family, about the ranch," she said. "You had six weeks before we ever got married to tell me. While you were in physical therapy, we talked all about my life, about my family. You said you didn't have one." Her usually soft voice had risen with every word she threw at him.

"Dusty Chaps doesn't," he said.

"Wow," she murmured. "So I'm not the only one who doesn't know who you are. You don't know either."

That jarred him nearly as much as finding out about her pregnancy had. Twins...

Did he know who he was? After he'd left the ranch for the rodeo circuit, he had pretty much created a whole new identity for himself. It was almost as if Dusty Haven had died long before Dale had. Maybe he hadn't changed his name just because he hadn't wanted to be associated with his mother. Maybe he'd changed his name so he could disassociate from his life, from all the tragedies, from the guilt he'd felt for leaving home when Dale and Jake had stayed.

But Dale and Jenny's accident had taught him that it wasn't possible to escape from all the loss and pain. He wasn't mourning just their losses, though.

"Apparently, I didn't know you very well either," he said. "You knew something tragic had happened, that I had to go home, and instead of waiting for me to call you later, like I'd promised I would, you took off. You packed up and left without even talking to me, without even finding out what that tragedy was. Instead of being there for me…" Like he'd needed her so badly. His voice husky with his emotions, his pain, he continued. "You *ran* away. Why?"

She flinched as if he'd slapped her, and a twinge of regret gripped his heart. Maybe he shouldn't have been so harsh with her, but he'd been out of his mind with worry about her in addition to being out of his mind with grief over losing his twin, the person with whom he'd been the closest until he'd gotten married.

"I was worried about you after you rushed out of the apartment like you did, without even telling me where you were going except home," she said. "That's why I called Tom after you left, trying to figure out where *home* was, so I could join you. He had no clue either, but he sent Traci over to *comfort* me."

He snorted again at the thought of Tom's mercenary wife comforting anyone, most especially Melanie. Dusty had briefly dated the woman, but he hadn't had to go out with her more than a couple of times to realize that she was more interested in being with a famous rodeo rider than she was in being with *him*.

"Instead she showed me the picture you had showed her when you were dating…"

His brow wrinkled. "Picture? What picture?"

"The picture you kept in the chest with your trophies," she said. "The family portrait."

"Dale and Jenny and the boys?"

She nodded.

He hadn't showed it to Traci, but she must have snooped around his place while they were dating and found it. He hadn't displayed it because whenever anyone had seen it, they'd always assumed it was him, and when he said it wasn't, they'd asked too many questions.

Traci hadn't asked him about it though, and neither had Melanie. Apparently, they'd just made assumptions, like everyone seemed to do about Dusty.

"Because I didn't know that you had a twin,

I thought that was you in the picture," she replied, her voice sharp with her defensiveness now. "I thought that that family was yours. That you were already married."

"I married *you*," he said.

"I didn't think our marriage was real then," she said. "I don't even know now if it is. I didn't marry Dusty Haven. That's not the name on the certificate."

"My name is legally Dusty Chaps now."

And she flinched again. "You gave it all up. Your family. The ranch. Even your *name*. You're the one who ran away, Dusty, who's been running all these years."

He couldn't deny it, but he hadn't been running away. He'd been running toward his dream. She was the one who'd run away, from him, from their marriage. He was more than defensive now. He was furious. "You were happy to believe Traci," he accused her.

She blanched. "Happy?"

"You were happy to think the worst of me and have your confirmation that no man can be trusted, just like good old Shep. I'm not your father, Melanie. You shouldn't have thought the worst of me." And it hurt so much that she had, that she'd believed he'd lied and cheated and scammed her.

Tears stung his eyes again, but these tears weren't over the death of his twin, these were over the death of his marriage. And his chest tightened with that loss just as it had over the loss of Dale and Jenny.

He couldn't stay inside this room with her, couldn't stay with her without giving in to those tears, to his grief. So he finally jerked away from the door, then he yanked it open and, feeling a lot like his seven-year-old nephew, did just what she'd accused him of doing. He ran.

MELANIE WAS NEARLY as stunned by his departure as she'd been by his arrival. As stunned as she'd been that day Traci had come over to comfort her. Like Dusty had said, she'd been little comfort when she'd gone immediately for that chest and pulled out the portrait to show her.

The portrait of his home. Of his family...

Or so the woman had claimed, and had probably actually believed, just like Melanie had. She hadn't been happy to think that, but she hadn't realized there was another explanation, that Dusty had a twin who was so identical to him they were impossible to tell apart. All she'd seen was the man she'd thought was her husband clearly in love with the woman in his arms and with the children gathered around them among hay bales in a barn.

Dusty hadn't given her a chance to share with him now how stupid and betrayed and devastated she'd felt. He'd just run off without giving her a chance to defend herself. She hadn't known about Dale. She'd just accepted that Dusty had lied to her, that he'd tricked her. That he was already married with children...

And that he'd abandoned them like he'd abandoned her when he'd run off that morning. He'd left first.

But he really had had a family emergency. She hadn't realized what that was until she'd arrived at the ranch. Bruised, as Miller had been when she'd met him at the hospital, she hadn't consciously recognized him from that portrait, but she'd connected with him so deeply that maybe on some level she had. She hadn't known when she'd taken the job that Dusty's twin and sister-in-law had died, and his nephews had been injured. She hadn't known he'd had any family at all because he had lied to her about that.

He had lied to her every time she'd tried to delve deeper into his past, into his life before he'd joined the rodeo. He'd acted as if, like her, the rodeo life was the only one he'd ever known.

She hadn't been wrong to take off like she had, to turn off her cell service, to not call him...until she'd learned the truth. But once she'd found out that his secret family wasn't a wife and kids but brothers, nephews and a grandmother, she hadn't known what to do.

Just like she didn't know now. Instead of running after him, she sat on the bed, staring at her open door, at the empty hallway. But it didn't stay empty for long.

A long shadow crossed it, and she drew in a shaky breath. He'd come back.

But it was Jake who appeared with Miller at his side. The boy's face was red and swollen from tears. She jumped up from the bed and rushed to him. "Are you all right?" she asked as she grasped his thin shoulders. "What happened? Is your leg bothering you?"

He didn't say anything, just kept crying, the sobs racking his little body. She knelt on the carpet and drew him into her arms, clasping his trembling frame close to her.

She stared up at Jake, questioning him with just a look, but he shook his head. "He wouldn't talk to me. I thought you might be able to reassure him..."

Of course. She eased back and cupped her young patient's face in her hands. "Miller," she said. "It's not your fault that I fainted. I am the adult. I know that I need to eat. You didn't do anything wrong. You did everything right."

That seemed to mean a lot to him, that he'd done nothing wrong. When they were doing the exercises to strengthen his leg, he made certain that he was doing them exactly the way she'd taught him. And Emily had mentioned that he got very upset if he missed a problem on homework or a test, that he never wanted to do anything wrong.

Melanie was worried the boy thought he was somehow responsible for the accident that had taken his parents, that had nearly taken his leg. But anytime she tried to talk to him about it, he shut her down, just like he must have shut down Jake when he'd tried to comfort him.

The seven-year-old sucked up some tears and snot, blinked his hazel eyes until they cleared, and focused on her face. "Are you really married to Uncle Dusty?" he asked.

Apparently, she was…if he had legally changed his name. But could she believe him? Could she believe anything he told her when he'd kept so much from her? She was not about to dump those doubts on a little boy, so she nodded.

And now Jake expelled a breath. When she glanced up at him, he stepped back, but he didn't leave them alone. He was clearly still worried about his nephew, or maybe he was worried about her as well. Jake Haven was a good man, one who took his responsibilities seriously; he cared about the ranch and most especially about his family.

"Are you going to leave with him?" Miller asked.

She stiffened. "Did he leave already?"

"I dunno..." Miller shrugged. "But he always does. Uncle Dusty only ever stays at the ranch for a couple of days, and usually just around holidays, before he has to go back to the rodeo."

She leaned forward and pressed her lips against Miller's crinkled brow. "I'm not leaving," she assured him. "I'm staying here as long as you need me."

He threw his arms around her neck and clasped her tightly. "Then you're going to be here forever..."

Her heart flooded with warmth, with love, for this sweet boy. All the boys were wonderful, but Miller was extra special to her. They'd bonded in that hospital room when they'd both been feeling so very alone.

"I'm not leaving you now," she assured him. "But I don't know if I can stay forever."

He eased back and nodded. "I know," he said and, with a wisdom far beyond his young years, he murmured, "Nothing lasts forever."

No. It didn't. At least not for Melanie...

Her honeymoon sure hadn't lasted. And her marriage was unlikely to last either. But if she wanted to leave Dusty permanently, she would have to leave the ranch too.

Even though he'd run away from it right out of high school, Ranch Haven was Dusty's home, not hers. Just as this was his family, not hers—even though she appreciated them far more than he seemed to.

She wouldn't have left them for any reason. And if she had...

She certainly wouldn't have lied about having them. She wouldn't have denied their existence. No. Dusty didn't deserve them.

But they weren't hers to keep...no matter how much all of them had come to mean to her.

CHAPTER SIX

DUSTY DUCKED INTO the dim light of the big horse barn. His heart hammered in his chest, and his lungs burned with exertion not just from running out here but from his effort to hold back his sobs. He'd already cried so much over losing Dale and Jenny and Melanie…

If it hadn't been clear to him before, it was clear to him now that he'd lost her the same day he'd lost his twin. No. He'd lost her earlier, when he hadn't told her the truth, when he hadn't been honest with her about having a family and a home. He'd done that so she wouldn't think badly of him for leaving them for the rodeo. But apparently she'd thought even worse of him.

She'd thought he'd tricked her into a relationship—that he'd already had a wife, a family—when he'd married her. His stomach churned with how terrible a person she'd believed he was. Sure, he'd made some mistakes, some *big* mistakes, but he'd never purposely tried to deceive her.

He just hadn't wanted her to think less of him for not helping with the ranch, for running off to the rodeo like his mother had. Obviously he'd been right to worry about Melanie's reaction because she had leaped to the worse conclusions about him. That he was a bigamist. That he'd abandon a wife and children.

Pain jabbed his heart at how easily she'd believed those horrible things about him. He was hurt now. And angry...

Not just with Melanie but also with his grandmother. He'd been so angry that he hadn't stopped when he'd passed her suite even though the door had been open. He'd glanced inside and seen her sitting on one of her easy chairs with that little dog curled up on her lap. She'd seen him, too, but she hadn't called out to him either.

He'd deal with her later. Right now he had to deal with what his brothers had kept calling him about... Midnight. He walked farther into the barn, down the wide aisle between the horse stalls. He whistled softly.

And a horse arched his head over the stall of his door, his glossy black coat and mane glimmering even in the dim light of the barn.

"Here you are," Dusty murmured as he approached the bronco.

The horse stared at him with those big dark eyes, and it was as if the animal was looking right inside him. It had been like that the first time they'd met, when Midnight had tossed him off his back without much effort. The animal had seemed to laugh at him for being cocky enough to think he could ride him when no other rider had been able to.

In their second matchup—after the accident, after Dusty had confirmed that Melanie had moved out without talking to him—Midnight had somehow seemed to sense his pain. Maybe he'd felt it as well. It was as if the horse had pitied him so much that he'd given Dusty the win. As sweet as that victory had been, it had been hollow too. Empty.

Sure, it had reminded Dusty of how much he loved to ride, how much he loved the rodeo, and maybe that was what had hurt. Because he knew he probably had to take off the rest of the season.

At least.

There was no way he could focus on riding while his nephews were hurting so badly. They weren't the only ones missing Dale and Jenny. Once he'd ridden Midnight, Dusty hadn't been able to call the one person he'd always shared everything with. Dale. Even his wedding...

He'd called Dale after the elopement. Instead of judging him for being too impulsive, Dale had congratulated him sincerely. He'd been happy that Dusty had found the woman he loved like Dale had loved Jenny.

Once Dusty had fallen for Melanie, he'd understood his twin more. He'd known why Dale had made the decisions he had, to marry Jenny Miller after graduation and stay at the ranch. To let Dusty chase his rodeo dream alone.

That dream had grown to include Melanie.

He pressed his hand to his chest, feeling for the ring dangling from the chain tucked inside his shirt. And beneath that ring, his heart ached.

Midnight arched his neck as if reaching for him. Dusty stepped closer to the stall, and Midnight bumped his head against Dusty's, knocking his hat to the ground. "Hey there, boy," he murmured to the bronco as he reached up and ran his hand along the velvety hair on the horse's head. "I hear you've been causing trouble around here..."

A groom had been injured. Dusty felt a flash of concern and regret over that, although Jake had assured him that the young man was fine now. During one of Dusty's calls with his brother, he'd also learned that Caleb had been hurt trying to get into the horse's stall. The little boy was clearly enamored with the animal. Dusty couldn't blame the kid; he was too. He continued to stroke the horse's head.

"You're a tough one," Dusty told him. "You make people earn your trust." A gasp slipped out of his lips as he realized that Melanie was the same way because of her father, because of all of Shep's lies and deceptions. She made people earn her trust too.

How had Dusty convinced her to marry him? He wasn't sure how he had. But he knew now that he'd blown it. By not being completely honest with her, he'd destroyed the little trust she'd reluctantly given him, and he was unlikely to earn another chance to win it.

"How do you do that?"

The question startled Dusty, and he whirled around to find Caleb holding out the hat Midnight had knocked off his head. Usually the bronco reacted to anyone's arrival, but he clearly recognized and liked the little blond boy. He let out a nicker and bobbed his head over the stall door in Caleb's direction.

"How do you do what?" Dusty asked him.

"How do you earn Midnight's trust?"

"I think you already have," Dusty assured him as he took the Stetson from his small hands.

That wasn't all Caleb held, and Midnight must have known it. His eyes seemed to widen at the sight of the bunch of carrots in the little boy's grasp. Caleb used a booted foot to kick a pail over, then stood on top of it so he could reach the horse.

Midnight carefully took the bunch of carrots from the boy, who giggled at the brush of the horse's lips against his skin. Dusty smiled at their sweet interaction. "You figured out the way to his heart."

If only he could reach Melanie that easily. Convince her to give him another chance. But would she be able to trust him again? Could he trust *her* again? Or would some part of him always wonder if she'd run at the first sign of trouble, like she had this time? Without trust, their relationship had no hope of surviving. But they would have to relate to each other for the sake of their children, their unborn twins.

Dusty was going to be a father...

He still hadn't processed that, couldn't quite believe it. They'd gotten married so quickly that they hadn't talked about having kids, about starting a family. All that had seemed so far into the future…

They'd only been focused on each other during those idyllic weeks of their honeymoon. But the honeymoon was over now; it had ended months ago.

"Uncle Dusty!" Caleb tugged on Dusty's hand as if he'd been seeking his attention and hadn't received it. "You think Midnight loves me?"

Dusty nodded. "I'm sure he does." If only Dusty could understand human emotions as easily as he could those of animals…

But before he could figure out how Melanie felt about him, he had to work out his own feelings. He'd loved her when he'd married her, and he loved her during their honeymoon. But he didn't love that she hadn't given him a chance to explain anything. That, instead of waiting for him, she'd run away.

Just like his mother had run away from the family without explaining her real reasons for leaving. If they'd known…

He sighed.

And Caleb squeezed his hand as if offering reassurance. "It's okay, Uncle Dusty," Caleb said. "Midnight still loves you too."

A smile tugged at Dusty's lips.

"You know you can love more than one," Caleb wisely explained. "And Midnight loves a lot of us now. He loves Uncle Jake and Uncle Ben…" He huffed out a breath. "But he sure doesn't love Uncle Baker."

Dusty chuckled. "Well, Uncle Baker doesn't like the ranch much, and Midnight probably senses that."

"I love the ranch," Caleb said.

And it was clear that the kid did. He might not have been born a Haven, but he'd been born to live at Ranch Haven.

"Do you love the ranch?"

"*Love* it…" he hedged as he considered the question. He'd spent a lot of years resenting it, resenting that Dale had stayed here instead of leaving with him. Maybe it wouldn't have been so scary, so hard, to break into the rodeo scene if he hadn't been alone.

Maybe that was why he'd never mentioned his family to anyone at the rodeo, including Melanie, because he'd resented how they hadn't supported his dream, how they'd instead judged him to be just as irresponsible as their mother. For years, he'd believed what they all had, too; that she just hadn't wanted the responsibility of raising her children or working the ranch anymore.

And he'd thought he was like her because he hadn't wanted those responsibilities either. That hadn't been Mom's real problem, though. No, she'd thought she was too responsible.

His head pounded with all the recent revelations he'd learned. The latest one had shocked him the most.

He was going to be a father. To twins…

Caleb grasped Dusty's hand a little more tightly. "I'm glad you love the ranch too," he said, misinterpreting what Dusty had meant. "Uncle Jake taught me to ride horses, but I want you to teach me how to ride Midnight and bulls and—"

"Whoa, little guy." Dusty chuckled at the kid's enthusiasm. Caleb was too young, but Dusty didn't want to be the one to dash the little boy's dreams. He knew how important dreams were, especially when you were young. If he hadn't had his dream, he might not have survived losing his dad, then his mom taking off afterward. But his dream had given him something to focus on besides his pain, his loss. Caleb had already lost his dad, so maybe he needed his dream as much as Dusty had. "We better ask your mom first," he told the little boy.

Caleb's slight shoulders slumped with defeat. "She'll say no. That I'm too little. How old were you when you started training for the rodeo?"

"I was smaller than you," he admitted and smiled at the memory. "Your uncle Dale and I used to ride hay bales in this barn…while we roped other hay bales…" And each other and their brothers.

"Riding hay bales is easy for me," Caleb said. "Little Jake is still too little to ride them, though. He fell off once."

Dusty was definitely out of his element here, with knowing what the appropriate age was for kids to do things. How was he going to manage with his own kids? How was he going to be a father when his own had only been alive for the first nine years of his life?

"Like I said, we better talk to your mom," Dusty said. Katie was obviously doing a good job raising her sweet little boy.

"Let's ask Daddy Jake," Caleb suggested.

Jake was a stepfather now. And from Katie's reaction to his speech at their welcome home party, Dusty suspected his brother might be a father, as well, in the near future.

How far along was Melanie? When was Dusty going to become a father?

He shouldn't have run out on their conversation; he still had so many questions. But he'd needed a moment to compose himself, to process everything he'd learned. That she'd thought so little of him, even less than his family did; that he could have had a whole secret family of his own...

He sucked in a breath and forced down that touch of betrayal. He was actually feeling better now, and he didn't know if that was because of Midnight or Caleb.

The little boy was tugging on his hand again, pulling him toward the open doors of the barn. "Maybe we should ask Grandma Sadie..." Caleb suggested.

"I do have to talk to Grandma Sadie," Dusty said. About so many things...

WHEN HER BEDROOM door closed behind Jake and Miller, Melanie released a ragged breath. She hadn't been alone for more than a minute since Dusty's arrival at the ranch earlier that afternoon. While she wanted to make sure that Miller was all right and that he wasn't afraid she was going to leave him, she needed a moment to herself to make sure that she was really all right.

To deal with her fear...

She was afraid of so many things. She was

afraid that the mistake she'd made might not have been marrying Dusty but leaving him without giving him a chance to explain anything to her.

He'd had his chance just now and, instead of explaining, he'd accused her of wanting to think the worst of him, of using any excuse to leave him.

To run away…

Was that what she'd done?

Her legs shaky yet, she didn't feel like running now. She walked instead back to her bed and sank down onto the soft mattress. She hadn't had more than a couple bites of that cookie Miller had brought her, so she hadn't raised her blood sugar enough. She needed to get something more to eat. But first, she needed more than a minute to herself.

A knock on her bedroom door had her sighing. Who was it now? Miller? Had he slipped away from Jake who'd convinced him to let her rest?

She couldn't turn him away if it was Miller. But if it was Dusty…

She definitely needed to rest and to eat before she was strong enough to deal with him and with all the emotions that he brought out in her.

"Melanie," Taye called out through the door. "Are you all right? I've brought you up some things to eat, to boost your blood sugar back up."

Taye…

She was the youngest of all the women Sadie had hired to help with her grieving great-grandsons, but she was by far the most nurturing of them.

"Come in," Melanie called back as the door was already opening.

Of course, Taye would want to see for herself that she was all right. And the cook only seemed to believe that people were all right if they were well fed. It wasn't Taye who walked through the door first but Emily. Taye followed her, trailed by Katie.

"We all wanted to check on you," Katie said with concern as she closed the door behind them, shutting them all inside with Melanie.

"We wanted to check on you and then interrogate you if you're feeling better," Emily admitted with her usual bluntness. She sat next to Melanie on the bed and asked, "Are you all right?"

Tears rushed to Melanie's eyes, but she nodded. She'd grown up an only child, with most of that childhood spent on the road, so she had no siblings and few friends. Until she'd come to the ranch…

While she wasn't very familiar with close relationships, Taye, Emily, and especially Katie, felt more like sisters to her than friends. Taking care of these boys together over the past two months had bonded them so deeply. She blinked against the tears again and whispered, "I'm so sorry."

"For what?" Katie asked as she sat on the other side of Melanie and closed her arms around her.

Her kindness released Melanie's tears.

While she sobbed, Emily answered for her. "For not telling us that she's married to Dusty."

"Not that you need to apologize to us," Taye added. "We totally understand that you're a private person…"

"And this is your private business," Katie said. "You don't have to tell us anything, but if you'd like to talk…"

The pressure on Melanie's chest, the guilt she'd felt over not being forthcoming with them, eased. "It's not that I haven't wanted to tell you all," she said.

"But you didn't know how?" Katie asked.

She shook her head and focused on Emily, who would understand the best. "I was too proud. I didn't want to admit to how stupid I'd been, marrying someone I barely knew..." Her voice cracked. "You all knew him better than I did, and I'm his wife."

"I understand," Emily assured her.

Melanie had a lot in common with Emily because they both struggled to trust anyone and they were both very proud. Emily had been pitied in school because, after her single mother died, no other relatives or foster families would keep her, and she'd wound up living with one of her teachers. Emily had hated feeling like a charity case.

While people might have felt badly for Emily's situation, she had been in no way responsible for it. Melanie wished she could say the same, but that wasn't true of her and Dusty. She hadn't had to even go out with him let alone marry him. But she'd been crushing on him for years, watching him ride at every rodeo and listening to all of his interviews. And once she'd gotten to know him better during those six weeks of physical therapy, or so she'd thought, she hadn't been as scared of falling in love with a rodeo rider as she'd once been. Because she'd already fallen for him. And then he'd proposed...

She'd thought he'd fallen just as hard for her.

She'd believed that with that much love, they could make their marriage work.

"I was such a fool…" she murmured as humiliation overwhelmed her. She, of all people, should have known better…after how foolish her mother had been to fall for her father's lies over and over again.

"Why do you feel that way?" Taye asked, setting the lunch tray on the nightstand. "But before you answer us, drink this orange juice, and have some of this soup." She pushed the glass of juice into Melanie's hand.

Her fingers trembled a bit, but she wrapped them more tightly around the glass and drank. Taye took the empty cup from her and replaced it with a bowl of beef stew. "Eat it before it gets cold."

The bowl was warm in Melanie's hands. Worried that the women fussing around her might spoon-feed her if she didn't eat, she quickly fed herself. And when the bowl was empty, Taye took that too. When she set it on the tray, she reached for something else. But Melanie held up a hand. "I'm feeling full…"

"And she has a story to tell," Emily said.

"If you want to," Taye said with a pointed glance at the blond teacher.

Melanie sighed and nodded. "I would

have told you before—I should have told you before—but everybody was always talking about how Dusty would never get married and settle down."

Katie smiled. "And he was already married to you. You should have told us how wrong we were."

"That's the thing," Melanie said. "I didn't know who was wrong. If you all were or if I was…" She shrugged. "I didn't even know if we were really married because I'm not married to Dusty Haven. I'm married to Dusty Chaps."

Emily laughed. "Who? What?"

"That's his rodeo name," Katie said. "I've followed his career for years. He's doing really well for himself."

Melanie nodded. "Really well."

"I was so glad he achieved his dream of becoming a champion rider," Katie continued. Since she'd dated Jake when they were in high school together, she knew his brothers very well.

"You don't think he should have stayed and helped Jake, like Dale did?" Melanie asked with surprise. Jake had quit college and sacrificed his relationship with Katie to take care of the ranch and his younger brothers. While

Dusty, according to his family, had taken off as soon as he'd graduated high school.

"That was Dale's choice," Katie said. "To stay, just like it was Jake's to quit college and break up with me." Her green eyes dimmed with sadness, but she quickly blinked it away and smiled. "Besides, I wouldn't have had Caleb if things hadn't happened like they had."

Melanie admired Katie for so many reasons, but most of all for her strength; she was so incredibly resilient and such a good mother. Melanie hoped she could handle parenting as well as Katie did.

"I thought Ben was selfish for not helping more," Emily said. "He didn't quit college like Jake did when their grandfather died."

"He had a full scholarship for that Ivy League college, and Jake and Sadie were adamant he couldn't give it up," Katie interjected.

Emily nodded. "I know that now, and I really respect that he only gave up the ranch because he wanted to take care of the entire town of Willow Creek. He wants to revitalize it and carry out all the plans for it that his great-grandfather had." Ben had followed in the footsteps of Sadie's father, who'd been mayor of Willow Creek for years.

Taye chuckled. "You already sound like a politician's wife."

If Taye had said that a couple of weeks ago, or even a couple of days ago, Emily would have glared at her. But now she just grinned and said, "Good." Then she focused on Melanie again and insisted, "So tell us everything."

And because these women were more like sisters than friends and because she trusted them, Melanie told them everything that had happened between her and Dusty, and everything that she'd thought and worried about since finding out that she was pregnant. She didn't want to raise her babies alone, but she didn't want to force Dusty to be a father when it was clear that he'd barely been able to be a loving uncle to his orphaned nephews.

But was that because of her? Because he'd been looking for her? She knew that he'd called her family and friends because they'd urged her to call him back. But she hadn't been ready to talk to him then. She wasn't really ready now.

"Oh, Melanie," Katie murmured as she hugged her again. "I'm so sorry you've gone through all that alone."

"That's my fault," she admitted. "I realize now that I could have talked to any of you."

"To all of us," Taye told her.

Emily nodded, but not particularly vigorously. She was the one who'd prodded Melanie the most to talk, so confused, Melanie quirked a brow.

"What?" she asked the young teacher who never usually hesitated to speak her mind.

Emily shrugged. "I don't want to upset you…"

"You won't," Melanie assured her.

"I just wonder why you didn't talk to Dusty," she said.

"After I saw the picture?" Melanie asked. She tried to draw in a deep breath but that panic she'd felt at the time was back on her chest, pressing on her. She'd been so devastated. So shocked…

"Yes, obviously it wasn't him," Emily said, "and you would have known that if you'd talked to him."

Emily was so candid, that was exactly how she thought. But Melanie hadn't been raised with straightforward people. "I believed he had no family, so I didn't know about Dale. I didn't know that Dusty had an explanation—"

"But if you would have talked to him," Emily repeated.

Tears of regret stung Melanie's eyes.

"I'm sorry," Emily said. "I'm not judging you. I understand—"

Melanie shook her head...because, evidently, Emily did not understand. "My dad was a cheater," she said then cleared the tears from her throat and corrected herself. "*Is* a cheater. But no matter how many times my mother has caught him, she stays with him because he always talks her into it. I didn't want to give Dusty that opportunity to sweet talk me into giving him another chance, like my mom always does. And the thought of being the other woman..." She shuddered. "Of putting another woman through the pain my mother has been put through..."

"But you aren't the other woman," Emily said. "You are the woman he married. Once you realized that when you moved into the ranch, why didn't you call him?"

Melanie felt that rush of anger she'd felt then. "I was mad at him, mad that he lied to me and claimed he had no family. I was mad that I didn't even know his real name. But I think I was the maddest that he wasn't here for his nephews, for his family..." If that was because he'd been searching for her in person as well as calling around, she wouldn't be able to hang onto that self-righteousness any longer.

Emily nodded more vigorously in agreement. "I get that," she said. "I understand being wrong about someone. I was wrong about Ben. I thought he was a shallow charmer, but I had misjudged him. He's a much better man than I thought he was." She smiled brightly.

Melanie cringed at the twinge of envy she felt for Emily. "According to what I learned since staying at the ranch, I misjudged Dusty the other way."

"Or did you?" Emily asked. "Maybe everyone else is wrong about him. I wasn't the only one who didn't realize how good a man Ben is."

"No, you were the only one," Katie said.

"I think his winning the election for mayor proves that," Taye pointed out.

Emily laughed and shook her head. "No…"

"You really were," Melanie added. Ben and Baker had jobs and responsibilities in town, but they still gave their nephews and the ranch more time and attention than Dusty had. And Dusty wasn't even riding right now. But apparently, he'd been looking for her as well as calling her family and friends. Emily was right. Melanie should have talked to him before now. But she'd been so afraid of getting her heart broken again. Now she was all talked out. "I think I need to rest," she murmured.

"Of course," Taye said. "Take a nap."

She doubted she would be able to sleep, but she definitely needed some time to herself. To think… And to process all the feelings rushing over her, stealing her breath and making her heart pound with that panic she'd felt when Dusty had gotten that call and rushed off to his family…

But now she realized that he wasn't the only one she didn't really know. She didn't know herself anymore. She didn't know what she wanted or what she was capable of.

Could she forgive him for the secrets he'd kept? Could she ever trust him again?

And, more importantly, could she ever trust herself?

CHAPTER SEVEN

SADIE FLINCHED AS the cuff tightened around her arm, but that was just a mild discomfort compared to everything else she was feeling. "You shouldn't have made such a fuss," she admonished Lem, who'd followed through on his threat to have Baker check on her.

"He was right, Grandma," Baker said. "Your blood pressure is up, and your pulse is racing too."

"And why wouldn't it be with all the excitement of Dusty returning and revealing he's already married?" she asked.

Baker snorted. "Like any of what happened today surprised you," he said, his topaz eyes assessing her. "You knew Melanie and Dusty were married before you hired her, didn't you?"

"Of course she did," Lem said, but almost as if he was proud of her. Then he added, "So if it isn't the excitement, what could be causing her blood pressure to be high?"

She sighed and admitted. "It often is. My doctor wants to put me on heart medication."

Lem gasped.

"And you thought I didn't have a heart," she teased him.

He shook his head. "I know you do, Sadie March Haven, and it's so big that it overrules your head sometimes and gets you into trouble."

Old Lem knew her much better than she'd realized. But then, he'd known her longer than anyone else alive had. They'd grown up together. But they were supposed to have grown old with other people. Lem with his sweet, beloved Mary, and she with her husband, Big Jake.

She should have realized when she'd lost first her sons and then her husband that things didn't always work out how they were meant to—and maybe that was going to be the case with Dusty and Melanie. While Lem had gone to get Baker, she'd seen Dusty walk past her door on his way out. But he hadn't stopped.

Where had he gone? And was he ever coming back?

As if just thinking about him had conjured him up, Dusty appeared in the doorway, leaning against the jamb. But his body was tense, his jaw taut, as if he was clenching it. He radiated his disapproval.

"Your heart is going to get you in trouble if you don't listen to your doctor," Baker admonished her. "And you—" He pointed at his brother. "Her blood pressure is up, so don't upset her."

"Don't upset her?" Dusty asked. "I better leave then." And he turned around and left.

And she wondered…was he angry with her about more than Melanie? Could he know about what else she'd kept from him—what she'd kept from all of them?

"I now pronounce you man and wife," the Elvis impersonator said.

A smile twitched Melanie's lips; she found it all so funny. So surreal…

Then Dusty leaned down and kissed her. And she realized what she'd done. She hadn't just fallen for a rodeo rider; she'd married him…

Melanie jerked awake from the dream, from the memory she often had of that day. Her wedding day. For even then it had felt like a dream, even as it had been happening, even as they'd been getting married…on their very first date. But she'd known that while she'd been working with him on his injury, she'd fallen from infatuation into love with him.

She huddled under the warmth of the blankets, in the comfort of the soft bed, and marveled that she'd managed to take the nap that Taye, Emily and Katie had urged her to take. That was probably due to the food coma she'd fallen into after eating that entire bowl of hearty, delicious stew Taye had brought her.

Yet her stomach rumbled now as if it was empty. How long had she slept? Blinking, she cleared the sleep from her eyes and her mind, and peered at the clock next to her bed. Hours; it was nearly dinnertime—no wonder she was hungry again.

Knowing now how easily her blood sugar level dropped, she wasn't going to miss another meal. She had more than herself to worry about now. She ran her hands across her stomach. She had the babies.

She must have gotten pregnant very soon after their wedding. When she'd taken Miller to Sheridan to have his cast removed a couple of weeks ago, she'd seen a doctor herself and had an ultrasound. She was even further along than she'd suspected: fourteen weeks—and carrying twins. She didn't want to raise her babies alone, but she wanted to make sure that everything she did was right for her children.

Was Dusty right for her children, even though they were his as well? Or would he hurt and disappointment them as her father had her so many times?

From how Dusty had acted after carrying her up to her room, he hadn't seemed overjoyed at the prospect of becoming a father. Having children wasn't something they'd discussed before getting married, but it was clear they had not discussed enough before they'd gone on their first date to that wedding chapel. Would they have the chance now to talk about their future?

With a sigh, she tossed back her blankets and dragged herself out of the warmth of her bed. After using the bathroom, she sauntered down the back stairwell toward the rumble of voices coming from the kitchen. Once again, she couldn't discern Dusty's voice among the others. Had he left?

The minute she stepped into the kitchen that rumble fell to an eerie silence, and everyone stared at her. Everyone included her husband, who jumped up from the seat he'd taken at the table. Her face heated until her skin fairly burned with self-consciousness.

"Are you all right?" Dusty asked.

No. And he was the reason why, but she just politely nodded. "Yes."

Miller scrambled off the bench where he sat with his brothers and Caleb, and rushed to her side. "Are you sure, Miss—Aunt Melanie?" he asked. "You were sleeping for a long time."

"I was much more tired than I realized," she admitted.

"You will be," Baker said, "being pregnant with twins. You need to get your rest." The youngest of the Haven brothers usually didn't come to the house for meals. He hadn't eaten with the rest of the family even during the two weeks he'd been living at the ranch to help out while Jake and Katie were gone. Was the paramedic worried about her?

Miller clasped her hand and tugged her toward the table. "Sit down," he said with concern. "You need to sit down."

Dusty held out a chair near him, but Miller pulled her right past her husband over to the bench.

She smiled at the little boy and assured him, "I'm fine, Miller. Really. I feel so much better after my nap." She smiled at Taye, too, who, with Emily and Ben's help, was setting steaming serving bowls on the table. "And after my big bowl of stew."

"I'm sure you're already seeing a doctor," Baker said, "so you might want to give them a call and just make sure everything's okay."

A little chill raced down her spine that maybe the paramedic was concerned that there was something else going on with her. Something other than low blood sugar. Unfortunately there was: stress.

And that increased as everyone continued to study her. She knew they were all concerned and curious. But she was uncomfortable, her face flushing with more embarrassment, partly because she had only seen a doctor in Sheridan once during her pregnancy. She needed to get a local doctor of obstetrics in Willow Creek... if she intended to stay in Willow Creek.

Miller hadn't released her hand even after she sat beside him on the bench. For him, she had to stay in Willow Creek; the poor kid had already lost too much.

"This is why she didn't tell us what was going on," Emily pointed out. "You're all staring at her." The teacher shuddered, as if reliving those times in school when everyone had stared at her.

Melanie smiled at her with gratitude. Emily really did understand her the most.

Her friend asserted, "So let's let the woman eat in peace."

Just as the kids usually jumped to obey her, the adults did now as well. Even Sadie picked up her spoon again while Mr. Lemmon, sitting next to her, hadn't even put down his. He had become a fixture at the ranch for meals. He claimed it was because Sadie had stolen his favorite cook from the town diner when she'd hired Taye. But Melanie suspected that Ben's matchmaking plan might have been starting to work with the elderly couple.

Ben chuckled. "I see someone's in bossy-teacher mode." His fiancée glared at him, and he chuckled again. "Hey, no complaints here. I like it when you get bossy."

Instead of arguing with him like she used to before their engagement, Emily agreed. "I am in bossy-teacher mode, so, on that note, I'd like to have a family meeting after dinner in the ranch business office."

"Family meeting?" Caleb asked, his voice quavering with excitement. As an only child, like Melanie had been, it was clear that he loved being part of a big family now.

"Are we going to talk about Uncle Dusty

teaching me to be a rodeo rider?" Caleb asked. He turned to his mother then, his eyes filling with confusion. "I thought you said we had to wait a few years before we could have that discussion."

Ben grinned. "That's not what we're going talk about, buddy. Just boring stuff that really wouldn't interest you or your cousins."

"So this meeting is just going to be for the adult half of the family this time," Emily told the boys with a smile.

"What does that mean?" Caleb asked again.

"It means you, Ian, Miller and Little Jake will be watching movies with Mr. Lemmon in the playroom," Emily elaborated.

Dread gripped Melanie. Was this meeting going to be about her and Dusty? She wasn't about to address his entire family regarding their situation when she wasn't entirely sure what she wanted.

A divorce or…

It wouldn't matter what she wanted if Dusty didn't want the same things. But apparently she wasn't going to get the chance to talk to him privately, if all of his family was going to be present.

"I'll help you, Mr. Lemmon," Melanie offered.

"I'll be helping too," Taye said. "So you're not outnumbered."

Mr. Lemmon smiled but insisted, "I don't need any help."

"He handles a lot more kids than this every holiday season with no issues," Ben reminded them of his deputy mayor's moonlighting role as the town square Santa Claus.

Miller's hazel eyes widened as if understanding was dawning on him that Santa Claus might actually be dining with them and not at the North Pole. To distract him, Melanie said, "Looks like you're done with dinner, so why don't you and I help Miss Taye clean up the kitchen while everyone else has that meeting."

Taye shook her head. "You're family, Mel. You need to be part of it. I'm just the cook."

"No, you're not," Sadie said with a glance at Baker.

And Melanie realized that Katie and Emily and Jake and Ben had all been right this entire time. Sadie had hatched some scheme to marry off all her grandsons to the women she'd hired to help out with her great-grandsons. Melanie had saved her some trouble because she'd married Dusty before she'd come here. She'd married him before she'd even known who he was. Clearly, Sadie had known about her.

But how? Nobody else in Dusty's family had. Maybe he'd told his twin, and his twin might have told their grandmother before he'd died.

She winced as a pang of regret struck her that she'd never met Dale and Jenny. From everything she'd heard about them, they sounded like such a loving, devoted couple as well as wonderful parents. She would have loved to have gotten to know them, but Dusty had denied her that chance when he'd denied having a family. Her anger with him surged up again.

"What's this *family* meeting about?" Dusty asked, his eyes chock-full with suspicion as he stared at Ben. "If you're just going to interrogate me—"

Ben shook his head and murmured to his fiancée, "And you once accused me of being self-involved…"

Dusty's face flushed with color, and Melanie felt a twinge of sympathy for him. Given how shocked everyone had been by his return and the revelation that she was his wife, it wouldn't be any surprise if this meeting was to interrogate them.

And she didn't blame Dusty for his questioning; she didn't want to be interrogated either.

Emily pitched her voice lower. "I'm the one who actually wanted to talk to all of you."

And the tension eased from Melanie's body. About the wedding...

This was probably about the wedding and about the dilemma Emily was going to have leaving the ranch once she married the mayor and went back to her job as a schoolteacher in town. The school year would be starting up again before they knew it, and all the boys wanted Emily here. They'd really grown attached to her over the past couple of months, and her not living at the ranch, not being here for them twenty-four seven anymore, could devastate them emotionally. They were still dealing—or perhaps not dealing—with the deaths of their parents.

While Melanie needed to talk to her husband, she was willing to wait. The boys needed to come first—with all of them. Then she felt something...like a little flutter inside her stomach, and she remembered there were more children to consider than just the boys. She had babies she had to think about too. Babies she didn't want to raise on the rodeo circuit like she'd been raised.

She wanted more for them. More for herself. But all Dusty had ever wanted was the rodeo. Would he give it up for them? Could she even ask him to do that after everything they'd been through?

DUSTY HADN'T APPRECIATED Ben calling him self-involved, but he couldn't deny that he had been. He'd taken off after the funeral because he'd been looking for his wife. And apparently if he'd stayed, she would have come to him.

No. She hadn't come here for him; she'd come here to get away from him. Because she hadn't known who he really was...

He wasn't sure he knew either—not now that his twin was gone and he wasn't riding. Dusty felt lost. He'd felt lost since Dale and Jenny had died and Dusty had left Melanie behind in Vegas while he'd flown home alone.

He felt lost now...as he walked down the gravel drive bathed in the pinkish hue of the setting sun. Of course he knew the way to the ranch office. When Willow Creek had planned to tear down the old schoolhouse years ago, Grandma had bought the building from the city and had it moved out to the ranch.

Dusty had hesitated to walk out to the building because he was still not entirely convinced that this meeting wouldn't turn into an interrogation. But once everybody else had headed for the schoolhouse after dinner, Dusty started walking toward it too, and he caught up with Melanie now, who'd slowed her pace as if she'd wanted him to catch up to her.

At dinner, his wife had seemed to avoid even looking at him. But now she spoke to him, softly, as if she didn't want the others to hear them. "Are you okay with my being at this meeting?" she asked, and she turned toward him, staring up at him.

That soft light bathed her face, making her skin glow. His breath caught for a moment at how beautiful she was, even more so now than he remembered. His pulse quickened. Nobody else had ever evoked the feelings in him that she did; the intensity of joy and of pain.

"Dusty?" she asked, her voice cracking, and he realized he hadn't answered her.

He'd been too struck by her beauty, as he always was. "Of course I'm okay with you being here," he said. "Why wouldn't I be?"

"Because this is your family," she said with a glance at the others who'd slowed their pace as well. Was everyone dreading this meeting or were they eavesdropping?

"They're your family too," he reminded her. And in the weeks she'd lived here, she'd clearly come to mean a lot to all of them, especially Miller.

The little boy hadn't avoided looking at him during dinner; instead, he'd kept glaring at Dusty. The only time the kid hadn't been glaring at him was when he'd been glaring at Baker or at his younger siblings. The seven-year-old only seemed to smile at Melanie. Apparently, the kid had fallen for his physical therapist just like Dusty had all those weeks ago.

"Are you sure this won't be uncomfortable?" Melanie persisted.

He shrugged. "I don't know. Might be...if they start questioning us."

She shivered despite the warmth of the summer evening. "I already talked to Katie, Emily and Taye."

"So you've already been interviewed?" he asked.

She glanced at the women walking ahead of them and nodded. "You haven't?"

He sighed. "Not yet."

He'd spent all afternoon expecting an inquisition from his brothers. But maybe Caleb being constantly at his side since they'd returned from the barn had saved him. Caleb had certainly saved Dusty earlier when Ian had asked him where his mom and dad were. Clearly, the five-year-old's short-term memory had not returned from the concussion he'd gotten in the accident. With the emotion choking Dusty, he wasn't sure he would have been able to answer Ian, but Caleb had.

Caleb wasn't with him now. He was surprised Melanie was; that she continued to walk beside him.

"Maybe they thought you'd left," she said softly.

He tensed. "Is that what you thought?" he asked.

"You ran out of my room earlier," she reminded him.

Running out of rooms was another thing he had in common with Miller. Dusty's face burned with the wave of embarrassment for how he'd acted, but he'd been about to fall apart...thinking about all his losses.

Even now, with Melanie walking beside him, he felt a greater distance between them than he had when he hadn't known where she was. And he wasn't sure if it was a distance, like her distrust of him, that would ever go away.

"I know we need to talk some more," he said. About so many things...

The babies. Their marriage. The ranch. The rodeo.

"But I don't want to do it with all the family present," he continued.

She nodded. "I don't either…" She glanced toward the others who were just ahead of them, climbing the steps to the schoolhouse. "Let's just focus on this meeting, on the boys, for now."

She hurried up then to join the others inside the schoolhouse. And Dusty wondered if she wanted to talk about their marriage at all. About their future…if they even had one.

CHAPTER EIGHT

EMILY HAD WAITED to call this meeting until Jake and Katie had returned from their honeymoon. And then there had been that big reveal this morning, that Dusty and Melanie were married...

It was good that the rodeo rider had returned to the ranch. For Melanie's sake and for their unborn twins'.

Emily had called this meeting in the interests of the boys, and she couldn't wait any longer to address her concerns. She barely waited until Dusty and Melanie stepped through the doors before she began. "I hope you all don't think that I've overstepped calling this meeting," she started.

"Of course you haven't," Sadie assured her. "You were right that we're all family."

And the older woman was probably thrilled that all of her family was back at the ranch. Emily wasn't so sure that Sadie's matchmaking scheme was going to be as successful as she would like, though.

While Baker had joined the meeting, he and Taye were at opposite corners of the big open area inside the schoolhouse. And while Melanie and Dusty stood next to each other, they seemed totally unaware of one another, like there was a mile between them. The married couple seemed closed off to each other while the newlyweds, Jake and Katie, held hands.

And Ben...

Her heart fluttered at just the thought of him as well as his touch. He stood beside Emily, his arm around her waist offering his support. Always...

She'd already brought up her concerns about Ian and Miller and Little Jake to him. Now she needed to share them with everyone else. "I'm worried about the boys," she said.

Katie paled and Jake tensed. "Did something happen while we were gone?" he asked, his voice gruff, likely with guilt for taking just those two weeks off from the weight of his responsibilities.

Emily shook her head. "Nothing bad happened," she assured the concerned uncle. "In fact, I think Ian is making great progress. He actually aced a test of things that I taught him since his concussion."

Jake's brow furrowed. "But that doesn't make sense if his short-term memory is still affected..."

"If," Ben stressed. "We don't think it is anymore."

Dusty cleared his throat and said, "But he asked me where his mom and dad were earlier today."

Emily nodded. "Yes, he still does that, and I think he knows..."

"Then why..." Dusty trailed off as if his throat filled again.

"I don't know," Emily said. "I'd like to have a friend of mine, the psychologist at the school where I work, talk to the boys, if that's all right with everyone else."

"It's overdue," Ben said. "We should have had them in counseling before this."

"They tried at the hospital," Sadie reminded them. "But the boys didn't want to talk to anyone. At that time, Little Jake wouldn't speak at all. And Ian..." She shook her head.

Emily hadn't been around then. Sadie hadn't hired her to come out to the ranch until two weeks after the accident. "Beth Lancaster is really good," Emily promised. "She'll get them talking without them realizing it." Just as Mrs. Lancaster had gotten her talking when she was a kid.

"Mrs. Lancaster talked to Caleb after we first moved back to Willow Creek," Katie said. "She was very sweet with him." Katie had moved back after her first husband, Caleb's father, had died.

"She's still there?" Baker asked. "She was there when we were kids."

Emily nodded. She and Baker were in the same grade growing up—though back then, everyone had only known her as the girl with no family, if they'd known of her at all. "She would be happy to come out to the ranch and talk to Ian and Miller and Little Jake."

"Thank you, Emily," Jake said. "Thank you for looking out for our boys."

Our boys...

That was how she thought of them. Tears stung her eyes with emotion that Jake had included her like that, like she was already family even though she'd just gotten engaged to his brother.

"I thought you called us out here to talk about your wedding," Katie said.

"I wish we could get married tomorrow," Ben said, "but we'd like to make sure that the boys are doing well first, that we're doing all the right things for them."

And that was why Emily loved him so much. He was willing to put his happiness on hold for his nephews. Ben Haven was a good man.

She'd misjudged him so unfairly.

Was Melanie doing the same thing with Dusty? Had they all assumed that the rodeo rider was like his mother and that he wasn't going to stick around?

"I think the best thing for the boys is that their family—their entire family—continues to rally around them," Sadie put in. "We all need to continue staying here at the ranch."

Ben sighed and shook his head. "Why did I suspect you were going to suggest that?"

"Oh, I realize you and Baker will have to go into town frequently for your jobs," Sadie admitted. But now she focused her intimidating gaze on Dusty. "But everyone else can stay here at the ranch."

Emily wasn't certain yet that she could, or if she'd have to return to town for the upcoming school year to keep her job. She'd been putting off asking Principal Kellerman if he would give her just a little more time off to stay at the ranch. If he wouldn't, she'd have to choose whether to go back or to resign and stay at the ranch. But she would wait to make her decision until after Beth Lancaster talked to the boys. Their well-being was her priority now. Besides, the new school year didn't start for several weeks.

Dusty uttered a ragged sigh. "Why don't you give the meddling a break for a while?" he asked his grandmother. "Remember that it hasn't always worked out well for you when you try too hard to control people." He stared at her with such intensity.

All the color suddenly drained from Sadie's face, and instead of saying anything, she turned on one of her boot heels and stalked out of the schoolhouse.

And Emily suddenly realized that despite living at the ranch the past couple of months, she didn't know her fiancé's family as well as she'd thought she had, for there was clearly something else going on here.

She waited until she and Ben had stepped out of the office to follow Sadie back to the house before asking, "What was that about?"

Ben shrugged his broad shoulders. "I have no idea. Must be something between her and Dusty, probably that she figured out somehow that he was married. I can't say I blame him for being angry with her for not telling him that Melanie was here this whole time."

Never wanting any secrets between them, Emily had shared with her fiancé what Melanie had told her and Taye and Katie that afternoon.

He tightened his arm around her. "I would have been out of my mind if I hadn't known where you were all that time…"

She suspected that Dusty might have been as well. But what was he going to do now that he'd found his wife?

Was he going to stay?

Was he going to prove everyone wrong about him, or was he going to leave and prove them right?

DUSTY STARTED TO head out of the schoolhouse after Sadie, Ben and Emily, but Baker grasped his arm and stopped him. "What was that about?" he asked. "I told you to take it easy on her."

A pang of guilt struck Dusty hard. "I know," He sighed with regret. "I didn't mean to upset her. I just wanted her to back off a bit. You should be thanking me. You are undoubtedly next on her hit list."

Color flooded Baker's face. And he glanced

at Taye Cooper as she headed out the door with Melanie. "Well, it didn't sound like you were talking about me," Baker said.

And he hadn't been.

"What were you talking about?" Jake asked, joining them after his wife hurried to catch Melanie and Taye. "Ben and I have no complaints about her meddling. In fact we think it worked out quite well."

"You have only yourself to blame for this." Baker gave Dusty a pointed look. "If you had told us about Melanie, we could have told you that she was here. But you never said a word about being married."

"Why not?" Jake asked. "Katie said you were married for a month before the accident even happened."

Here was the inquisition he'd been dreading. Fortunately, this firing squad consisted of only two members of his family instead of all of them. There was more family than Dusty's brothers even knew about, but that wasn't his secret to share with them.

Dale would've understood that—he'd kept Dusty's secret about his wedding. Well, he'd kept the secret from their brothers. Had he told Grandma? Or had Sadie tapped another source? Was she keeping tabs on him? Dusty wouldn't doubt it.

But he shouldn't have doubted Baker about her blood pressure. He should have been careful not to upset her.

"I made a mistake," Dusty conceded.

Jake's breath hitched. "That's an awful thing to say. Melanie's a wonderful woman," he said earnestly. "The boys adore her. Katie loves her and—"

"I do too," he interjected.

And the oldest and the youngest of his brothers stared at him in shock. They weren't the only ones—he was shocked too. While he was aware he'd fallen for her, and that was why he hadn't been able to let her go once his physical therapy had ended, he wasn't sure those feelings were quite as strong now that she'd run out on him. Without waiting for him to explain. Or to apologize…

Which he hadn't actually done yet because he'd been so upset that she'd left, that she'd disconnected her cell service, that she was pregnant and hadn't even let him know…

As annoyed as he was with Melanie, he still had feelings for her. Attraction. And stronger feelings…especially when he'd seen how close she was with his oldest nephew, how much she cared about all of the boys.

"Of course I love her," Dusty said. And it was still present tense. But was it enough to overcome all their mistrust of each other?

"You do love her," Jake murmured as if surprised.

"Why else do you think I married her when I'd sworn I was never going to do that?" Dusty asked. "I didn't want to lose her." But then he had anyway because he hadn't been completely honest with her.

Would she have married him if she'd known everything? Would she stay married to him now that she knew? She seemed to think the same way the rest of his family did, that he was shirking his responsibilities. While the ranch hadn't necessarily been his responsibility the past eleven years, it was partially his now, just as caring for his orphaned nephews was. Miller, Ian and Little Jake had needed their family close. Despite giving Grandma a hard time, Dusty couldn't argue with her that the boys needed all their family rallying around them with love and support.

Guilt squeezed his heart that he hadn't been there for them like he should have been, like

Dale would have wanted him to be. Dusty had a lot of apologies to make.

But not to his grandmother...

She could have brought him back sooner if she'd only told him that Melanie was here.

"Seems like you lost your wife for quite a few weeks," Baker said, needling him more like Ben would have. Apparently, the paramedic and the mayor had spent too much time together while Jake had been on his honeymoon.

Jake shook his head. "I've always told Ben that he's the most like Grandma, but I think you're the one who is," he told Dusty.

Offended at the comparison, he sucked in a breath. "What? How? I don't meddle in anyone's life."

"No," Jake agreed. "Except maybe your own."

Dusty hadn't meddled; he'd just messed it up. Maybe so much so that he wouldn't be able to fix it again.

"You're like Grandma because you're both so pigheaded," Jake explained.

"Says the man who insisted on quitting college and giving up the love of his life to come home when Grandpa died," Dusty said.

"Somebody had to," Jake remarked.

And even though he hadn't been at college like Jake and Ben when the original Big Jake had passed, Dusty flinched at what felt like a personal jab. Grandma had insisted that Jake and Ben both stay in college. Jake had ignored her, as he usually did, while Ben had stuck with his original dream of pursuing his political science degree and becoming mayor of Willow Creek. Nobody had questioned Ben's decision or knocked him for making it. But when Dusty had finished high school and left for the rodeo, he'd heard the comparisons to his mother and the recrimination. Maybe it wouldn't have been so bad if Dale had left with him, but Dale had insisted on staying in Willow Creek and helping Jake with the ranch.

Dale had been the good twin. That was how Dusty had felt for the past eleven years because he'd figured it was how everyone else had felt.

"What choices are you going to make now?" Jake asked him.

He wished he knew.

"I need a ranch foreman," Jake continued. "Apparently, the couple of candidates I had narrowed it down to didn't measure up to Baker's standards."

Dusty turned to their baby brother and raised his brows. "Your standards for what?"

he asked. "You've never wanted anything to do with the ranch." Like Ben, he'd always made it clear that he wasn't going to be a rancher.

For some reason their decisions had been respected. Maybe because Ben had become the mayor and Baker had become a hero first as an army medic and now as a firefighter/EMT. But nobody seemed to respect what Dusty had done, the titles he'd won, because all they ever did was compare him to their mother.

She'd had her reasons for leaving too, and they weren't the selfish ones everyone believed. But before he could share what he'd learned with everyone else, he needed to talk to Grandma.

"I don't have to be a rancher myself to recognize that someone else isn't ranch material," Baker said. He shrugged his broad shoulders. He was only a year younger than Dusty, but Baker had always been their baby brother in size as well as age...until he'd had a growth spurt during his basic training for the army. Then he'd passed Dusty and Dale and had almost caught up to Big Jake.

"In fact, maybe that's what makes it easier for me to recognize it," Baker said.

"What about you, Dusty?" Jake asked.

Dusty studied his big brother's face. "What

about me? Would I recognize when someone is or isn't ranch material?" He shook his head. "I doubt it. I didn't think Dale would stay."

He'd thought his twin would leave too, that they'd stick together.

Dusty continued. "And I figured Baker was always protesting too much and that he actually loves the ranch."

Baker snorted. "Yeah, right."

Jake shook his head. "That's not what I meant. Do you think you could do the ranch foreman job?"

Tension gripped Dusty: here it was. The pressure his brothers had been applying over the phone during every one of the calls he'd had with them since he'd left Willow Creek after the funeral. They kept trying to coerce him into taking Dale's place. As if, because they'd looked alike, they'd had the same abilities.

But Dusty hadn't spent the last decade on the ranch like Dale had. While he knew animals, he didn't know the day-to-day operations anymore, and he wasn't sure if he wanted to learn them. Because then he would have to stay; he would have to give up the rodeo for more than a season. He'd have to give it up forever.

"Before you shoot me down like you usually do," Jake said, "take some time to think about it. Talk to your wife about it because I don't think Melanie's going anywhere. She's very attached to Miller, nearly as attached as he is to her. She has to stay."

What did that mean for their marriage? For them? Dusty definitely needed to talk to his wife.

"And I need to go," Baker murmured. "I've got to get back to town, back to my job."

Jake nodded in acceptance of *that* brother's choice. "Just make sure you come around more than you used to," he advised, "because Grandma is right about the boys."

They needed everybody. Some more than others…like Miller needed Melanie.

Jake was right that Dusty needed to talk to her, and not just about the foreman position.

HE'D STAYED FOR dinner and the meeting. Yet Melanie had no idea if Dusty intended to remain at the ranch or return to the rodeo before there were too many more events and he had no chance of catching up in the standings. More importantly, she had no idea if he intended to share her room if he stayed. They were husband and wife, and even though she knew more about him now than she had when they'd wed, he felt like a stranger to her.

On edge, she paced her bedroom, wondering where he was, what he was doing. After she, Taye and Katie had come inside the house, they'd headed upstairs to help Mr. Lemmon with the boys. As Ben had assured them, the old man had had no problem handling them all on his own. They'd been gathered around him like they usually gathered around Emily, as Mr. Lemmon told them a wild story about a woman who killed rabid wolves with her bare hands.

Katie had chuckled. "Maybe he's how that rumor got started."

"What rumor?" Melanie had asked.

"That Sadie killed wolves with her bare hands," Taye had explained with a wide smile.

Melanie didn't doubt that she could have when she was younger. But now the Haven matriarch looked her age, and not just because of her white hair but because of the sudden slump of her shoulders, the lines of weariness in her face. Maybe Dusty had had a point when he'd said that Sadie's efforts to control people hadn't always worked out well for her. Maybe it had exhausted her.

Melanie had been surprised that Sadie hadn't

had some snappy comeback for her grandson. Instead of fighting with him, she'd fled. That wasn't like the woman Melanie had come to know and admire and maybe fear a little. Even though she was showing her age now, Sadie was no less intimidating than someone who'd kill wolves with her bare hands.

She wasn't the only intimidating Haven.

With his big size and initially gruff demeanor, Jake had intimidated Melanie when she'd first arrived at the ranch too. And Ben, with his quick wit and sharp mind, had worried her. She'd figured he would be able to see right away that she'd been hiding something… like her marriage to his brother.

And Baker…

While he was the youngest in age, his soul felt the oldest, like he'd seen and experienced things that nobody should.

Melanie sighed as she considered who was the most daunting of all: her husband. Because he'd been the one man who'd convinced her to cast aside the caution with which she'd lived her entire life…until that day they'd eloped.

He'd been the one man she'd wanted enough to risk getting hurt. And he had hurt her…

But she suspected she'd hurt him too, when

she'd so easily believed the very worst of him, that he was a liar and a cheater.

So he probably had no intention of trying to share her life anymore.

Then a light knock rattled her door, startling her.

It could be anyone.

While the boys should have been in bed by now, Miller sometimes couldn't sleep and sought her out for the comfort he was too proud to ask for when everyone else was awake. She opened the door, but it wasn't a seven-year-old standing in the hall.

When he got older, Miller would look like this man—with his hazel eyes and golden-brown hair. They even had a slight limp in common now, which she noticed when Dusty stepped inside her room and closed the door.

"What…what do you want?" she asked, nerves fluttering inside her stomach. And why, at the same time, did her pulse quicken at the sight of him?

She'd thought she'd loved him, but she hadn't known who he really was.

"I just want to talk," Dusty said, as if assuring her. Had he misinterpreted her excitement as fear?

She actually was afraid—afraid that she

would let him get to her like he had before, to slip beneath her defenses and into her heart again. So she reminded herself, and him, "You didn't seem to want to hear what I had to say earlier today when you ran out on our conversation."

"Apparently, that's something we have in common," Dusty remarked. "Not giving the other person a chance to explain."

Guilt gripped her. "I'm sorry," she said. "I should have talked to you about that picture, about everything…" She had just been so afraid that she would have folded like her mom had done every time her dad had asked her to take him back. And every time her mom had, her dad had broken all the promises he'd made and hurt her again.

All of her life Melanie had watched her mother endure the pain and humiliation over and over again, and she'd vowed long ago that she would never put herself through that, that she would never give another chance to a man who'd broken her trust and her heart. When Melanie had learned how much of himself Dusty hadn't shared with her, he'd broken both.

"I'm sorry too," he said. "That's why I came up here to talk to you, because I realized I hadn't apologized to you. I was just so shocked when I found you here."

"Is that why you said what you did to your grandmother?" she questioned. "About her controlling people…"

"That's part of it," he said.

"But there's more?" she asked.

"I realize now that there's always more with Grandma," he said. "But I came up here to talk about us."

"Is there an 'us'?" she challenged. "You weren't honest with me…about anything…so what does that leave us? Just lies?" And two babies that were going to be born into a situation they hadn't chosen, that she wouldn't have chosen for them had she known everything.

"I didn't intentionally lie to you," he insisted.

His words eerily echoed ones she'd heard her father tell her mother when he'd been caught having one of his many affairs. The comparison chilled her, making goose bumps rise on her skin. She rubbed her arms.

"I just didn't know how to tell you everything," he admitted.

Her brows drew together in confusion. "I don't understand why you just weren't honest with me from the start," she said. "You could have told me about changing your name, about your brothers, about growing up on the ranch… about your life…" But he had shared none of that with her; he hadn't really shared anything with her but his love for the rodeo and what he'd professed to be his love for her. But if he'd really loved her, why hadn't he trusted her enough to be completely honest with her?

He took off his hat and ran a slightly shaky hand through his thick hair. "I didn't want you to think the worst of me," he said. "I didn't want you to look at me the way my family does…like I'm selfish for not staying to help Jake out with the ranch like Dale did. I didn't want you or anyone else to think I was like my mother. That's why I wanted to use a different name on the circuit."

His words, and the guilt on his handsome face, got to her, reaching inside to squeeze sympathy from her. If he'd been truthful with her from the start, she might not have looked at him that way, but after spending these weeks at the ranch without him helping out like everyone else had, she undoubtedly had looked at him like that. Like he was selfish. Unless there was more to the story?

"I was not running away from the ranch or from responsibilities," he continued, his deep voice hard with defensiveness. "I was running toward the dream I always had of joining the rodeo, the dream Dale had once shared with me before he backed out, before I had to chase that dream alone…"

As she heard all the emotions in his voice—the guilt, the resentment, the grief—her sympathy for him intensified. "You could have told me all that," she said, "if you'd trusted me…"

He nodded. "I could have. And you could have talked to me after Traci showed you that photo…if you'd trusted me."

Suddenly weary despite the nap she'd taken earlier, Melanie stumbled back and dropped onto the edge of her bed. And, Dusty, his handsome face taut with concern, dropped to his knees in front of her. "Are you okay?" he asked, and he reached up, cupping her cheek in his palm as he studied her. "Are you feeling faint again?"

"No." She shook her head, and the gesture caused her cheek to rub against his palm, against the row of calluses across it. He had the hands of a rodeo rider, the hands her father still had despite not being able to ride for years. The rodeo wasn't just something they did; it was who they were. His family didn't understand that, but she did. She knew it wouldn't be easy for him to give it up and stay at the ranch for his family or for her.

"You need to make an appointment with your doctor, like Baker said," Dusty advised her. "Make sure everything is all right with you and the babies."

"I know," she agreed.

"I want to go with you when you go," he said. "I want to be there for you, if you'll let me…"

"For how long?" she asked. "How long will you be here, Dusty, before you go back on the road?"

"Before *I* go back?" he asked. "You're not coming?"

She shrugged. "I don't know…"

"When we got married, I didn't think anything would change," he said. "I thought we'd keep traveling with the rodeo like we both always did, only we would do it together."

"How can you not see that everything has changed?" she countered. "And I'm not even talking about the pregnancy…" Though that had definitely not been planned. She had no idea how Dusty felt. And until she'd started working with Miller and moved into the ranch, she hadn't realized how much she loved kids.

He released a shaky sigh. "Of course I

know…that in that moment, when the accident happened…when I lost my twin… I knew that everything had changed. I knew I'd lost my best friend then. I didn't know I was about to lose my wife too."

She closed her eyes, unable to look at his handsome face contorted with pain over his loss. She kept thinking of what the boys had lost when their parents died; she hadn't considered what her husband had lost as well. "Dusty…"

CHAPTER NINE

DUSTY WAITED FOR Melanie to continue after she trailed off. But she fell silent while he stayed on his knees in front of her. He felt like he had that day he'd begged her for a date, and when she'd refused, how he'd been so desperate not to lose her that he'd proposed.

And even though he'd found her, he didn't know if he could stay here with her...if that was even what she wanted.

Could he give up the dream he'd had for so long? Could he take Dale's place at the ranch and work with Jake?

And, more importantly, could he ever regain Melanie's trust? Without it, their marriage didn't have a chance...even if she gave him another one.

Clearly, his not being open with her had put her off, just as he'd worried that it would. "I'm sorry," he said again. "I never meant to hurt you..."

That was the last thing he'd wanted to do.

His chest ached with a hollow feeling, like his heart had been ripped from it. Dale and Jenny's deaths might have caused that, but losing Melanie…that had made the pain almost unbearable.

Her brown eyes glistened as tears filled them, wrenching his heart even more. He ran his fingertips along the delicate line of her jaw. "Please…" he breathed.

"Please what?" she asked.

"Please don't cry," he murmured, hating that he'd caused her tears.

Her thick lashes fluttered and her eyes cleared. "Dusty…" But she trailed off again.

So he had to ask. "What do you want?"

He wanted her to say his name again. He wanted her to want him like he wanted her. Then they could figure out the rest of it—the ranch, the rodeo…

And he could take that ring off the chain and slide it back on her finger…

But before she could say anything, a scream shattered the tense silence between them. That scream of such fear and pain had haunted his dreams since he'd heard it last, when he'd been at the ranch just after the accident. When Little Jake had awakened from one of his nightmares…

Dusty had had weeks off from waking up to those heartbreaking cries. So he knew he should be the one to respond, to let the others rest. He scrambled to his feet and hurried out of the bedroom to the nursery just a few doors down from Melanie's room.

He pushed open the door and stepped into the dim light of the myriad stars the mobile projected on the ceiling. The little boy stood up in his crib, his chubby hands locked around the rungs of the railing. His mouth opened wide as another scream rent the air.

Dusty rushed forward and reached for his nephew, but the toddler clung tightly to those rungs yet. "You're all right, little man, it's just a dream," he crooned. Unfortunately, it wasn't; it was reality. That horrific nightmare had actually happened, and this little boy had lived through it.

The child released the railing and reached for Dusty, winding his arms around his neck so tightly he nearly choked him. "Da-da," he murmured with awe. "Daddy..."

Dusty froze at the sound of the little boy's voice. Those two weeks that he'd been here after the accident, the child hadn't made a peep beyond his nighttime cries. He hadn't been the happy, babbling baby that he'd been when Dusty had come home for Christmas just four months earlier.

But it wasn't just the sound of the little boy's voice that had made Dusty tense. It was what Little Jake had called him.

"Daddy…" the toddler repeated with awe as he pulled back and stared into Dusty's face.

"That's not Daddy!" Light flooded the room, illuminating Ian, who stood just inside the doorway, his body shaking with his anger. "That's not Daddy…" Tears glistened in his eyes.

And Dusty realized that Emily was right. Ian remembered more than he wanted to admit, maybe more than he wanted to face… until now.

Then he asked, "What are you doing here, Uncle Dusty? Where are Mommy and Daddy?"

That hollow ache in Dusty's chest intensified until he felt like he was being crushed, like a one-ton bull had stomped all over him. "They're gone," he lamented.

"Where did they go?" the boy asked. "Did they leave on a honeymoon like Uncle Jake and Aunt Katie?"

If he could remember that Jake had gotten married, he had to remember what had happened to his parents.

"Oh, Ian…" Dusty sighed.

Emily was definitely right. The little boy needed to talk to a counselor. He also needed his family around to support him. All his family. Grandma was right about that, just not about everything else…

Miller hobbled into the nursery then, his eyes narrowed in a glare when he looked at Dusty. Then he asked the same question Ian had. "What are you doing here?"

"Little Jake had a nightmare," he said.

The toddler was calm now, his big brown eyes wide as he stared in wonder at Dusty. Had his nephew realized who he really was yet?

"I mean, what are you doing here at the ranch?" Miller asked. "Did you come to take Aunt Melanie home with you?"

"Aunt Melanie isn't leaving," Dusty assured him. She hadn't answered his question earlier, but she hadn't needed to. It was clear she had a bond with Miller, one she wasn't going to break now. If ever…

Miller's shoulders slumped a little, with what looked like relief, as he released the breath he must have been holding.

"Is it all right with you if I stick around for a while?" Dusty asked.

"What do you mean?" Miller asked.

"Uncle Jake needs help on the ranch." Recognizing his nephew's prickly pride, Dusty didn't want to imply that Miller needed help even though he and his brothers definitely did. They'd been through too much for anyone let alone for such young children.

"You're going to give up the rodeo?" Miller asked, and he was clearly skeptical.

"I can't ride right now," Dusty answered as honestly as he could. He wouldn't be able to ride for worrying about his nephews and about his wife and their unborn babies.

"You limp too," Miller said. "Did you get hurt?"

Dusty nodded. "The first time I tried to ride him, Midnight hurt me," he admitted. "That's how I got close to your aunt Melanie." He owed Midnight some carrots, too, for giving him a reason to spend all that time with the beautiful physical therapist.

Surprise passed across his small face. "She helped you too?"

Dusty nodded again. "Yes, she did." She'd more than helped him; she'd made him do something he'd vowed that he would never do: marry. Not that she'd talked him into it. He'd had to talk her into it.

"But you still limp a little," Miller said.

Dusty sighed. "That's because I went back to ride Midnight again," he shared. "I stayed on, but it wasn't easy…" And he had reinjured his leg a bit. Would that happen every time he tried to ride? Maybe he should retire from the rodeo, but the thought of no longer doing what he loved, of giving up the dream he'd had for so long, intensified that ache in his chest.

"So the rodeo is hard?" another little boy asked, his blue eyes wide with curiosity and concern.

Dusty hadn't even noticed when Caleb had joined them. His focus had been on Little Jake, who still clung to him, and on Miller, who so warily studied him. And on Ian, who so confused him. Why would he want to be reminded about his parents' death over and over again? Or did he want so badly to forget they were dead that he kept pretending he had forgotten? Maybe then he could pretend they were still alive.

Dusty wished he could forget and pretend they were still alive too.

"Is it hard?" Caleb prodded him when he'd hesitated too long.

He didn't want to dash this little boy's dream, but he also wanted to be honest. So he nodded. "Yes."

"Then why do you do it?" Ian asked that question so matter-of-factly, as if when something was hard it wasn't worth doing. For Dusty, it was just the opposite—the harder it was, the more he wanted to do it. That was why he'd gone back for another round with Midnight.

Maybe it was even why he'd married Melanie, because, to him, marriage had seemed nearly impossible. But losing her like he had, not knowing all these weeks where she'd been, had made him rethink if going another round at marriage was worth that kind of pain. He'd felt like he had when his mom had taken off after his dad died; he'd felt loss and betrayal. She wasn't the only one struggling to trust again. He wasn't sure that he could either. Maybe this was one round he wasn't going to win.

"Yeah, why?" Miller asked, and he'd let down his guard a little to shuffle closer to Dusty.

Dusty had learned his lesson about not being completely honest with the people he cared about, so he answered truthfully. "Because I love it. I've loved it ever since my mom and dad brought me and my brothers to my first rodeo. I was just sitting in the stands then..."

But he'd felt more at home there than he ever had on the ranch.

"If you love it so much, why do you want to stay here?" Miller asked, and his small body had tensed again with pride. He probably suspected it was because of him and his brothers.

Recognizing that defensiveness in his nephew and wanting to diffuse it, Dusty replied, "I want to stay here because I love my family more." As he said it, he realized how true it was. As much as he loved the rodeo, his family had to come first now. And maybe always...

"So is it all right with you all if I stay?" he asked again, glancing around the room.

Caleb's brow furrowed beneath a lock of blond hair that kept falling in his eyes. He pushed it back and asked, "Why wouldn't it be all right?"

Dusty's chest expanded, like he'd been holding in his own grief over losing his twin, and it shifted inside him. "I look exactly like their dad," he explained to his new nephew. "We were twins. And if it's hard for them to see me because they miss him too much, I will leave." He turned back to Miller then. "Is it too hard for you?"

And he realized, too late, that it was the

wrong way to have asked that question. Because Miller, all snappy, shook his head vigorously. "It's not too hard for me!"

"Where did Dad go?" Ian asked, his hazel eyes full of confusion.

Was it real, though? Or was it his way of dealing or not actually dealing with his pain?

"Your dad and mom are in Heaven now," Dusty told him. "They've been there for months, Ian."

"What? Why are you lying?" he asked, his voice cracking with emotion.

"He's not lying!" Miller shouted.

And Little Jake, who'd been so still and quiet, began to cry again.

Dusty had stepped in to try to calm the children down, but all he'd done was upset them more. He'd known he could never take his brother's place, never be the father that Dale had been to his sons. Would he even be able to figure out how to be a father to his children when the twins were born?

MELANIE GASPED AT the sudden turn of mood within the nursery. She'd waved off Emily, Jake and Katie when they'd stepped into the hall to attend to Little Jake. She'd wanted to see how Dusty would handle the boys on his own. But now she was the one who rushed to his aide.

"Hey, guys," she said as she wrapped an arm around Ian and her other arm around Miller, pulling them close to her sides. Both their small bodies were stiff with their tumultuous emotions. Emily was right; they needed help, more help than even their family could give them. "It's late, and we all need to get back to bed."

"Look what you did!" Miller said, leaning around her to yell into Ian's face. "You woke up Miss Aunt Melanie, and she needs her sleep!"

"He didn't wake me up," Melanie said.

"Then *he* did!" Miller pointed at Little Jake in Dusty's arms. Or maybe at Dusty.

He hadn't woken her up, but he'd kept her awake many nights when they'd been together and after she'd left him. She'd spent so many nights worrying about what she'd done and what she would have to do eventually.

See him again...

Or was she actually seeing him for the first time? Here in this room with his grief-stricken nephews. She hadn't known this man existed. He'd been kind and charming with her, but with the boys, he'd displayed a level of sensitivity she hadn't thought he had.

He'd also been honest with them, more honest than he'd ever been with her. He loved the rodeo; she'd heard the reverence for it in his voice. But then he'd told them that he loved his family more.

Had he been honest then too? Or had he just told the boys something to make them feel better?

It hadn't. It had led to this latest skirmish between Ian and Miller—one of many since Melanie had brought Miller back to the ranch.

She needed to focus on them and on soothing their frayed tempers. "Nobody woke me up," she insisted. "But we're going to wake up everyone else in the house if we keep arguing." She swept her gaze around the room to include Caleb, who'd edged closer to Dusty and Little Jake. "You *all* need to go back to your beds now."

But Ian and Miller clung yet to her, until Miller shoved at his little brother, trying to push him away. Ian wrapped his small arms tighter around her, refusing to let go.

"Hey now, guys," Dusty said. "You're going to hurt your aunt if you keep squeezing her so tightly."

They both jerked away from her in alarm, and tears stung Melanie's eyes over their instant concern for her. "I'm fine," she assured them. "I'm not going to break."

Not anymore…

Their uncle Dusty had already broken her heart. Would she ever be able to trust him or anyone else with it again, besides these sweet little boys, his nephews?

Her nephews now, at least by marriage, and the nephews of her heart. She loved them so much. She squeezed Ian and Miller against her again and said softly, "Okay, let's get back to bed."

She glanced at Caleb too, who was leaning sleepily against Dusty now—apparently his new hero. When he and Katie had first come to stay at the ranch, the little boy had fallen hard for Mr. Big Jake, as he'd called him. Then when Jake and Katie had left on their honeymoon, he'd turned his hero worship on Ben. Now, he apparently had a new hero in Uncle Dusty. "You have to go back to bed too, Caleb."

But when she steered Miller and Ian out of the room, Dusty followed with Little Jake propped on one of his lean hips and the heavy-eyed Caleb propped on his other one. From his family she'd learned how infrequently he'd visited the ranch since he'd left for the rodeo, but he seemed very natural holding and comforting Little Jake. And he'd taken to Caleb right away too.

Maybe he would be a good father to their children. Maybe he could love them like he loved his nephews. Did he love her? Had he ever?

They went first to Caleb's room. When Dusty leaned down and gently deposited the child back in his bed, Caleb's eyes opened and he peered at Dusty through his bangs. "Will you teach me how to be a rodeo rider?" he asked.

While Melanie stared in alarm at the thought of Caleb trying to ride that dangerous bronco, Dusty chuckled. "Remember, your mom said you'll have that discussion when you're older." With his free hand, he pulled the covers up to the little boy's chin, and then, as if he couldn't help himself, he kissed the child's forehead. "Good night, little cowboy."

Caleb's lips curved into a sweet smile as he drifted off to sleep.

His new cousins were not as drowsy as he was. Their squabble had riled them up so much that they were still tense against her.

"Let's go to Ian's room next," she suggested. Ian was usually more malleable than Miller was. But he planted his feet and refused to budge.

"I wanna sleep in here with Caleb."

She doubted Caleb would mind or probably even notice since he was already sleeping soundly. So she nodded.

And Dusty pulled back the covers so that Ian could squeeze into the small bed with his best friend. Dusty leaned down to kiss his forehead too.

"It's okay," Ian whispered.

"What's okay?" Dusty asked.

"It's okay if you stay," Ian said. "I know you're not Daddy."

Dusty sucked in a breath as if the little boy had punched him. But he only nodded and stepped back from the bed.

Miller clasped Melanie's hand and tugged her toward his room. He was ready now to go to sleep. Or did he just want to get away from his uncle?

But Dusty followed them, and maybe all his walking around had rocked Little Jake to sleep because the toddler drooled onto his uncle's shoulder, dampening his shirt.

"I don't need to be tucked in," Miller insisted. "I'm not a baby like they are." But yet he clung to Melanie's hand.

"I won't tuck you in," Dusty assured him with a slight grin. And he leaned on the door frame as Melanie entered and pulled back the covers for Miller.

He warily eyed his uncle before slipping into bed. "You don't have to kiss me," he said. "I'm too old for that."

But he had no objection when Melanie brushed her lips, which were twitching with the urge to smile, across his forehead. A slight smile of his own stole across the boy's mouth. Then he whispered, "It's okay with me too."

"What is?" Dusty asked.

"If you stay."

"Are you sure?" Dusty questioned.

Miller's head bobbed against his pillow, and his lids drifted down. He sleepily sighed, "Yeah…"

Her heart swelling with love for the boy, Melanie brushed her lips across his forehead again. Then she turned back to the doorway, but Dusty was gone.

She straightened up and slipped out of Miller's room, pulling the door closed behind her. Dusty's deep voice rumbled in the nursery, and she stepped inside to find him leaning over the crib where he'd deposited Little Jake.

"Sweet dreams only, little man," Dusty murmured. Then he straightened and turned toward the doorway, toward her. But he said nothing until he joined her in the hall, pulling Little Jake's door partially closed behind him. Then he asked, "What about you?"

"What about me?" But she knew.

"Is it all right with you if I stay?"

Her pulse quickened at the thought of his living here with her. But then she reminded herself and him, "This is your home. Of course, it's all right for you to stay."

"It's your home now too," he said. And he gestured at the closed door to Miller's room. "Maybe more yours than it ever was mine."

She gasped. "That's an awful thing to say. Of course, it's your home. This is your family."

He sighed. "I know. I know. It's just that…"

"What?" she asked when he trailed off.

He shrugged. But his broad shoulders didn't relax; he was just as tense as his squabbling nephews had been. Like Miller had taken her hand, she took Dusty's and pulled him through the open door of her bedroom. Then she closed it and leaned back against it, and as she did, she worried that he might have gotten the wrong idea, especially when his eyes darkened and he entwined his fingers with hers.

Instead of pulling away, though, she savored his touch—the roughness of his hand against her softer skin. Her breathing quickened, and she started struggling for air at just the thought of how much love he had made her feel.

But then she reminded herself of the pain, though the hollow ache inside her was so constant that she needed no reminder. She pulled her hand free of his and hastened to explain, "I don't want to wake up the boys again. And it seems like there's something else bothering you."

He shook his head. "It's never easy for me being here, but it's even worse now."

"Because of Dale and Jenny's deaths?" she asked.

He expelled a ragged breath and nodded. "That's…gut-wrenching…"

"I'm sorry," she said with a twinge of guilt that she'd never expressed her condolences to him over his loss. "I can't imagine how hard it must have been on you to lose your twin." She didn't even have a sibling, so she had no way of knowing, but since coming to the ranch and seeing how his brothers and nephews interacted, she understood how special that sibling relationship was.

"My best friend," he murmured. "He was my best friend. I don't know how many times I've picked up my phone to call him before I remember that he's gone…" Tears glistened in his eyes until he blinked furiously and cleared them away. "And Jenny…" He cleared his throat. "She was so sweet that I couldn't even get mad at her when Dale chose to stay with her instead of coming on the road with me."

But she'd heard the resentment in his voice earlier; she knew he'd been upset that his twin had backed out of their childhood plan.

"I wish I could have met them," she said. She wished she had met all of them before the accident, before all this pain had become such a part of their lives.

"Dale knew about you," Dusty said and his lips curved into a faint smile. "And because Dale knew, I'm sure he told Jenny too. They had no secrets."

She steadied herself against the sting of his words. "That must have been nice…" she murmured. "They must have had a happy marriage." She doubted they could have the same. She had once doubted any marriage could be happy, especially when the rodeo was involved, but she'd fallen so hard for Dusty that she'd married him despite all her doubts and fears. She'd been right about them, but maybe Dale and Jenny had had one of those rare happy marriages.

"I'm sorry," he murmured.

But it didn't matter how many times he apologized; he couldn't undo the damage that had been done. So she drew in a deeper breath now and focused on what he'd been saying. "So Dale or Jenny must have told your grandmother about me," she mused.

"I don't think Dale told her, but maybe Jenny did. Or my manager..." He sighed. "Guess she's as good at finding out secrets as she is at keeping them."

A small groan of frustration slipped through Melanie's lips when she considered how she'd foolishly thought it all might have been a coincidence, her coming here to Ranch Haven. "I should be furious with her for bringing me here under false pretenses, over not telling me that she knew I was your wife."

"But you're not?" he asked.

She sighed. "I think Sadie's heart is in the right place." And now Melanie's heart was too, with Dusty's nephews.

Dusty snorted as if he doubted his grandmother's motives.

"Are you angry with your grandmother for bringing me here?" She thought of how he'd talked to Sadie during the family meeting, of the looks he'd been giving her even before that, as well as the sound he'd just made.

He sighed again, raggedly. "I'm angry that she didn't tell me she'd found you. But the bond you have with Miller...he needs that. He needs you, so I'm glad she brought you here."

What about him? Did her husband need her? Was that why he'd been looking for her?

"Why didn't you tell the rest of your family about me?" she asked. So often over the past several weeks, she'd wanted to scream when one of his family members had claimed that Dusty would never settle down, never marry, that he already was. But it had been so impulsive, and there was still so much she didn't know about him, so she'd kept her humiliation to herself. But now she asked him, "Are you ashamed of me?"

He gasped, and his hazel eyes went wide with shock. "Oh, God, no! Never!" he vehemently assured her. "I was ashamed of me. That's why I didn't tell you about my family. It's why I didn't tell my family about you because you didn't know about them, because I was keeping things from everyone…" He groaned. "Maybe Baker's right. Maybe I *am* the most like Grandma because I'm just as stubborn as she is. If I'd said something to any of them, I would have known where you were and I wouldn't have had to keep looking."

"I'm sorry," she said, reiterating the apology she'd given him earlier. "I shouldn't have canceled my cell number. I just didn't trust myself to talk to you." More like to listen to him and not fall for his lies. She'd thought a clean break was for the best. She'd avoided him because she hadn't trusted herself, and in doing so, she'd upset him. And he'd already been upset enough. She reached for his hand again and squeezed it. "And I'm sorry I wasn't here for you for the funeral."

"That was my fault," he said. "I should have brought you with me when I flew back right after Jake's call."

"I wish you had too," she said, her voice hoarse with the emotions rushing over her. "I could tell how upset you were, but you wouldn't tell me what was going on or where you were going."

"I was out of my mind from Jake's call about the crash, and I didn't know what to do, how to tell you about them…" He shook his head. "I'm sorry I made such a mess of things." He entwined their fingers again and stepped closer to her. Then he leaned down and brushed his mouth softly across hers.

And her heart slammed against her ribs before it began to pound furiously. She forced herself to pull back, to resist the attraction that had compelled her to impulsively marry a stranger.

"You didn't finish what you were about to say earlier," he reminded her. "You were talking about everything changing…"

"It has," she said. "It's all so complicated now."

"Does it have to be?"

She ran her hands over her stomach. "We don't just have ourselves to think about right now," she said. "We have to focus on the boys and…" And their unborn babies.

"If it was just us again, like it was those first weeks after we got married, what would you want?" he asked. "What do you want, Melanie?"

His love. His devotion. But even if he offered it, she wasn't sure she could accept. Not now.

"I don't know," she admitted.

His throat moved, as if he was struggling

to swallow something, and he asked, "A divorce?"

She tugged her hand free of his and ran it over her stomach again, over their babies.

"Not now," he said. "I want us to be married when they're born but..."

"I don't know," she said. "I don't know if I could ever trust you again."

He flinched as if she'd slapped him.

And then she added, "I don't know if I could ever trust myself again." Maybe that would be the harder thing for her to fix.

He was silent a moment. "Is it really okay with you that I stay here?" he asked.

Her still madly pounding heart seemed to jump inside her chest at the thought of sharing such close quarters with him. She shook her head to clear her mind.

And he looked once again like she'd slapped him. "Then I'll leave in the morning."

"No!" she said. She couldn't bear the thought of him leaving his nephews now. Or her... "I just meant that I don't want you staying in this room with me."

"Oh..." He sucked in a breath and nodded. "Of course. I understand." He reached around her then, for the handle to the door. "I'll find somewhere else to stay on the ranch."

He opened the door and stepped out into the hall, and she pushed the door closed with her body and sagged against it. If she didn't lock him out now, she might do something crazy… like pull him back inside with her, like try to recapture those blissfully happy weeks right after their wedding.

Was that why her mother always forgave her father? Why she always gave him another chance? Because she loved him too much to let him go no matter what he'd done?

Her cell phone vibrated against the surface of her bedside table, drawing her away from the door where she might have stayed slumped with exhaustion and confusion if not for the call.

The screen lit up with the caller's identity: Mom. She quickly swiped to accept. "I was just thinking of you," she said with wonder. They'd always been close, never more so than during that week and a half after she'd seen that portrait of the family she'd thought was Dusty's. She'd stayed with her parents until Sadie had offered her the job at the ranch. Maybe her mother had somehow sensed that Melanie needed her now.

"Good," her mother said. "I'm about to board a plane to Wyoming."

"Where in Wyoming?" Melanie asked with alarm.

"Sheridan, the airport closest to Willow Creek," she said. "I've left your father."

So maybe her mother had finally reached her limit for forgiving...

Melanie hoped not, because she needed her mother to forgive her; she hadn't told her anything she'd learned since coming here. Like her husband's real identity...

Or that she was pregnant.

And she felt a pang of regret and panic. Maybe she had more in common with Dusty than she'd realized. Maybe she shouldn't have cast stones at him when she'd been keeping secrets of her own.

CHAPTER TEN

IT WAS LATE. And despite how long the day seemed since his return to Ranch Haven, Dusty knew he wasn't going to be able to sleep, at least not inside the house. Melanie was too close, and he was too tempted to fight for another chance, to fight for their marriage, for them.

But he didn't want to pressure her, especially when he wasn't entirely certain he could give her everything she needed, everything she deserved. Like the security of the ranch or even his trust. He wasn't sure that he could trust her not to run away from him again when he needed her most, like he'd needed her when Dale and Jenny died. But when he'd called her from the hospital, she hadn't picked up.

She hadn't been there for him then or all these weeks since. She'd been here.

He slipped outside into the comfort of the darkness, into the warmth of the summer night, and he walked around the ranch.

He could have saddled a horse and taken a ride. But despite not being able to sleep, he was tired, and he didn't want an animal to get hurt because he wasn't alert enough to danger. Even now, in the distance, he could hear coyotes howling. He lifted his gaze to the sliver of the moon that barely penetrated the darkness, and he was tempted to howl as well.

He felt a little wild, a little out of control, a little helpless. He didn't know how to fix the mess he'd made of his life. If only Dale was around...

They'd talked nearly every day but for the last four weeks he was still alive, when Dusty had limited their calls to when Melanie was at work.

Dale, who'd loved Jenny so much from the first moment he'd met her, had assured him that he understood that honeymoon phase. He'd still been in it with Jenny even after all the years he'd known her. He was the one who'd first pointed out to Dusty that he'd fallen for the physical therapist he couldn't stop talking about, and he had encouraged Dusty to date her. "Or if she's a wonderful as you say she is, you should just marry her."

Dale must have been joking about the marriage, though, because he had never done anything impulsive. Even his decision to stay at the ranch, to marry Jenny, those were decisions he hadn't made lightly.

At least, that was what he'd told Dusty when he'd been so angry with him for going back on their plan, for reneging on their dream.

And Dusty had realized that the rodeo had really only been his dream. He'd lived it now, so maybe it was time to retire. To give it up…

To take the job Jake had offered as ranch foreman?

Thinking of the position reminded him of the cottage where Jake had lived until the accident. Even though Dale had had the job title, he'd lived in the ranch house with Jenny and his family while Jake, the general manager of the operation, had lived in the foreman's cottage.

Jake would undoubtedly stay in the house now since his family was growing. But what about his old place?

Gravel crunched under Dusty's boot heels as he walked down the path toward it. It had to be sitting empty now, but as he approached it, he heard what sounded like another scream. It wasn't as high-pitched and hysterical as Little Jake's had been but lower and more guttural, like that of an animal in pain. He glanced around, searching the shadows for that wounded animal. Maybe the coyotes he'd heard moments ago had injured something. As he neared the cottage, a motion light on the porch came on and dispelled the shadows closest to it, revealing someone moving around inside.

Dusty found himself at the door, pounding on it until that dark shadow appeared behind the glass panes and the door drew open. Wariness finally had his body tensing, ready for a fight—one he should have considered he might have when confronting an intruder.

"What are you doing here?" Baker asked, his voice raspy, as if he'd been sleeping...or uttering those noises Dusty had heard.

"What are *you* doing here?" Dusty asked. "I thought you left earlier, right after the family meeting. You said you had to get back to town."

Baker yawned. "It was already getting late, and I was tired. I figured I'd leave early in the morning."

"But what are you doing *here*?" Dusty asked. "Out in the foreman's cottage?"

Baker's broad shoulders lifted and dropped in a weary shrug. "I've been staying here while Jake and Katie were on their honeymoon. I didn't feel comfortable in the house. Grandma brought in all those women to help with the boys…"

Dusty bristled. "One of those women is my wife," he said. "Do you resent them stepping in and getting so close to the boys?" Or was his little brother worried about one of those women getting too close to him, like Katie had Jake and Emily had Ben? A smile twitched at his lips.

"No," Baker said. "I think they're all better for the boys than we are. At least me…" His chest expanded as he drew in a deep breath. "They're doing more for them than I can."

Dusty's eyes narrowed. "What do you mean? Because you're busy with work?"

Baker nodded. "Yeah, that's it."

But it wasn't. And Dusty knew it. "That's not what you meant," he said. "What do you mean? Why can't *you* do more for them?"

"Because I think I remind them of the accident," he said. "You might have forgotten that I was first on the scene…" His voice cracked. "But the boys haven't forgotten…or forgiven… me for not saving them."

Was that why Miller seemed so angry with Baker, even angrier than he was with his brothers and with Dusty? "I haven't forgotten that you were the first one there," Dusty assured him, his heart aching for what his younger brother must have seen, what he'd gone through trying to save them. When Dusty had gotten to the hospital that day, Baker had still had their blood on his clothes and a tortured look on his face that had never really left it. Clearly, he was never going to forget.

Was Baker worried that he reminded the boys of the accident? Or was he worried that the boys reminded him of it?

"That must have been horrible," Dusty said. He'd once lost a friend at a rodeo when a bull had trampled him; it had been so hard to see that and not be able to save him. But a family member… He shuddered.

And Baker stepped back. "You're cold. Come inside."

"It's not cold out," Dusty said. But he crossed the threshold and shut the door of the little cottage. It was dark inside, and Baker didn't reach for any lamps, almost as if he preferred the darkness. "Was that you that I heard?" he asked. "Were you yelling?"

It had been more than that, but Dusty knew that his little brother was a lot like Miller, very proud.

"You heard yelling?" Baker repeated as if surprised that Dusty had called it that.

He must have been aware of his nightmares. Maybe that was why he'd chosen to sleep out in the foreman's cottage and not because of the women or the little kids. He hadn't wanted his nightmares to wake up the rest of the house like Little Jake's nightmares did.

"Yeah," Dusty said. "I heard it. If you ever want to talk about it…"

Baker snorted. "I'll reach out to Mrs. Lancaster," he said, referring to the school psychologist.

But Baker wasn't a little boy anymore, no matter how much Dusty and their other brothers taunted him about being the baby of the family. Baker was a man. A man who'd gone to war abroad, and as a first responder at home, he'd gone to war when he'd tried to save his own family.

"Do you mind if I crash here tonight?" Dusty asked because Baker seemed to have made a proprietary claim on the cottage. "I don't want to wake anyone up looking for an empty bedroom right now."

"Sure," Baker said, and he almost sounded relieved, as if maybe he didn't really want to be alone like he pretended.

"Not that I'm all that tired," Dusty said. "In case you want to talk…"

Baker chuckled. "You want to play shrink?"

Dusty shook his head. "No. I'm not qualified for that. Heck, I probably need one myself…"

Maybe talking to someone could help him figure out how to have all the things he wanted: his wife, the rodeo, and more importantly, his wife's trust again. Because he knew he'd never have her if she couldn't trust him.

But he understood how difficult that would be for her to do now, after he'd failed her. Because he felt the same way, that she'd let him down.

"Well, don't look at me for any counseling," Baker told him, "especially if it's marriage counseling. I have no interest in that institution."

"Have you told Grandma that, because I think she has plans for you."

Baker snorted again. "She can plot and scheme and manipulate all she wants. She's not making me do what she wants like she has Jake and Ben."

Yet here Baker was…staying on the ranch…

Maybe not in the main house, but he was here. And for some reason, even though Jake had returned from his honeymoon, Baker seemed reluctant to leave.

Was it possible he loved the ranch more than he would admit? Maybe more than he was even aware?

Was it possible that Dusty cared about it more than he realized? That he could give up the rodeo and be happy here like Melanie seemed to be?

MELANIE AWOKE WITH a start, finding herself lying atop her covers, fully clothed. She hadn't thought she'd fall asleep; she'd been waiting for her mother to call her, to let her know she'd landed.

But because she hadn't wanted to wake anyone else in the house, Melanie had turned down the volume of the ringer. When she grabbed her phone from the bedside table, she noticed the missed call. And then the text.

It's late. I checked into a hotel near the airport. I'll see you tomorrow when you pick me up.

The address for the hotel was included in the text. Melanie gritted her teeth. While she loved her mother, she wasn't sure she could bring her here to the ranch. Dusty had assured her that it was her home, too, now—maybe even more so than his—but she didn't know if she believed it, if she felt that way.

For so long she'd doubted that her marriage was even real. And now...

Now that she knew it was legal, it felt even less real to her because she wasn't sure that it could last, that they wanted the same things for the future.

Her phone vibrated again. Mom...

She swiped to ignore. Just for a moment.

Just until she had time to talk to everyone. Her fingers trembled a bit when she texted: I'll call you soon.

Once she figured out how she was going to handle this. Chances were that her mother was already booking a return flight to Vegas. She could never stay away from Shep for long. He usually persuaded her to forgive him before she had her bags packed.

This time she'd made it to the plane. She'd made it to Sheridan. Melanie jumped up from the bed and hurriedly got cleaned up and ready to go.

Her mother needed her support now, just like she'd offered it when Melanie had left Dusty. As she descended the back stairwell to the kitchen, she heard the excited chatter of the children and the deeper rumble of adult conversations. But not Dusty's voice…

Maybe he'd already gone out to the barn to take care of that bronco that had been too dangerous for anyone else to handle…until Jake and Ben had gained his affection. How in the world had the thing ever trusted Dusty enough to let him ride it? To win it?

When she stepped into the kitchen, all conversation ceased. "Sorry I slept in," she murmured.

"Understandable," Taye returned. "You needed the rest."

Melanie nodded. "Did Dusty come down yet?"

Taye shook her head. "And I wouldn't have missed him."

Melanie knew that; Taye was always the first one up. She made Jake's breakfast and packed him a lunch before he started out for his day, which usually started at dawn. Yet he was sitting at the long table today, next to his wife and stepson.

"You haven't seen Dusty?" he asked Melanie.

She shook her head. "Not since he tucked in the boys last night."

"Not me," Miller said with a slight scowl. "I don't need tucking in."

If he'd meant to offend Caleb or Ian, they were unconcerned as they played with brightly colored paddleballs that Katie and Jake must have brought back from their Hawaiian honeymoon. Miller's sat next to his plate, untouched, just like his food. Was he still upset from last night?

Was he upset about Uncle Dusty being here? As upset as she was… She might be even more upset that after he'd explained everything to her, she'd wanted to forgive and forget…especially when he'd kissed her. She'd wanted him to stay, not just at the ranch, but with her. Then that fear had overcome her again, that fear that trusting him again would lead only to more disappointment and heartbreak.

He'd kept so much from her that she couldn't help but wonder what else he'd kept. And even if he hadn't, she would probably never stop wondering and worrying…

She would probably never trust him not to hurt her again. And she wasn't certain her heart would mend after another break. It ached even now from the cracks that were just beginning to heal. Could she risk it again?

Her stomach churned, reminding her too

much of the nausea she'd suffered every morning for too long. She was starting her second trimester now and had thankfully gotten over that. Or so she'd thought.

"Sit down," Taye insisted. "You need to eat." She put a full plate of toast, scrambled eggs and sausage next to Miller's.

"Thank you," she said. Maybe the food would settle her stomach. She slid next to Miller on the bench and squeezed his shoulders. "You need to eat too," she told him.

And he obediently picked up his fork and attacked his small stack of pancakes.

"And you call me the kid whisperer," Emily said to Taye. "I think Melanie's earning that title too."

Taye smiled. "I think you're both going to lose out to Mr. Lemmon."

Sadie, sitting at the head of the table, snorted. "That old fool is too deaf to *whisper* about anything." But she smiled, and her voice softened as she spoke of her former nemesis.

Melanie was new to Willow Creek, so she had no idea what reason Sadie would have had to dislike the man or vice versa. But she knew they'd known each other a long time. A lot could have happened between them. But they seemed to have been letting that animosity go now as it gave way to a sweet friendship.

Lem wasn't here today. He rarely was for breakfast as he worked in town with Ben, deputy to Ben's position of mayor. Ben wasn't here either, for the first time in a couple of weeks. Baker's absence was the norm.

But Dusty...

Even though he'd just returned, his absence seemed the most remarkable, at least to her. And maybe to Miller. Nonetheless, the little boy was eating now.

She needed to tackle her breakfast too. But first she had to ask Sadie, "Would it be all right if I take today off and borrow one of the ranch vehicles?"

Everybody stopped talking again, and Miller stopped eating, his fork suspended over his plate with a bite of pancake dripping syrup. "You're taking a day off?" he asked as if he didn't understand what that meant.

It felt strange to Melanie to ask for one; she hadn't since Sadie had hired her. But helping Miller's physical recovery wasn't a job to Melanie, not anymore. Not since she'd bonded with him that first day in the hospital.

"My mother flew into Sheridan last night to

see me," she said. She wasn't certain that was all her mother wanted.

Pick me up...

That made it sound like she intended for Melanie to take her somewhere. Here?

"That's wonderful," Taye said with a smile, but it was almost as if she was forcing it. And her blue eyes glistened slightly. Then she blinked, and she looked fine.

Had Melanie just imagined it? Probably.

Emily was the one who'd lost her mom when she was around the same age as Miller. She was the one who should have looked wistful because she could never see her mother again.

Melanie had missed hers. "Yes, it is," she said. Even more so if Juliet Shepard had finally decided to leave her husband. Melanie's father would be fine. Shep always landed on his feet. When an injury had ended his rodeo riding days, he'd become even more acclaimed as an announcer than he'd ever been as a rider. Though Melanie had often wondered if that was what had led to his cheating, that disappointment over the career he'd loved being taken from him.

Would that happen with Dusty if he gave up the rodeo he loved so much? Would he resent her as much as Shep resented his physical limitations?

"We'd all love to meet your mother," Sadie said. "Please, bring her here to the ranch."

Her stomach flipped at the thought of having to tell her mother everything she'd kept from her, let alone having to do it at the ranch. "Uh, I'm not sure that's such a good idea," she admitted.

"Why not?" Sadie pried.

"Well, I don't know how long she's planning on staying," Melanie replied. She hadn't had the chance yet to talk to her, to find out what Shep had done that had finally been the last straw for her mother.

If it was actually that at all, or if she was already reconsidering. She glanced at her phone, at the time, not the text from her mother. "I really should be going. Do you mind if I borrow a ranch vehicle?"

"You're not borrowing a vehicle," Jake said, and she might have been alarmed had his tone not been kind. "You're family, Melanie. The ranch is yours now too."

"Yes, it is," Sadie said. "So please bring your mother home with you. She's welcome to stay as long as she likes."

Tears stung Melanie's eyes at their kindness,

and at the thought of having a home. She and her mother had rarely stayed at whatever house Shep had rented for them; they'd usually traveled with him on the circuit. Maybe her mother had thought that would keep him honest and faithful. It hadn't.

Melanie blinked away her tears and smiled. "Thank you," she said. "I'll talk to her and find out her plans."

"Can I go with you?" Miller asked.

She was torn between wanting the boy to feel secure but also knowing she needed to have a serious conversation with her mother about Shep, and about the secrets Melanie had been keeping from her. "Uh…"

"I need your help today, Miller," Jake said.

"You need my help?" Miller asked skeptically.

"Yes, you need to bring me up to speed about what's happened around the ranch the past two weeks," he said.

"I can do that, Daddy Jake," Caleb offered.

Jake smiled. "Yes, you can, but it's very helpful to have different perspectives."

"Different what?" Ian asked.

"Points of view," Jake explained. "Miller might have noticed something you didn't notice. I'm sure you were in different places at different times, so you saw a lot of different things."

"I saw a lot of Uncle Ben kissing Miss Trent," Caleb said.

Everyone laughed, even Emily, though her face got a little pink. And Melanie breathed a little sigh of relief that no one had witnessed Dusty kissing her. They were married, and it would have been expected...except that everything about their marriage had been unexpected, including the marriage itself.

Miller leaned against Melanie's side and murmured, "I'd rather go with you than talk about Uncle Ben and Miss Trent kissing. Can I, please?"

Her mother would have no objections to Miller joining them; she loved kids and would have had more had she been able. But fertility issues, and maybe Shep's infidelities, had kept her from having any more.

Melanie wanted—needed—to be able to talk freely, though.

"Hey, Miller," Jake said. "We're done talking about kissing. We'll go for a nice long ride around the ranch. I've not been able to ride with you since your cast came off."

Miller jerked his head toward his uncle then and grinned. "A long ride?"

Jake nodded. "Yeah, I have to inspect the ranch. And we have to find Uncle Dusty." He sounded doubtful. Did he think Dusty had left again?

Had he?

CHAPTER ELEVEN

HIS WIFE WAS GONE. AGAIN.

By the time Dusty had finished cleaning out Midnight's stall and gone up to the house, Melanie had left.

"She's gone?" Dusty repeated what Taye had shared with him the minute he'd stepped into the kitchen.

She nodded. "Everybody thought you were too," she said as she waved him to a stool at the long kitchen island. She set a plate of biscuits and gravy in front of him, steam rising from it.

He narrowed his eyes at the plate. "You must not have." Or she wouldn't have had food waiting for him.

"I saw your truck outside," she said. "Melanie probably saw it when she left too."

Melanie wasn't the only person missing. Taye seemed to be the only one in the house since it was eerily quiet.

"Where did she go?" he asked, his heart pounding fast and hard at the thought that she might have taken off again, that he might have to figure out where to look for her next. This was why he worried about trying too hard to win her back—because he would never know for certain if he really had, or if she was going to take off at the first sign of trouble. Even though he knew the truth now, he couldn't forget how abandoned he'd felt when his mother had left, just as things got tough, how devastated he'd been. Like when he hadn't been able to find Melanie. He wasn't certain he could survive another desertion.

"Her mother flew into Sheridan, and she's going to pick her up," Taye explained, her voice a little raspy, as if she'd gotten emotional. But then she focused on him again and arched a dark blond brow. "She didn't tell you?"

He shook his head. "No." But she hadn't told him anything for more than two months; she hadn't even talked to him at all until yesterday.

"I'm sorry," Taye offered sympathetically.

He sighed. "It's my fault," he said, owning his mistake. "I..."

"Screwed up!" Sadie said as she joined them in the kitchen.

He glared at his grandmother, not that she was wrong. He'd been about to admit as much himself. But he wasn't the only one who'd messed up, and Dusty wanted to call her out on her hypocrisy. Baker had left that morning before Dusty had had a chance to ask him just how precarious Sadie's health actually was. As irritated as he was with her, he didn't want to hurt her...even though she'd hurt him.

"I screwed up too," the older woman admitted with a humility Dusty hadn't thought she possessed.

He expelled a shaky breath, releasing some of his resentment of her along with it.

"I'm sorry," she said now. "I should have told you where she was, and I should have told her that I knew who she was."

Dusty nodded in wholehearted agreement. "Yes, you should have."

"I was afraid that she would leave if I did," Sadie explained.

That, he could understand, especially now, with Melanie leaving the morning after his arrival. Had her mother really flown into Sheridan? And just her mother?

What about Shep? Juliet rarely left her husband's side except when he was working, and even then she hung around the rodeo as if reluctant to let him out of her sight. That was the lack of trust that Melanie didn't want to live with, and neither did Dusty.

"What about me?" Dusty asked. "Why didn't you tell me?"

Sadie sighed now and settled onto a stool next to his at the island. Her shoulders slumped as she propped her elbows onto the stainless-steel top.

"I... I'll leave you two alone," Taye murmured. "I have shopping to do anyway."

"You can..." Sadie began, but the young chef had already hustled out of the room "...stay." She sighed again.

It was clear to Dusty that his grandmother had become very attached to these women she'd hired. Something about Taye even reminded him of Sadie; maybe it was her intuition. Sure, she'd seen his truck in the driveway, but how had she known when he'd show up in the kitchen?

"Eat," Sadie insisted. "Before it gets cold. Taye's cooking is..." She uttered another sigh now but this one was almost lustful.

He took a bite of the biscuit, soaked with chunky sausage gravy, and moaned with pleasure. "She is really good," he proclaimed, and he regretted that he hadn't paid more attention to dinner the night before. But he'd still been in shock over finding his runaway bride at the ranch.

Sadie nodded. "That's why that old fool Lemmon keeps coming around."

One of the few things Dusty had noticed at dinner the night before was that Lem had seemed more interested in Sadie than in his plate. "Okay," he murmured around his mouthful. "If that's what you want to believe…"

"I believe in you," Sadie said. "I knew you'd come back to the ranch."

"I would have come back sooner if you'd told me my wife was here," Dusty pointed out.

"I wanted you to come back on your own," she explained. "And I was being stubborn because I was irritated that you'd kept your marriage a secret from all of us."

"I told Dale," he said. "Is that who told you?"

She shook her head. "Your twin would never betray your confidence," she said. Then she chuckled and added, "Now, your manager…"

Instead of laughing with her, Dusty huffed now as his irritation with his grandmother returned with such force that his stomach turned. "How can *you* judge me at all for keeping secrets?" he asked.

The color in her face receded, leaving her skin starkly pale. "You *do* know…" she murmured.

He nodded.

"How?" she asked.

"When I was looking for my wife, I found my mother," he said.

She arched a brow and asked, "How? Did you just accidentally stumble across her?"

He shook his head. "No. I sought her out. I actually had her number for years. Someone on the rodeo circuit gave it to me."

Shep. In a moment of weakness, Dusty had asked for it, knowing that if anyone had her number, it would have been that womanizer. Shep had insisted that he'd never been involved with her. As an announcer, he had contact information for all the riders, even the ones who'd retired long ago, like she had. Dusty shouldn't have worried about running into her on the circuit when he'd joined because she'd retired before he started. Shep had wondered why he'd wanted her number, but Dusty hadn't admitted she was his mother, just an old acquaintance.

He hadn't called her until that day at the hospital when he'd confirmed that his twin was gone. For all the good that call had done him. That was why, just before returning to the ranch, he'd tracked down where she was living. As angry as he'd been with Darlene over deserting them all those years ago, he'd been more upset that she hadn't been there for Dale and Jenny's funeral.

"You called her?" Sadie asked, her voice slightly hoarse.

He nodded. "I thought she deserved to know that one of her children had died."

Sadie flinched, and he felt a twinge of guilt and alarm.

"Are you okay?" he asked with concern, and he reached out and covered the hand she'd fisted against the countertop. "We don't have to talk about this now." But he wanted to talk about it, not just with her but with his brothers as well. They all deserved to know the truth.

"I... I can't..." Sadie choked out, and she jumped up from the stool, pulling her hand from beneath his.

He'd never known his grandmother to not face something head-on, no matter how painful it was. And she had to know what else his mother had told him, whom she'd told him about.

"We do need to talk about it, though," he told her. "With everyone."

She nodded. "I know. Just give me a little time..."

That was the same thing his mother had asked for when he'd appealed to her to come to the ranch, to see her sons, to meet her grandsons. She'd shaken her head and pleaded for a little time. Time to prepare herself? Or more time to grieve the son she'd lost before getting the chance to reconnect?

Because of that, she shouldn't have wanted to waste another minute before reconnecting with the rest of them. After finding where she'd been living, Dusty had been even more determined to find Melanie. But unlike with his mother, whose location he'd tracked down through old rodeo friends of hers, nobody had helped him find his wife. Not her friends. Not her family.

Not his family.

That pressure was back on his chest, pushing hard on his lungs. The pressure he'd felt when he'd been searching for her. What if she didn't come back today? But she had to, if not for him, at least for Miller and his other nephews.

When she'd run away months ago, it had been from Dusty, not the ranch. She would be back. She had to be back.

"SHE'S NOT COMING BACK!" Miller shouted the minute Dusty walked in the door that evening, after he'd spent the day working the ranch with

Jake while trying not to worry that this very thing was going to happen.

Small fists struck Dusty's chest and stomach as Miller launched himself at him. "It's all your fault! It's all your fault! I wish you never came back!"

Instead of pushing his nephew away, Dusty wrapped his arms around the boy and pulled him closer. "What's wrong? What's going on!"

"Aunt Melanie isn't coming back," the little boy said, his voice cracking with his tears. "And I know it's because she doesn't want to see you."

The kid was smart and had obviously figured out that Melanie hadn't been happy for her husband to come home.

"Miller," Emily said. The teacher's voice held exasperation and concern as she rushed down the hall, with Taye and Ben following close behind her. "Aunt Melanie told you herself when she called that her mother needs her—"

"I need her!" Miller interrupted, and tears slipped down his face, which was already red and splotchy from crying.

Dusty regretted now the extra time he'd taken at Midnight's stall. He should have come back sooner, should have been here when Melanie called.

"She promised to be back in the morning," Taye added.

"People lie," Miller said. "People lie all the time."

Dusty's brow furrowed. How did the kid know that already? Who had lied to him? Had Grandma shared her secrets while Dusty had been out?

The little fists stopped pummeling him as Miller jerked back and ran up the stairs to the second story.

"What's going on?" Dusty asked.

Emily uttered a shaky sigh. "We should have gotten the boys help before now…"

Ben slid his arm around his fiancée's slim shoulders. He must have driven back to the ranch after spending his day at city hall because Dusty hadn't seen him earlier. "That's not your fault," Ben assured her. "It's ours." And he shared a pointed look with Dusty.

He didn't deflect or defend himself. There was no defense. He should have been here for his nephews. As Dale's twin, he felt even more responsible for the boys, and even guiltier for not being here.

Emily started toward the stairs. "I'll go talk to him."

Dusty shook his head. "No. I will."

"Are you sure?" Ben asked skeptically. "He seems to be taking this out on you."

Dusty focused on Taye then. "Should he be?" he asked, figuring that the cook, with her intuition, might know the real reason that Melanie wasn't returning.

She shook her head. "No, I don't think so. It sounded like her mom's going through something..." Her voice trailed off as it got raspy. She cleared her throat and continued. "And Melanie just didn't want to leave her."

Dusty groaned. "Shep..." He must have done something that had really upset his wife, enough for her to finally leave him.

Melanie's father was the reason that she struggled so hard to trust anyone, and with good reason. Now Dusty's odds of ever regaining her trust had just gotten worse. Maybe he could regain his nephew's, though.

"I'll talk to Miller," he said. More than anyone else, he identified with the boy's fear that Melanie wouldn't return. They both loved her.

MELANIE HADN'T INTENDED to go back to the ranch. At least not tonight, not with as upset as her mother was. But when she'd called and Miller had gotten on the phone, he'd sounded even more upset than Juliet was with Shep.

Melanie glanced across the console of the van at her mother, who sat quietly in the passenger seat, staring out the side window. Her image reflected back in the glass. Juliet Shepard was a beautiful woman with thick, curly, dark hair and big dark eyes, and a figure that women much younger than her envied and tried to emulate. Her mother was in her mid-fifties but looked thirty, except for the furrow between her brows, the worry lines.

And Melanie hadn't even told her everything yet. She hadn't had the chance. Her mother had been talking nonstop since Melanie had met her at the hotel, until now, until she must have finally talked herself out.

Melanie was stunned by what she'd revealed. While she'd feared, when Traci had showed her that picture, that Dusty had a secret family, her mother had proof that Shep had one.

At least a son...

Maybe more children than that. There had always been rumors. But now her mother had proof.

"Are you all right coming back to the ranch with me?" Melanie asked again. She'd had to come back for Miller, but she hadn't wanted to leave her mother alone.

"As long as you're sure it's okay with your employer," Juliet said.

And Melanie stiffened. She needed to tell her everything. "Um…"

Juliet turned toward her then. "It is okay with them, right?"

Melanie nodded. "You will be very welcome there."

Her mother reached across the console and squeezed her arm. "Thank you," she said.

"Of course. You're always going to have a place to stay with me," Melanie assured her. Just as her mother had taken care of her in those several days that Melanie had been so devastated after Dusty had left for home.

"Thanks for that too," her mother said. "But thank you for giving me the strength to leave him."

"How did I do that?" Melanie asked, wonder in her voice. She'd been trying for years to point out that her mother would be better off alone than in a relationship with a man she couldn't trust. But Juliet had never listened to her before.

"You showed me," Juliet explained. "When

you left Dusty, despite how much you love him. You showed me what true strength is."

Melanie groaned. She would have closed her eyes then, too, but she needed to focus on the road. This close to the ranch, there were no streetlamps; only the van's headlights illuminated the narrow country road.

"What?" her mother asked with concern. "What's wrong? Are we lost?"

She had felt lost especially in those first days after Dusty had left their apartment so abruptly. But not anymore...not since his return to the ranch. "No, I know the way."

To the property. But could she and Dusty ever find their way back to each other? Would they ever be able to trust one another again?

She sighed.

"I could drive, sweetheart," Juliet offered. "If you're tired."

Melanie could feel her mother's scrutiny, her concern.

"I've been rattling on and on about myself, about your father," her mother said. "And I haven't asked how you've been. If it's getting any easier..."

Maybe she hadn't asked because she'd already seen that answer on Melanie's face, and she hadn't wanted confirmation that leaving a man you loved was the hardest thing to do.

"We're not far from the ranch now," Melanie said. So she needed to tell her. "And I am tired, Mom, because I'm pregnant. With twins."

Juliet gasped. She looked stunned momentarily before asking, "Are you okay? Is your health okay?"

Melanie thought so, but her little fainting spell yesterday had raised enough concerns that she knew it was past time that she found an obstetrician in Willow Creek. "Yes."

"Oh, sweetheart…what are you going to do?"

Melanie expelled a shaky breath. "I have no idea," she admitted.

"We'll figure it out together," her mother assured her. "You're not alone."

"No," Melanie said. "I'm not alone." She drew in a breath now, bracing herself for what she had to share. "I'm with family at the ranch."

"That's sweet," her mother said. "That you've gotten so close to everyone. I've loved your stories about the boys and about the other women who work there. Katie and Emily and Taye. I can't wait to meet them, and Sadie. That woman sounds quite formidable."

"She's really not…" Melanie murmured. "And she was very adamant that you are welcome and can stay as long as you want."

Her mother smiled softly. "That's so gracious. She must really appreciate your work with her great-grandson."

Melanie nodded. "She does. But…" Regret weighed heavily on her, making her shoulders slump from the burden of it. She wished she'd told her mom everything. Maybe she hadn't because she'd known what a coward she'd been when she hadn't given Dusty the chance to talk to her. When she'd been staying with her mother and Dusty had called there, her mom had urged her to take his calls, had said how tortured he'd sounded.

Her mother's hand tightened on her arm. "But what?"

"She's also Dusty's grandmother," Melanie said. "The picture that I saw…it was Dusty's twin and his wife. And Miller and Ian and Little Jake."

Her mother's stunned expression was back as she took a few moments to process what Melanie had revealed. Then she blanched. "So Dusty's twin is who died."

Melanie nodded. "He and his wife." She'd

told her mother about the horrible accident, just not about everything else.

"But you said Dusty had no family…"

"I didn't know…" Melanie said. "Until I got here."

"That was several weeks ago," her mother said. "And Dusty's still been calling me, still been trying to find out where you are. You're with his family and he doesn't know?"

"He does now," Melanie said.

Her mother's brow creased. "Why didn't you tell me?"

"He just got home yesterday," Melanie said.

"No, why didn't you tell me weeks ago that you were wrong about that picture?" her mother asked, and she sounded hurt now.

"I felt stupid for jumping to conclusions," Melanie admitted. "And I wasn't sure if it changed anything. He still hadn't told me about the ranch or his brothers and nephews and grandmother." She sighed. "I didn't even know his real name."

"What is it?" her mother asked.

But Melanie didn't have to answer because the van headlights illuminated the sign on the gate as she turned into the driveway. Ranch Haven…

Her mother stayed silent then, maybe in deference to the darkness of the ranch house.

It was late. Everyone had gone to bed, so they were quiet as they carried her mother's suitcase up the back steps. "You can share my room tonight," Melanie said as they entered it. "And we'll find you an empty guest room tomorrow."

She didn't want to wake anyone now.

"What about Dusty?" her mother asked.

Melanie shrugged. "I have no idea where he slept last night." Or where he was tonight because her room was empty but for her and her mother.

"You haven't taken him back?" her mother asked. "Now that you know the truth?"

Melanie shook her head. She wasn't even sure he really wanted her back. "There were too many secrets..." she murmured.

Her mother arched a dark brow. "Yes, there were, and he wasn't the only one keeping them. You should have told me all of this."

Melanie was glad now that she hadn't. Her mother might not have had the strength to leave Shep if she hadn't believed Melanie had been justified when she'd left Dusty.

"I'm going to check on Miller," she said. He'd sounded so upset during their phone call.

Fortunately, she hadn't had her cell on speaker, or her mother would have heard him yelling that she wasn't coming back because of Uncle Dusty, that it was all his fault. She didn't want to cause any more of a rift in that relationship than there already was.

"Can I come?" her mother asked. "I'd like to see him. You talk about him so often and with such love. In fact, he's the only thing you've really talked to me about." Tears glistened in her mother's eyes.

Melanie hugged her. "I'm sorry, Mom." About so many things.

Her mother gently squeezed her back before releasing her. "You need your rest. You and those babies, so let's check on Miller and then go to bed ourselves."

Melanie led her mom the short distance down the hall to the little boy's door and quietly turned the doorknob. She didn't want to wake him if he was asleep, and she hoped that he was sleeping. But as upset as he'd sounded, and without her to comfort him, she wasn't sure that he would have been able to.

The light from the hall spilled into the room and across the relaxed face of the little boy. His eyes were closed, his long lashes lying against his cheeks. He wasn't alone, though, for that light illuminated another face, of a handsome man, his eyes closed, as well, his hair, the same golden brown of Miller's, tousled against the pillow they shared.

Dusty's long muscular body was contorted and probably partially in the crack between the small bed and the wall. There wasn't really enough space for both of them in there, yet Dusty had stayed with his nephew.

"Oh…" her mother whispered. "That's so sweet…"

Tears stung Melanie's eyes as love overwhelmed her…for both Miller and her husband. This was the man she'd married, the man she'd thought Dusty was before she'd determined she hadn't really known him at all. He was humble and sweet and kind.

He was also a rodeo rider. Could he give that up for his family, for the ranch, for her and their babies?

And did she want him to make those sacrifices even if he was willing? Could she take him away from what he loved so much and trust him not to resent her for it? Was that why her dad had cheated so often? Because he'd resented no longer being able to ride? If Melanie gave Dusty another chance, would they wind up just like her parents?

CHAPTER TWELVE

DUSTY KNEW EXACTLY what he wanted: more
sleep. But as he rode the ranch early the next
day, he should have been grateful that he'd
managed to get any at all while sharing that
tiny bed of Miller's, with the boy continually
jabbing him with his elbow or his knee. The
kid had been so upset and worried that Melanie wasn't coming back; he hadn't been the
only one.

Instead of lying to him, like Miller had accused everyone else of doing, Dusty had admitted his concern. "I'm worried about that
too." He'd also been worried about her making that long drive on her own, especially after
having fainted the day before. He hadn't shared
that worry with his young nephew.

"If you want to, because you can't sleep
or something, you can stay in here with me,"
Miller had offered as he'd pulled back his blankets to invite Dusty to share that small bed.

He hadn't been able to refuse. He hadn't had

to be back at the ranch long to realize that the kid had let few people past his guard after the accident. Melanie actually might have been the only one.

So Dusty hadn't been about to turn down the olive branch the little boy had offered, and he'd folded his long body to fit next to the anxious child on the mattress. Miller had eventually fallen asleep after Dusty had, at the kid's urging, told him several stories about stupid things he and Dale had done when they were kids. The trouble they'd gotten into switching places in school and even trying at home, although they'd never fooled Grandma Sadie. Just Grandpa Jake a few times. Quite a few times...

His lips curved into a smile as he thought of Grandpa Jake. The original Big Jake...

The new Big Jake glanced over his shoulder at Dusty and narrowed his eyes beneath the brim of his hat. "Your mood improving?"

Dusty's Appaloosa followed Buck, Jake's buckskin quarter horse, across a pasture as their riders checked the fences. The horses were more alert than Dusty was, though. He squinted against the brightness of the sun bearing down on them.

His brother must have interpreted his look as a glare because he mumbled, "Guess not."

As well as being tired, Dusty was a little irritated with his brother. "We could cover more ground if we weren't riding together," he said. Again. He'd told Jake that when his older brother had come up to him at Midnight's stall earlier that morning. Too early.

"But who would find you when you fall asleep in the saddle and topple off your horse?" Jake asked.

"I'm not going to fall asleep," he said, especially not now, since he was getting frustrated. "And I know my way around this ranch too. I won't get lost." But he didn't think that was the reason for Jake's insistence on riding together. This felt more like an on-the-job audition, which was how Baker had interviewed a couple of prior candidates for the ranch foreman position.

Dusty wasn't sure he even wanted the job, but he was insulted that Jake intended to try him out and test him for the position, as if he doubted that he was actually qualified for it. And maybe he wasn't; because, like he'd been trying to tell everyone, he wasn't Dale. They were not interchangeable.

"I don't know…" Jake returned. "You've been gone a long time, and a lot has changed."

"Has it?" Dusty quipped. While there were a few new varieties of cattle in the pasture and some horse breeding, the ranch looked much the same to him.

"You can't see how the ranch has expanded?" Jake asked, stunned.

"Where?" Dusty asked. "Did you buy more land?"

"We have enough land," Jake replied, looking offended.

"Are you sure?" He'd recently learned that a ranch within an hour's drive was going up for sale. It was nowhere near the size or condition of Ranch Haven but it had some verdant pastures, mostly because they hadn't been used for so long.

"I'm sure," Jake replied—shortly.

"Then what's expanded?" Dusty asked.

"We're raising a lot more head of cattle, and we're breeding quarter horses now too."

Dusty shrugged. "Still no bulls? No broncos?"

Jake snorted. "Why would we breed those?"

"For rodeos," Dusty replied. "There's a big market, and a lot of money to be made." It was why Dusty had sent Midnight home to the ranch—in hopes of getting Jake to see the possibility of doing it themselves.

"The ranch is doing well now," Jake said.

Dusty knew there had been some lean years in the beginning, when Jake had first taken over after Grandpa's death. But he and Dale had worked hard to make it prosper.

"I know," Dusty said. "I just think you're missing some opportunities."

"Me or you?" Jake asked. "Who's missing what opportunities? Are you missing the rodeo? Or could you be happy here as the ranch foreman?"

"I'm not Dale," Dusty reminded him, although he doubted his oldest brother needed the reminder. Dale had been Jake's best friend too. Maybe they'd been even closer than Dusty and Dale because they'd both loved the ranch so much. "I'd want to do some things my own way," Dusty said. If he stayed…

"That's not the issue," Jake said. "You know rodeo, but ranching is totally different."

"I know livestock," Dusty said. "Bulls. Horses. I know that ranches that cater to rodeos make a lot of money. Midnight can make us a lot of money."

"We're lucky Midnight hasn't cost us a lot

more," Jake said, "and I'm not talking about just money. He's dangerous to be around."

Dusty snorted. "Surely, you can't say that anymore. You and Caleb and Ben have tamed him." As much as a bronco like Midnight would ever be tamed.

Jake smirked as if he wasn't convinced.

"I have an angle on a mare that I'd like to use for breeding with him," Dusty said, excitement coursing through him as he remembered finding her. He still couldn't believe where she'd been and how valuable she was. "She's a little pricey, but she'd be worth it."

"You want to buy her?"

"I want the ranch to buy her," Dusty said. "I want to expand to supplying animals for rodeos." He and Dale had discussed the idea several times, but clearly, from Jake's surprise, Dale hadn't mentioned it to their oldest brother.

"Not everything is about rodeo," Jake insisted. "And I sure as heck don't want to cater to them."

"Because of me or because of Mom?" Dusty asked. And he knew that he needed to tell the rest of his family what his mother had admitted to him. Whether they believed her or not, they deserved to know the reason she'd left. He still wasn't sure that he believed it, but at least she'd told him. She'd wanted to be the one to tell everyone else, but Dusty wasn't going to wait for her to come around like he'd been waiting since he was nine years old for her to come home.

Like he and Miller had waited for Melanie to come home last night. Taye had assured him, when he had found her in the kitchen this morning, that Melanie and her mother had made it safely back to the ranch the previous evening.

He'd expected that pressure on his chest to ease then, that he'd be able to breathe a little easier knowing she was all right. But *they* weren't all right, so neither was he.

He'd thought the weight that had nearly smothered him for the past several weeks would ease once he knew where she was. But even though he knew now where she was, he had no idea where *they* were in their relationship, in their marriage, so that burden was just as heavy as it had been since that morning Jake had called him with the horrible news. Just like Melanie had said—everything had changed.

In that moment, Dusty had known that his life would never be the same. He'd lost his twin, which had felt like losing part of himself. And even though he'd come back home, he still felt lost, like he didn't even know who he was anymore or what he wanted.

MELANIE STRUGGLED TO open her eyelids, which felt so heavy with fatigue. She and her mom had gotten back late the night before, so she hadn't set her alarm. She'd wanted to rest; she knew that being pregnant with twins, she needed more sleep. And less stress.

At least she could control her sleep. She probably would have let herself slip deeper into it if she hadn't had the sensation that someone was staring at her. Probably her mom.

They'd shared her bed, which fortunately was bigger than the one that Dusty had shared with Miller last night.

Warmth flooded her heart as she thought again of how the man and the boy had looked cuddling together in that small space. Like father and son…

She touched her stomach then, rubbing her palm over it. Soon…he would be a father. She would be a mother.

But would they ever be a family?

With a sigh, she opened her eyes and peered up into the face leaning over her. While her mother had few wrinkles, this person had none except for the slight crease in his brow as he stared down at her with his hazel eyes.

"You came back," Miller declared.

And a twinge of regret struck her heart that he'd been worried she wouldn't.

"I told Uncle Dusty that you would," he said.

Maybe he wasn't the one who'd been worried; and given how she'd disappeared on her husband without any explanation, she couldn't blame him for being concerned. She could still blame Dusty for not being completely honest with her...though she was beginning to soften regarding that as well. She hadn't been very forthcoming with her mother, and she and Juliet had always shared everything. Maybe that hadn't been a good thing for a daughter to hear the things about her father that she'd heard at such a young and impressionable age. Maybe that was why she struggled so hard to trust anyone, even herself.

"I told you that I would come back," Melanie reminded him. She reached up and touched his sweet face. "I wouldn't lie to you." She knew how badly it hurt to have someone you cared about shatter your trust.

He nodded. "I know."

"I hope you do," she said. It was clear the little boy needed someone he could trust. Had he begun to trust his uncle Dusty? Was that why they'd been together last night? She should have been happy that they'd bonded, but she was worried that Dusty might let down the little boy like he'd let her down.

She glanced around the room then. "Did you meet my mom?" she asked.

He nodded. "She's really nice. She's downstairs helping Miss Taye bake."

Melanie smiled. "Yes, she's very sweet." That was why she'd kept forgiving her husband. Or was Melanie the reason? Had she made sacrifices for her? For their family?

What sacrifices was Melanie willing to make for hers?

Because when these babies were born, they were going to be a family. He was their father; she their mother. And it didn't matter whether or not they were together, they would always have that bond of being parents to the same children.

Miller leaned down and hugged her.

And this bond…

With these beautiful children. His nephews. She wanted to stay a part of their lives no matter what happened between her and Dusty.

She wanted to stay at the ranch. She was more certain of that than she was of her mar-

riage. She wasn't certain that she could stay
with Dusty...not unless she could find a way
to trust him again. To trust herself again...

THERE WAS A time not long ago when Sadie
would have opened the door to Lem Lemmon
standing on her front porch and then slammed
it in his wrinkled face. Now she opened the
door, grabbed his arm and jerked him over
the threshold. Then she slammed it behind
him and tugged him down the hall to her private suite. She pulled him inside with her and
slammed that door too.

"Okay, we're alone," she announced after
releasing a shaky sigh.

Lem's throat moved as if he were choking
on something. "I had no idea this was what
you wanted when you called and told me to
get my butt out here."

She grimaced. "What are you talking
about?"

He wiggled his bushy white eyebrows up
and down over blue eyes that twinkled with
mischief. "Me. You want me, Sadie March
Haven."

She snorted with derision even as heat
rushed to her face. "You know the only thing
I want with you is..." Somebody to talk to,

somebody who understood, like Lem understood her, who'd suffered the same losses, who'd lived the same lives, who knew the same people.

That person had once been Big Jake, but he'd died a dozen years ago. And she hadn't realized how lonely she'd been until Lem had started coming around and she'd had someone to talk to, to *really* talk to…

Her pulse quickened a little with the realization, and she shook her head, vanquishing the crazy thought. She knew why her grandson Ben had started bringing his deputy mayor around the ranch; he'd wanted to give her a dose of her own matchmaking medicine.

But she was not about to take it.

No. She was the most stubborn of all the Havens, except maybe for Dusty and for…

She released a shaky sigh and closed her eyes against the sudden rush of tears.

"What's wrong, Sadie?" Lem asked with what sounded like genuine concern, and his hands gripped her arms, as if he was worried that she might keel over if he didn't hold her up.

"Dusty knows…"

"Of course he knows," Lem remarked. "He

was bound to realize that the physical therapist you hired for Miller is his wife."

She opened her eyes and glared at him. "I'm not talking about that." That felt like old news now…after the conversation she'd had with Dusty the day before. "He found Darlene."

"His mother?" Lem asked.

Sadie nodded.

"How is she?"

She shrugged. "He didn't really say, and I didn't really ask because there was something else…"

"What?" Lem asked with more concern, and his hands, which were surprisingly strong despite his age, tightened around her arms.

"I think she must have told him about Jessup…" Her heart ached just saying his name.

Lem sucked in a breath. "You never talk about him."

She shook her head. It was too painful.

"So how did she know?" Lem asked.

She sighed. No doubt Darlene had learned about him from her husband, Sadie's younger son. "I'm sure Michael talked about him. Jessup was his big brother. He loved him so much. He missed him so much."

"So do you," Lem said, and he moved his

hands from her arms to close around her back. He pulled her against him. "I'm sorry, Sadie. What did Dusty say?"

She shook her head. "Nothing really…but I promised I'd talk to him and the rest of the family, that we'd talk about…" Her throat felt as if it was closing, choking her with emotions she'd tried to bury so long ago, long before she'd buried Michael and then Big Jake.

"Do you want me to watch the little ones again while you talk to your grandsons?" he asked. "What do you need from me?"

Tears stung her eyes at his kindness. Ever since their first day of elementary school, they'd been rivals, competing for the best grades and the friendships of their classmates. They'd rarely had kind words for each other, but when it had mattered, like when Michael and then Jake had died, Lem had been there for her. And when his beloved Mary had gotten sick, she'd tried to return the favor.

But until now she'd never realized what they were: friends. And she closed her arms around him and just held on for a moment. And it was nice. Nice to have a man hold her again.

"What do you need?" Lem asked again.

Because he was that kind of man, the kind that stepped in and stepped up; it was why he'd been mayor of Willow Creek for so many years after her father retired.

It was why he was here now.

She pulled back and sucked in a breath, trying to steady herself. "I can't talk to any of them yet until I know…"

"Until you know what?" he asked. "About how much Dusty knows?"

She shook her head. "I need to know what happened to Jessup."

He had to be dead. With as sick as he'd been and all the years that had passed…

He had to be dead. That was why Dusty's comment had struck such a nerve when he'd talked about his mother. When he'd said, "I thought she deserved to know that one of her children had died…"

Sadie deserved to know, too, but she didn't. She'd spent the past forty-two years wondering what had happened to her firstborn, where he was buried…

"Help me find out what happened to my son," she pleaded to Lem. She'd tried for years to find him, but she hadn't been successful.

Then she'd tried for years to forget him, but she hadn't been successful at that either. That was the one thing she and Big Jake had never really talked about; their runaway son. She hadn't wanted to know if he'd blamed her as much as she'd blamed herself. And she'd been able to tell how much he'd been hurting and missing him without ever having to ask him.

"I need to know," she said.

Lem didn't argue with her. He didn't point out how impossible a task she'd asked him to help her with; he just nodded. And she knew that she'd appealed to the right person. He would help her find out the truth.

Somehow...just as he'd bested her so many times over the years of their rivalry, he would best her this time. He would find out what she hadn't been able to; he would find her missing son.

CHAPTER THIRTEEN

As THE DAY had worn on, Jake had worn on Dusty's nerves more and more until they were so frayed that he felt like Midnight, who reared up the minute Dusty neared his stall after he'd tended to the Appaloosa.

He was surprised that Jake hadn't supervised his work, offering critiques or easier ways of doing things, like he'd kept doing all day. Dusty had felt like a dumb kid to his older and wiser brother. Now he understood how Baker had felt growing up as the youngest, why he'd complained all these years about how his older brothers had treated him like a baby.

Of course, Baker hadn't put his complaint in those words since he was at least a teenager, but for the first time Dusty understood how he must have felt. Inadequate.

If Jake had treated Dusty that way while he was growing up, Dusty hadn't noticed. But then, he'd been so focused on his dream, on his plan of leaving for the rodeo, that he hadn't paid much attention. He'd known he wasn't going to be at the ranch or even in Willow Creek for long, so it hadn't mattered. Nothing had mattered to Dusty but the rodeo.

Now he was married. He had a wife. Babies on the way. And orphaned nephews to worry about. And big shoes to fill if he decided to take Dale's job.

If Jake was still considering him for the position...

Dusty felt like he'd failed the tests Jake had not-so-subtly given him today. He didn't see the ranch the way that Jake did. The way that Dale had.

While Dale had been Dusty's twin, he'd been much more like Jake in disposition and in their love of the ranch. Dusty cared about it, but it wasn't his whole life, like it was Jake's—or had been Jake's until he'd married.

And it was clear Jake was willing to let someone else carry the load of the responsibilities for the ranch...as long as that person agreed with him on how to run it. Dusty thought the family business could be more, that it could earn a nationwide reputation for raising rodeo livestock, if Jake would open up his mind to the possibilities.

But his brother wasn't open to anything

rodeo-related. Was that because of Mom? Did he hold the rodeo responsible for her leaving? Did he hold it responsible for Dusty's leaving?

That wasn't the rodeo's fault; it was theirs. They'd each chosen to leave. The rodeo was his passion, but it hadn't forced him to leave. Mom had had reasons of her own...reasons that the rest of the family deserved to know sooner rather than later. Maybe it was time that Dusty called a family meeting, but first he needed to check in with his grandmother again, to make sure that she was physically and emotionally ready to have the conversation they all needed to have.

No more secrets...

Midnight reared up again when Dusty opened his stall. The bronco had proven to be empathetic before; maybe he could feel the frustration building in Dusty, maybe it was putting him as on edge as Dusty felt.

Or was Midnight just mad that he hadn't been getting the time and attention that a magnificent animal like him deserved?

"I know, I know," he told the horse. "You're getting bored hanging out in this stall with nobody giving you the challenge you crave." Dusty's right palm itched with the need to grasp a rope, to hold it tightly as he flew up and down on the back of a horse. This horse...

He'd flown up and down and off the first time...when Midnight had sent him right to Melanie. And the second time... Dusty had sent Midnight here, not even knowing that Melanie was already at the ranch.

He rubbed his palm along the horse's jaw. "You are a magnificent animal." The horses he could breed...

The mare wouldn't be available much longer, not with as valuable as it was and with as much as the owner seemed to need money. Dusty needed to put in an offer. He could afford her. But where would he put her? Jake had shot down his plans, and he clearly wasn't happy about Dusty sending Midnight here either.

"Can I ride him now?" a small voice asked. "Can I?"

The horse didn't rear up like he had for Dusty, instead he shifted and nickered as if delighted with this visitor. But then, how could he not be when the little blond boy brandished a bunch of carrots in his small hand?

"Are those for me?" Dusty teased Caleb.

Caleb glanced at the carrots and wrinkled his nose with disgust. "You want them? Miss

Taye and Grandma Jules just made a bunch of cookies."

"Grandma Jules?" he repeated, confused, until it dawned on him that Caleb was talking about Melanie's mom, his mother-in-law, who was soon to be a grandmother. Apparently, Juliet was already embracing her new role.

"Aunt Melanie's mom," Caleb said. "She's really nice. And she really likes Miss Taye's cookies too. Have you had any yet?"

He shook his head, but he had no doubt they were exceptional like everything else Taye had cooked or baked that he'd eaten since he'd arrived. The ranch was much different now than it had been when he'd left right after the funeral. Those first two weeks after the accident had been lonely. Even with his brothers and nephews and Grandma in the house, it had felt empty because it had been missing two very important people. Dale and Jenny, and because Miller had still been in the hospital, they'd been missing him too.

Dusty glanced behind Caleb, but he must have come out to the barn alone. Ian and Miller and Little Jake weren't with him. Miller was probably glued to Melanie since her return. He felt a little pang of regret that he might have lost some of the ground he'd made up with his nephew.

"I'll bring you some cookies," Caleb offered, but there was a note to his voice and a spark in his blue eyes that alerted Dusty to the fact there might have been a catch. Then he added, "If you show me how to ride Midnight."

"Your mom said you need to wait to learn to be a rodeo rider," Dusty reminded him. "And even when that time comes…" Though he doubted it would, given how much Caleb's new stepfather resented the rodeo. "You might want to start out a little smaller. Midnight is a tough horse to ride."

"But you rode him."

Dusty sighed. "Yes, but I've been riding for years." And he had the scars and aches and pains to prove it. "And riding horses and riding broncos is very different."

"Will you show me?" Caleb asked again. "I mean will you actually show me how you rode Midnight? Will you ride him again for me to see?"

Dusty glanced back at the horse, who'd gently taken his bunch of carrots from Caleb's outstretched hand. But now the bronco eyed Dusty warily and shifted his hooves against the ground, as if he was considering rearing up. Midnight must have sensed Dusty's irritation with his big brother and his restlessness. The horse seemed restless too. Bored...

Dusty turned back to the boy and admitted, "I don't know if he'll let me do it again."

"Will you try?"

"I'll try, but only if you promise me that you won't," Dusty said. "Just like your mom told you, you have to wait until you're a lot bigger before you can learn how to be a rodeo rider and ride broncos and bulls."

Tears glistened in the little boy's blue eyes. "I don't know if I'll ever get big," he said, his voice cracking with emotion.

Concern gripped Dusty's heart, squeezing it tightly. He'd just met the child a couple of days ago, but he already cared about him. Did the kid have some medical ailment, some fatal diagnosis? "What do you mean?"

"Grandpa and Grandma O said I prolly won't get that tall. That since I'm just like my daddy, I'll be short like he was." The tears trailed over. "I love my daddy, and I like being like him. But I wish I could be tall like Daddy Jake."

Grandpa and Grandma O must mean Katie's parents. O'Brien. Why would they have said something so insensitive to such a little kid?

Irritated with the grandparents, Dusty assured him, "Don't worry about any of that stuff." The kid was only five. "Uncle Baker was puny all through school. He didn't grow until after he graduated from high school."

Caleb's eyes widened with shock. "Uncle Baker was puny?"

Dusty nodded. "That's why we all tease him that he's the baby. So, you could be like Uncle Baker and surprise everyone and be taller than Jake, or you might wind up being the same size your dad was. But your height doesn't matter. And it definitely doesn't matter in the rodeo. Some of the best rodeo riders I ever knew weren't very tall."

"They weren't?" Caleb asked.

Dusty shook his head. "Nope. One of the guys—'Shorty' everybody calls him—won more championship titles than any other rider."

"Than even you?" Caleb asked.

Dusty nodded. Since around the time when he was Caleb's age, he'd wanted to win more championships than any other rider in rodeo history. That had been his goal, and not for the fame but for the sense of accomplishment. Growing up in the shadow of his brothers Jake and Ben, and even Dale, he'd always felt like less than them.

He wasn't as big and strong as Jake or as smart as Ben or as good as Dale. But he was good at riding, at rodeo. And even more than that sense of accomplishment, he just loved it—loved the thrill and the challenge of it. He'd intended to pass Shorty with those championships, but he was already late joining this season. He probably had no hope of catching up in the points standing…even if he rejoined the circuit. And with the boys struggling and Melanie pregnant, he really had to sit this one out.

What about the next? And the next? Did he give them all up and take Dale's job on the ranch…if Jake deemed him qualified enough to work with him? And could he do it and ever be truly happy again?

"I'm going to have more championships than Shorty someday," Caleb professed.

And Dusty smiled at how much the little boy reminded him of himself at that age. He'd been so enthralled and determined to ride. It was all he'd dreamt about, all he'd thought about, but maybe he'd done that so he hadn't had to think about everything else, about his dad dying and his mom leaving and then Grandpa Jake…

"Whatcha doing?" Jake asked as he joined them, his eyes narrowed and slightly hard as he studied Dusty. "Trying to get my son to run off and join the rodeo with you?"

Dusty shook his head. "You worried I'm looking for payback for you talking Dale into staying here with you?"

He'd said it in jest, but Jake's brow creased at the words. "Is that what you think?" Jake asked. "That I talked him into it?"

Dusty shrugged like it didn't matter, but it had bothered him in those lonely early years. And now that Dale was gone, it upset Dusty more that they hadn't had that time together, traveling the circuit like they'd planned. "It bothers me that we didn't follow through on the dream we had as kids," Dusty admitted. "We were going to take off together after high school but then…"

"Then he fell in love," Jake said. "Love can change all your plans."

Love had changed Dusty's plan of never getting married. Once he'd fallen for Melanie, he hadn't wanted to ever let her go. But while he'd committed to her, her actions so soon after their wedding had made him question her commitment to him. Even though she was pregnant now, was she committed to their relationship, to their family?

"HAVE YOU CHANGED your mind about staying?" Melanie asked her mother, who'd paused at the top of the stairs leading down to the kitchen. While dinnertime was still a half hour away, Melanie only had to listen to know the family was already gathering in the kitchen.

"No, not at all," Juliet assured her. "I just need a minute…"

"It can be overwhelming with all the kids and people," Melanie said. She understood. As a naturally quiet and shy person herself, she'd had to get used to the commotion of the ranch. But now she loved it and everyone and everything that lived in the house. "And Feisty…" The little dog yapped excitedly as if conversing with her humans.

Her mother shook her head. "It's not that. I like Feisty, and I like Sadie too…" She trailed off, obviously leaving something unsaid.

"What is it, Mom?" Melanie asked with concern.

Her mother had seemed to enjoy the day, spending much of it with Taye in the kitchen and with the children in the playroom. Maybe keeping busy had helped take her mind off leaving Shep because she hadn't mentioned him once today. That didn't mean she wasn't thinking of him, though.

Melanie hadn't spoken of Dusty when she'd been at the ranch, but she'd thought of him always, not just when his family had brought him up or called him. He'd never not been on her mind.

"I'm nervous about seeing Dusty," her mother admitted. "He kept calling to talk to you, and I refused to tell him where you were even when you were staying with me. I thought he'd lied to you, and that he had a wife and children."

Pain and regret caused Melanie to wince. But if Dusty had told her he'd had a twin, she would have known that the picture had been Dale's family portrait. And she could've told her mother that too.

Juliet continued, "I had no idea what he was going through, that his twin had died, and I feel terrible that I was so short with him, so rude, and now I'm staying at his house."

"He won't be mad at you," Melanie assured her. He hadn't even been all that angry with Melanie, and maybe he should have been. She'd jumped to conclusions and then not even given him a chance to explain. She'd run away.

Just like they'd run off to get married without really thinking it through beforehand. If they'd taken more time, if they'd dated, maybe they would have had a chance to get to know one another better. To know whether or not they were even right for each other.

When her mother had learned of their elopement, she'd been concerned, but she'd also been happy for them. She'd known Dusty from the rodeo; or at least she'd known what little Melanie had known about him. She'd even thrown them a party to celebrate their marriage.

Her mother hesitated yet again at the top of the stairs until a deep voice spoke from the hall behind them.

"Juliet, I'm so glad you're staying at the ranch."

"Dusty!" Her mother blanched. And then she was turning and hugging him. "I'm so sorry about your brother and his wife. So sorry... about everything..."

"Me too," Dusty said as he hugged her back.

Envy gnawed at Melanie that they could forgive and forget so easily.

"I'm so glad you're here," he said again. But he wasn't looking at her mother now; he was staring at Melanie.

Was he glad she was here? Had he been worried, like Miller had said, that she wasn't going to come back to the ranch?

"Uncle Dusty! Uncle Dusty!" Caleb called

out from the bottom of the stairs. "You have to come down and tell everybody that you're going to ride Midnight. They don't believe me."

Melanie gasped. "You're going to ride Midnight?"

He nodded, and excitement glinted in his eyes just as it did whenever he talked about riding. "Yes. I think he's getting restless. It'll be good for him."

Was he talking about the bronco or himself? Was he already getting restless, wanting to return to the rodeo?

"It might not be good for you," she warned him. "I noticed that you're limping again."

He grimaced and reached down to squeeze the back of his thigh. "Midnight made me work for it when I won him."

"You really won that bronco?" Juliet asked. "Shep had somebody's cell phone video of you riding him, and reported about it, but nobody knew for sure if the owner had actually honored your bet."

"The horse has been here for a while now," Melanie said. "Your leg should be better than it is." But it clearly wasn't. "You really shouldn't ride him until you're completely healed." She didn't want him getting hurt again, any more than she wanted him hurting her if she gave him another chance. Did he want that chance with her or just with the bronco?

"I'll be fine," he said.

"Uncle Dusty!" Caleb called out again.

Dusty squeezed around them to descend the stairs to the kitchen.

"He misses it," her mother murmured. "Just like your father still does. The challenge of riding a bronco, a bull..."

Melanie knew he loved it, and when they'd gotten married, she'd understood that and hadn't wanted to take him away from it. She'd become a physical therapist specializing in treating rodeo riders because she'd always felt so badly for her dad having to give up riding. She'd used that as an excuse for her dad's bad behavior, just like Shep had. But now that she was pregnant and away from the rodeo, she didn't want to go back to that life of traveling. It had been hard enough on her mom to do it with one baby, but with two...

As the thought of trying to manage that passed through her mind, an odd sensation passed through her stomach...like a cramp. And she flinched. She was glad now that she'd followed Baker's advice and had scheduled an appointment with an obstetrician in Willow

Creek. Fortunately, the office had had a cancellation for tomorrow. She was relieved that she could get in so soon and make sure everything was all right with the babies. She already knew that everything wasn't all right with her, not since Dusty had found her.

She followed her mother down to the kitchen where everyone had already gathered around the long table. Jake was holding up a hand to wave down the volume and excitement of the little boys thinking they were going to have a live rodeo on the ranch.

"Uncle Dusty is going to have to wait for his rematch with Midnight until Uncle Baker has a night off," Jake said, "so that we have a paramedic on hand."

Melanie wasn't sure if Baker was working or just avoiding the house again. He was probably especially worried that his grandmother had only him to focus all her matchmaking efforts on now. Sadie didn't seem very focused on anything tonight. Instead of engaging with her family, her head was down as she stared at her plate. Mr. Lemmon, sitting beside her, stared at her with concern, which raised Melanie's concern. She wasn't just worried about the older woman; she was thinking about her husband.

Jake seemed concerned about him too, but maybe more with potentially setting a bad example for the young boys than Dusty getting hurt again.

Looking around at Caleb and his nephews, Jake said, "Riding broncos is super dangerous."

Dusty was obviously unconcerned as he uttered a derisive chuckle. "If Midnight gives me a hard time, Melanie can make me as good as new again," he said. "She's done it before." His gaze met hers and held it, and something fluttered inside her again.

"Is that how you two met?" Taye asked.

Dusty continued to hold her gaze, and the look in his gold-flecked eyes had warmth flooding her...because that look was the one he'd given her before, when she'd thought he'd loved her. And that flutter in her stomach now moved to her heart. She took a steadying breath at the intensity of her feelings for him.

"I knew Melanie from around the rodeo circuit for years, but I didn't get to know her until she became my physical therapist," Dusty said. "She wouldn't give me the time of day until I'd gotten hurt."

"So you fix rodeo riders?" Caleb asked her, his blue eyes wide with awe. While Caleb was always sweet with her, and especially with Emily, he usually reserved his hero worship for the Haven men.

She smiled. "I try to help them." But her smile slipped away as she acknowledged that some were beyond her help; that when they had to give up riding, like her dad, they were devastated.

She'd become a physical therapist because she hadn't wanted anyone to have to give up what they loved doing. She wanted to help them get better so they could keep going. So how could she ask Dusty to give up the rodeo? To give up his dream? Especially when she wasn't sure what she could give him in return.

Her trust?

Her heart?

She wasn't sure she could risk getting hurt again.

CHAPTER FOURTEEN

DINNER HAD ENDED too quickly for Dusty. He'd been enjoying it all so much: the excited chatter of the boys, the delicious food, and the glances he'd exchanged with his wife. He'd missed her, had missed just looking at her and hearing her soft voice and feeling the warmth of her smile.

She was so beautiful. Inside and out...

But dinner and dessert had ended, and the table had been cleared. Grandma and Lem had already left the kitchen. Sadie had looked tired, as tired as Melanie looked with the dark circles beneath her eyes. Grandma was showing her age and her stress. He shouldn't have brought up his mother, shouldn't have brought up... what she clearly didn't want to talk about, what she'd never talked about...

Emily and Ben ushered the boys upstairs for baths while Katie helped Taye clean up the kitchen. Melanie and her mother stood at the foot of the stairs. He wanted to call her back, wanted to talk to her, but then Jake was gripping his arm and tugging him through the French doors onto the patio. "I want a word with you…" his oldest brother said.

Dusty groaned. "You had a lot of words with me today. What did I do wrong now? Wasn't I chewing the right way, the way Dale would have chewed?" He cringed at the petulant sound of his voice. They would start calling him the baby of the family if he kept acting like it.

Jake groaned. "This isn't about Dale. It's about you and that dang bronco. The last thing Caleb needs to see is you riding Midnight. He's going to be even more convinced that he can do it too."

Dusty shook his head. "Don't you think that already occurred to me?" He probably understood Caleb better than anyone else on the ranch—because Caleb was as obsessed with that bronco as Dusty had been. Midnight was the reason Dusty had needed physical therapy in the first place. "I already told him that riding broncos is harder than he thinks. Tomorrow night, I'll *show* him that it is."

Jake released a shaky sigh. "Okay, I thought you were just trying to show off."

Offended, Dusty sucked in a breath. There

were times that he purposely put on a show, but that was when the stands were full and he knew he had the win. With Midnight, he never knew if he had the win, and he never knew if he might get hurt. "Who do you think I am?" he asked.

"A championship rodeo rider," Jake said. "That's all you ever wanted to be."

"And why is that such a bad thing?" Dusty asked. "Why was it okay for Ben to stay in college and go into politics? Why was it okay for Baker to join the army—" He interrupted himself with a chuckle and shook his head. "Never mind, of course that was okay. What everyone else did was…"

"What do you mean?" Jake asked, confusion lacing his tone. "What are you trying to say?"

Dusty shook his head again and repeated, "Never mind." His family was probably never going to get it, not even when he told them about their mother, about her real reason for leaving them, and how it had had nothing to do with the rodeo.

He turned away from his brother and stared out across the sun-soaked backyard. The big patch of grass gave way to a field of wildflowers and colorful weeds. But none of that was as beautiful as the sight Dusty had stared at during dinner; nothing was as beautiful as his wife.

He released a shaky sigh now.

"What did you mean?" a soft voice asked.

It wasn't Jake's deep rumble.

Startled he whirled around to find that his brother had gone back into the house while Melanie stood on the brick patio behind him, her brown eyes warm as if the sunshine had heated them too.

"I didn't know you'd followed us outside," he said with surprise.

"I didn't mean to eavesdrop," she said. "I just wanted to tell you that I was able to schedule an appointment at the doctor's tomorrow."

Concern drew him closer to her, had him reaching out to cup her cheek in his palm. Dark circles rimmed her heavily lashed eyes. She looked exhausted. "Are you feeling okay?"

She nodded. "Just tired. But Baker was right. I should get checked out."

"Thank you for telling me," he said. "I want to go with you."

She hesitated a moment. "If Jake needs your help on the ranch, my mom can go with me."

That might have been what she preferred, but these were his babies too. And she was still his wife...even if their marriage was on shaky ground. Would she ever wear his ring again or would it forever dangle from that chain around his neck?

"I want to be there," he said. "And I think Jake and I could use a break from each other."

"Already?" she asked. "What's wrong?"

"Me," he said. "I'm not Dale." That hollow ache in his heart intensified, and he closed his eyes against it.

Melanie reached out to him now; he felt her arms closing around him. "I'm sorry," she said. "I'm sure that he doesn't mean to make you feel that way."

Dusty shook his head. "I think he expects that just because I look like Dale, I *am* like him." He opened his eyes and met her gaze. "But Dale and I couldn't have been more different from each other. And because of that, it was always like he was the good twin who made all the unselfish choices, and I was the bad one who thought only of myself."

"Dusty!" she said, and she tightened her arms around him, holding him close.

Maybe she was holding him together because he felt like he was falling apart.

"It's true, Melanie. Over the past two months, you must have heard what they all think of me, that I'm like my mother, just because I fell in the love with the rodeo."

"That's what you meant," she murmured, "when you said that it was okay for Ben to stay in college and for Baker to leave the ranch for the army..."

He nodded and eased away from her, his hands on her slender shoulders. Maybe she could understand what he'd struggled to understand himself all these years. "It was okay for Ben to want to be mayor and for Baker to become a firefighter, but for me to join the rodeo...that made me like my mother...that made everyone think I'm irresponsible and selfish." And because all of his family seemed to think that, he'd worried that they might have been right about him. His chest ached with that hollow feeling, with the fear that he would never measure up to his brothers in his wife's eyes or in her heart.

"Oh, Dusty," she breathed. "I'm sorry..."

And he knew why she was apologizing, because she'd thought the same way they all had. That ache in his heart intensified with pain, and he felt all over again that she'd betrayed him, just like his mother had all those years ago.

He sighed. "And you know, the sad thing is

that my mom didn't leave us or the ranch for those reasons."

Her brown eyes widened with surprise as she stared up at him. "You've talked to her?"

He nodded. "It turns out that it was easier for me to find her twenty years after she took off than it was for me to find my wife."

She flinched, and he did too, as a jab of regret struck his heart. "I'm sorry," they said in unison.

Then Melanie blinked and cleared her eyes, and asked, "Was she still with the rodeo?"

He shook his head. "No. She's living on a ranch not far from here," he said. He couldn't believe she'd been so close and had never reached out to any of them, that she hadn't even come to the funeral. When he'd called her about Dale's death, he'd had no idea then how close she'd been, but she'd claimed to have a good reason for not coming. "I saw her just a few days ago." Before he'd come home. And he'd been reeling still from everything she'd told him when he'd discovered his wife in the kitchen. That she had been here nearly the entire time he'd been looking for her.

"Oh, my…did she know about Dale?"

He nodded. "I had called her from the hospital."

"So you've been in contact with her all these years?" she asked, and her body stiffened as if she'd realized what he had, that he'd still not told her everything.

He shook his head. "Not until that day," he said. "I had her number, but I'd never used it." He hadn't thought there was anything she could have said that would make him forgive her. And maybe that was why Melanie had shut off her phone and run away. Because she hadn't thought there was anything he could say to earn her forgiveness or her trust?

Had she been right?

She reached out to him now and cupped his cheek in her hand. "I'm sorry...that must have been so difficult."

He nodded and released a shaky sigh, remembering how devastated his mother had sounded on the phone, nearly as devastated as he'd been.

"Have you told your brothers?" she asked.

"Ben and Baker know that I talked to her, and that I told her about Dale. But they don't know that I've seen her in person or where she is." So close that it wouldn't even take an hour to see her again after all these years...

"Are you going to tell them?" Melanie

asked, and there was a note of disapproval in her voice.

He didn't want to add to her disappointment in him, but he shook his head and told her the truth. "Not yet. I promised I'd give her some time to come to grips with Dale and Jenny's deaths. I think she has some other stuff going on in her life too. She wouldn't let me inside the house…" Like she'd been hiding something, or someone, from him despite everything else she'd shared.

"They need to know," Melanie said. "Secrets have a way of coming out."

"I know." And now Sadie did too. "And I agree that some of those secrets need to come out soon." If he'd known for the past twenty years what he'd learned recently, he might have felt differently about so many things. Even about himself… "My mother blames herself for my dad dying."

"I don't even know how he died," she said. "Everybody just says a ranch accident."

"He fell off a tractor and it ran him over," Dusty said, his heart squeezing as he remembered. Fortunately, he and his brothers had been at school, so none of them had seen the accident, just the ambulance driving away with the lights off as the bus had dropped them at the ranch.

Melanie's dark eyes filled with unshed tears and sympathy. "That's so sad, Dusty. I'm sorry. How can she blame herself for that?"

"She was on the tractor with him and thinks she distracted him," Dusty said. Darlene had seemed so broken with guilt and grief even after all these years. "It was still really hard for her to talk about it. She thought we all blamed her for his dying, like she blamed herself. She thought we all hated her, so she left... not because she loved the rodeo but because she didn't know where else to go. She'd lost everything...even herself."

Dusty had felt that lost when Dale and Jenny had died and then Melanie had disappeared. And he wasn't entirely sure if he'd found himself yet or if he ever would, even if he returned to the rodeo he'd loved...

Because if he went back, what else would he lose?

MELANIE FELT BAD leaving Miller behind again when she left the ranch. But she didn't want him at her doctor's appointment in case anything was wrong with the babies or with her.

"Don't worry about Miller. He'll be fine,"

Dusty assured her from the driver's seat of his truck.

At least the seven-year-old knew that she was just going into Willow Creek and not as far as Sheridan, and she'd promised that she wouldn't be gone long.

"He told you himself," Dusty reminded her of the assurances the little boy had made just moments ago.

"Pregnant ladies have to go to the doctor a lot," he'd told her. "I remember Mama doing that when she was pregnant with Little Jake."

His mention of Jenny had surprised Melanie because he rarely talked about his parents and only if someone else, usually Ian, brought them up.

Dusty must have been aware that she was still concerned about his nephew because he reached across the console and squeezed her hand.

Her skin tingled from that contact, and she held her breath at her reaction. At the reaction she always had to him.

She forced herself to turn away from the rear window and her view of the ranch. "Will you be fine?" she asked. She was still in shock over everything he'd told her the night before. She hadn't wanted to leave him, had wanted to spend the night in his arms like she used to, but then her mother had called out to her. Miller had finished his shower and had been looking for her.

She glanced into the side-view mirror and caught a glimpse of him standing on the porch, watching them drive away, and she felt a pang of regret.

"I'll be fine," Dusty said, "once I know you're fine. And Miller will be fine too."

"Emily said that the school psychologist will be able to make it out to the ranch later this week," Melanie shared. "Hopefully, the boys will talk to her." Maybe Melanie needed to talk to her about her trust issues too. Her daddy issues...

How had she let herself fall for a rodeo man? She knew how hard the life was; she'd lived it herself. She didn't want that life for her children, but she didn't want to make Dusty give up something he loved. After their talk last night, she also didn't want to make him feel guilty about loving it, like the rest of his family did.

Dusty groaned. "I didn't think about that... that they might need psychological help. My brothers and I didn't talk to anyone after our dad died. I don't think we really even talked to each other about it. That's why I don't get why my mom thinks we blamed her."

"Maybe because she blamed herself, she thought everyone else would too," Melanie suggested.

"Guilt…" Dusty concurred. "I understand that. I feel so bad that I took off after the funeral. I kept calling to check in on the boys, but it wasn't the same as being here for them like you were. It's no wonder that Miller is so attached to you."

"I'm attached to him too," Melanie said. "I know I shouldn't have gotten so involved, but I think I fell for him before I even realized he was your nephew. And then when I met the others…"

"Those kids are pretty special," Dusty agreed.

"Your whole family is," Melanie said.

His handsome face contorted with a slight grimace. "Except for me…" he murmured.

"Don't…" she whispered. She reached across the console now and gripped his forearm, which was lightly dusted with golden hair that tickled her skin, making an almost involuntary shiver pass through her. He affected her so much…even when he wasn't trying. He was the most special of them all to her.

"Don't what?" he asked.

"Don't beat yourself up like that," she said. "You're not the bad twin…just because you chose to do something other than the ranch with your life." Despite all the distance still between them, she was grateful he'd confided in her. "And you need to tell your brothers about your mom, so they know the rodeo wasn't the reason she left."

He nodded but he didn't speak, as if he were struggling to keep his emotions in check.

An hour later, he did that again. When he stared stock-still at the blurry images on the screen of the ultrasound machine and listened to the two little blips that were the heartbeats of their babies.

Melanie's heart beat a little stronger, a little harder, as it seemed to swell with the love flooding it. Love for her babies…

Did Dusty's heart feel like that too? Was he falling in love with those blurry images like she was? Was he falling in love with her again?

Because she felt closer to him in that moment than she had even since those early days of their marriage.

They had made these babies together. Twins…like him and his brother.

Was that why he seemed so emotional now?

Because they reminded him of Dale? Would these two grow up like he and his brother had—as best friends?

Would they grow up?

"Are they all right?" she asked, her heart rate faster now with fear. She'd been afraid before of losing Dusty, of getting hurt, but if she lost these babies…

My children…

"Everything looks good," the doctor said as she studied the screen. "I would say fourteen—almost fifteen—weeks along."

"What about their mother?" Dusty asked the question. "How is she?"

Warmth flooded Melanie that he was worried about her, that he cared. And she felt a flash of guilt for how she'd run away from him, for how she'd hidden from him all these weeks. She hadn't been fair to him, just as his family hadn't been fair to him.

"We've taken blood," the doctor said. "But our lab isn't that fast. It'll be a couple days before we have the test results back. But given what you've said about your morning sickness, your brother-in-law was probably right about the low blood sugar…" A smile curved the woman's lips, like when Melanie had first mentioned Baker.

And earlier, in the waiting room, Dusty had pointed out the firemen calendar on the wall of the reception area. Baker was July, and even though it was still June, the calendar was dog-eared, as if it had been turned to that page often. They'd assumed the office staff had been ogling his picture and had shared a chuckle about how embarrassed Baker would be if he knew that.

The doctor shook her head, as if clearing away her thoughts of Baker, and continued. "Coupled with low blood pressure, it explains the fainting. You need to add some more iron to your diet and get a lot of rest."

"She's still working," Dusty said, "with my seven-year-old nephew."

"Miller," Dr. Clark said. Like everyone else in Willow Creek, the young obstetrician was aware of the Haven family tragedy.

"He's doing all the work now," Melanie assured them both. "It's the easiest job I ever had." Physically. Emotionally, it was the toughest. She couldn't help Miller heal what hurt most on the boy, his broken heart. She couldn't bring back his parents for him; all she could do was make it easier for him to walk.

Dusty's mouth curved into a slight smile. "You are amazing," he proclaimed.

"You all are," the doctor remarked, "with how you've stepped up to take care of those boys. As some people know, not everyone is so willing to do that."

Dusty's face flushed, and he shook his head, obviously unwilling to accept praise for something he hadn't done. "I wasn't around, like I should have been," he admitted.

Melanie hated the guilt that she heard in his deep voice and saw on his face, especially when she was the reason that he hadn't been around. Because he'd been searching for her. And she had been in the last place he'd expected to find her.

"That was my fault," Melanie said.

The doctor's brow furrowed as she glanced from one to the other. But she didn't pry. Instead, she handed Melanie a wad of tissues. "You can clean off the goo now and get dressed. I'll call you when the lab results come back. In the meantime, just make sure that you eat well and often, and get plenty of rest."

Melanie nodded. "I will."

"And stop at the reception desk to schedule your next appointment," the doctor added. "We need to see you at least once a month to monitor your blood pressure and check on you and those babies."

"Thank you, Dr. Clark," Melanie said.

"Yes, thank you," Dusty added, but he was staring at the screen of the ultrasound machine again. The machine had shut off with the image frozen on the blurry peanut-sized outlines of their babies sharing one sac. Identical twins, like he and Dale had been. Had he realized that? Was he thinking of the twin he'd lost?

The doctor slipped out of the room, closing the door behind her. And Dusty jumped a little, as if she'd startled him.

"Are you okay?" Melanie asked him.

He nodded. "Yes, of course." And he reached for the wad of tissue she'd been holding and gently wiped the goo from the skin of her swelling belly.

She shivered in reaction to his touch, to his tenderness, and their eyes met and held. And he was looking at her that way again, like he loved her. She was tempted to pull his head down for her kiss, like she had so many times in those first four weeks that they'd been married.

But she remembered where they were and that she needed to exchange her paper gown and drape for her clothes. She shivered again.

And Dusty shook his head, as if he was

just waking up from a dream. "I'm sorry," he said. "You're probably cold. You need to get dressed. Should I step out?"

He had earlier when the nurse had given her the paper things to wear for the ultrasound. He'd stepped into the hall, giving her privacy to change. He'd been just as respectful and sweet right after their wedding, offering to give her as much time as she needed before making love.

His patience and sensitivity had made her want him even more than she already had. If only they'd been more prepared…

But she glanced at that screen and her heart swelled with love for her babies. They hadn't been planned, but they were very much wanted.

"I'm sorry," she said.

"It's fine," he said. "I understand." And he reached for the door handle.

"No, I mean I'm sorry that…" She couldn't even say it because she really wasn't sorry. She was happy that she was pregnant even as sick as she'd been that first trimester.

"About them?" he asked and shook his head. "No, don't be sorry."

"I'm sorry that we didn't talk about it, that

we didn't plan, that everything's caught us so much by surprise," she explained.

"That was my fault," he said. "I rushed you into marriage, and you didn't even have all the facts. You didn't know everything you should have known about me."

She still wasn't sure if she knew everything yet, but she certainly knew more than she had when she'd said, "I do."

"And then I rushed off back here like I did, leaving you alone to cope with that morning sickness." He shuddered like he had when she'd first mentioned it to the doctor.

"Katie was there for me," she assured him. "She helped me through it."

He shook his head. "It should have been me."

"You didn't know where I was," she reminded him. "And that's my fault. I should have called you." She should have talked to him, at least given him that chance to explain.

"Everything is my fault," he insisted. "None of this is yours." Then he opened the door and stepped into the hall, to give her that privacy she really didn't want, at least not from him.

She thought about how wrong his family was about him, how wrong he was about himself. He didn't run from responsibility. Instead, he took responsibility for things and situations that weren't his fault.

Dusty Haven was a much better man than anyone—including himself—gave him credit for, which he proved when she joined him in the hall.

"Let's go shopping," he said.

"For what?" she asked.

He gestured at her clothes, at the blouse she'd barely been able to button over her belly. "For you. You need some things." His voice cracked with emotion, and then he continued, "And they'll need some things."

"They won't be here for months yet," she said. And where would *here* be? At the ranch?

She wanted to stay, but she needed to find out what Dusty wanted too. Did he want to be part of their children's lives—part of hers? And could she find it within herself to let him back in?

Maybe first she needed to find out what she wanted—besides the babies. Because she wanted them very much.

And she wanted for them the childhood she'd never had, one where they felt secure and safe. Maybe that was what she wanted for herself, too, to finally feel secure and safe. She had a feeling that she would only find that within herself, though, and not at a place.

Not even at the ranch…

CHAPTER FIFTEEN

A BEAD OF sweat rolled down Dusty's back, between his shoulder blades. Maybe it was hot in the small shop crowded with maternity clothes and baby stuff, or maybe he was freaking out like he nearly had when he'd seen those images on the screen an hour ago.

He was going to be a father. To twins.

Boys or girls?

Oh, what if they were girls…

More heat rushed over him, making him sweat even more in his panic.

He knew nothing about women, which was probably partially why he'd blown it so badly with his wife that she'd run away from him. He wasn't sure where she was even now; she'd disappeared into a changing room some time ago with an armload of clothes.

If it was as hot in the shop as he thought, maybe she'd passed out from the stuffiness or from lack of food. They'd eaten a big breakfast before they'd left that morning, but it was close to lunch now.

Panicked over the thought of her lying on the dressing room floor, Dusty scrambled around the store, knocking into baby beds and changing tables and a rack of tiny clothes before he found the curtain behind which she'd disappeared.

"Melanie!" he called out to her.

And she must have heard the panic in his voice because she pushed aside the curtain and stepped out. "What's wrong?" she asked, her eyes wide with concern. "Has something happened?"

Her...

She looked so beautiful that his heart stopped for a moment before resuming at a frantic pace. She wore a sunny yellow dress that made her look even more like an angel than she already had. Her skin glowed, as if she were illuminated from within somehow.

"Dusty!" she said again, grasping his arm. "Are you all right?"

He didn't want to mislead her anymore, so he shook his head, just as his legs were shaking, and he felt a bit like he might be the one who passed out.

She steered him toward a rocking chair and

pushed him into it. "What is it?" she asked. "Are you okay?"

The one salesperson in the shop, an older woman, stepped out from behind the counter and started toward them. "Do you need anything? Water?"

The heat that rushed to his face now was from embarrassment. He shook his head. "No, no, I'm fine."

"No, you're not," Melanie chided.

And he felt another flash of panic that she was disappointed in him, that he'd let her down again just like he had when he hadn't been honest with her about his family. "I'm sorry," he said.

She smiled, but it was a bit wan. And her skin, while luminescent, was also pale. Alarmingly so…

"Are you okay?" he asked, and he jumped up from the chair to guide her down into it. "Do you need that water? Or something to eat?"

She pressed a hand over her stomach, which was more visible in the dress that skimmed over it.

And panic gripped his heart again. "Do we need to go back to the doctor?" he asked.

She shook her head. "No. I'm just…" She uttered a shaky sigh. "I don't know what to buy or how much or…"

"We'll get whatever you need," he said.

"I don't know what I need," she admitted. "I don't know what things or…" She gestured around the crowded store. "Or double what things…"

"Double…" he repeated as another bead of sweat trailed down his back. "We need double of everything."

She nodded. "But not for me. And we don't need to worry about furniture or stuff for the babies yet. I have nearly six months to go."

And he wasn't sure if she was trying to reassure him or herself. He nodded. "Yes, we have plenty of time to figure out what we need for them. And as for you, get it all," he said. And he touched her pretty dress. "Especially this."

She offered him a shaky smile, but it didn't quite reach her eyes. It didn't dispel the fear from them.

"It's going to be okay," he assured her.

Her eyebrow quirked slightly as she stared up at him. "I thought you were going to be honest with me from now on."

He sucked in a breath and nodded. "Yes. I am. I promise."

And she flinched. "Don't make promises you can't keep."

"Melanie…"

"Are you two all right?" the clerk asked, her eyes squinting behind the narrow lenses of her small glasses as she studied them.

Maybe she recognized Dusty, or maybe she was studying them so intently because she didn't.

Melanie jumped up from the rocking chair, gathered up the armload of clothes, and carried it to the counter. "I'd like to get these things," she said as she reached for her purse.

Dusty was already pulling out his wallet. "I'm going to buy them," he assured her.

The woman's narrowed eyes glanced at Melanie's bare ring finger, and her lips pulled together into a slight frown of disapproval.

Melanie must have noticed the look, as well, because her face flushed with embarrassment. And Dusty's spine stiffened as his entire body tensed with his own disapproval for this woman.

"My wife can't wear her ring because she's pregnant with twins," Dusty said. And he reached inside his shirt collar and pulled out the chain and the diamond wedding band that dangled from it. "So I'm wearing it until I can put it back on her finger."

The woman's face flushed now. "I—I didn't…"

"I didn't catch your name," Dusty interrupted.

"Imelda," the woman replied, her spine stiffening now. "And this is my shop."

He glanced around it. "It's cute," he said. "But we'll probably head into Sheridan when we need the rest of the things for the babies…" He sighed. "I'll just have to explain to my grandmother why, though. I'm sure you know her? Sadie Haven?"

The woman gasped now. "You're one of Sadie's grandsons?"

He nodded. "The black sheep of the Haven boys," he told her. It was probably already what she was thinking. "The rodeo rider…"

The woman's face got pale then. "Oh, I should have recognized you…" Her eyes filled with tears behind those lenses. "Your twin brother came in with his wife when they were expecting their first boy. I'm so sorry for your loss."

Tears stung Dusty's eyes and he felt shame for taking the woman to task like he had. He nodded. "Yeah, me too."

Melanie reached out then, entwined her fingers with his, and squeezed his hand. And for the first time in a long time, he felt comforted enough that the hollow ache in his chest eased a bit.

He still loved her. But was it fair to her when she deserved someone better than the black sheep of the Havens?

HE WAS WEARING her ring.

That revelation had stunned Melanie into silence, so she'd let him win the war to pay for her maternity clothes. She'd even let him pay for lunch at the diner in town, and now she understood why Mr. Lemmon ate so many meals with them at the ranch. Nobody's cooking measured up to Taye's. But Melanie ate because she knew she had to for the babies and because it gave her an excuse not to talk to Dusty.

Because she didn't know what to say...

No, because she was afraid of what she might say, that she might ask for her ring back. That she might ask for him back in her life in every way.

But they had to talk first. They had to figure out if they could trust each other again and if they could envision a future together with their children that would make them both happy.

Before she could think of how to broach that subject, though, Dusty spoke. "I'm sorry," he said.

She glanced across the console of his pickup truck at him. He'd apologized so many times, she had no idea why he was apologizing now.

"I realize I embarrassed you back there," he said. "I thought I could tell how that woman was looking at you and..." He groaned. "I was probably imagining it and I overreacted. I guess I've just gotten a little oversensitive to disapproval over the years."

"It really bothers you," she murmured.

He groaned again. "Not her. I shouldn't have said anything to her. I feel like a fool that I did, but I didn't want anyone treating you like..."

"Your family treats you," she finished for him. That was really what was bothering him, and it was why he hadn't told her about them and about the ranch. She understood that now.

"Like I'm a jerk just because I joined the rodeo."

"That's not your fault," she assured him. "That's your mother's...for leaving you all."

"I told you that she had her reasons," he reminded her.

She nodded, but she felt a bit like that woman in the baby shop, still disapproving. Her children weren't even born yet and Melanie couldn't imagine leaving them for any reason.

Dusty's nephews weren't even hers, and she was already missing them. She peered out the windshield then and frowned. "Where are we? This doesn't look like the way back to the ranch." She hadn't been to town but a couple of times over the past several weeks. To buy dresses for Jake and Katie's wedding and for Jake and Katie's wedding ceremony.

"I wanted to make a slight detour to show you something," he said.

"But, Dusty, we need to get back," she said, feeling a little anxious at the thought of Miller panicking. It had been hard enough to leave him, but to stay away any longer...

He reached across the console and touched her hand. "Don't worry about the boys," he said. "Jake was going to knock off early and take them all out for another long ride and a picnic lunch. We have plenty of time before they'll even miss us."

But she was already missing them. How could she leave them if Dusty wanted to go back to the rodeo circuit? How could she subject her children to that kind of life, always traveling, never setting down roots or making friends?

She couldn't do it.

She couldn't go back to the rodeo, and she couldn't stay away from the boys. "I don't want to leave my mom alone either," she said.

Dusty chuckled. "Nobody's alone at the ranch. I think she was going to go along on the ride anyways."

Melanie released a shaky breath. "That's good." Her mother had always loved to ride, and keeping busy with the kids would keep her mind off Shep. Maybe. It hadn't kept Melanie's mind off Dusty. But then, she'd had constant reminders of him with how much Miller and Ian resembled him.

"She seems to be doing well," Dusty remarked.

She nodded.

"How are you doing?" he asked.

She tensed. Were they going to have this discussion now? She wasn't sure she was ready.

"About your mom and dad," he hastened to add, as if he'd seen her panic or maybe because he wasn't any more prepared to talk about their future than she was.

She shrugged. "I don't know what to think

yet—because I don't know if she's going to change her mind again." Especially now that she knew that Melanie had been wrong to leave Dusty. Or had she been?

He hadn't had that secret wife and family she'd thought he'd had, but he'd had many other secrets he hadn't shared with her. Like this one...

"So where are you taking me?" she asked.

He'd pulled off the main highway onto a gravel road that cut between pastures on either side of it. The fences looked worn and the fields overgrown. This was definitely not Ranch Haven where everything was meticulously maintained.

"What is this place?"

"I'm not showing you the place," he said. He pushed back his hat and peered out into those pastures as if he was seeing it for the first time. "Though, it is going up for sale soon..."

Was he interested in it? "You're not sure that you even want to stay at your family ranch," she said. So he couldn't be considering a purchase of this one.

He sighed and nodded.

"You love the rodeo," she said.

And he nodded again.

His family didn't understand that, didn't understand how much it meant to him, how it was more than what he did but it was who he was. Shep Shepard's daughter understood— all too well.

It might mean more to Dusty than she and their babies did. She blinked against the sudden sting of tears and cleared her vision to focus on the house that was coming into view. Like the pastures, the two-story building was a bit rundown with peeling white paint, dirty windows, and baskets of dead flowers hanging above the rotting porch railing.

"Who lives here?" she asked, wondering if anyone did.

"My mother," he replied.

And she gasped. "You brought me to meet your mother?" She suddenly felt light-headed and turned toward him to find his face red, as if he was embarrassed. Maybe because he hadn't done that before…he hadn't introduced her to any of his family before they got married.

"I—I don't know if she's here," he said.

"Then why…"

"She's selling a mare," he told her. "I'll show you." He pushed open the driver's door and came around to open her door before she had even reached for the handle.

"You're showing me a horse?" she asked. Now she was even more confused.

"I think she'd be perfect to breed with Midnight," he said. "She comes from great stock, from a champion barrel racing horse. She's gorgeous." His face flushed even more, but now it was with excitement that shone in his hazel eyes.

He hadn't seemed this excited at the obstetrician's office or at the maternity shop. He'd seemed stressed then.

Tears of disappointment rushed to her eyes, but she furiously blinked them away. He reached for her shoulders, cupping them in his big hands as he stared into her face. His excitement was gone. Now he looked like he had then: scared.

"Are you feeling all right?" he asked. "I'm sorry. I shouldn't have brought you here."

"I'm fine," she said, and she was the one who wasn't being entirely truthful now. "I had some trouble being around animals during my first trimester...when the morning sickness was so bad. But I should be fine now."

He grimaced. "Forget it. The barn's not as clean as it should be."

She squeezed his forearms before pushing him back so she could step out of the truck.

"I'm fine." And she wanted to see the animal that had him so excited.

But now he was glancing toward the house, as if trying to peer inside to see if his mother was there.

"Are you going to knock?" she asked.

He shrugged. "She rushed out last time I pulled up, and there was a vehicle here then that isn't here now."

There were no vehicles around; nobody around.

"Are you sure we should be here?" she asked. "Is this her house or…"

He shook his head. "She talked about the owner like it was someone else and not her, so I don't think it's her place…"

"Do you think she left?" Melanie asked. "After you found her?"

He sucked in a breath. "You think she took off again?"

"I don't know."

"I hope not." He frowned. "I wanted her to talk to my brothers, to explain to them like she did to me about why she left us. But I wonder if she chose to leave again instead." He groaned. "And now I feel like that kid she left all those years ago."

Sympathy flooded Melanie's heart and she

reached for him, sliding her arms around him in a comforting hug. "I know."

He clasped her close for a long moment. "You do," he agreed. "You know how it feels to have a parent disappoint you."

She tensed at the thought that Shep wasn't the only one who'd disappointed her. She'd disappointed herself when she'd rushed into a relationship without thinking it through.

As if he'd noticed her stiffness, he pulled back and murmured another apology.

"Go to the door," she urged. "Knock. See if she's here."

He shook his head. "I'd rather see if the mare is still here," he said, and he took her hand and led her toward the barn. Like the house, the paint had peeled off, leaving the wood exposed to the elements that had stained with the rain and snow.

"There's a horse from a championship bloodline here?" she asked skeptically.

"The place wasn't always like this," he said. "Or at least that's what Mom—" He cleared his throat. "What Darlene said. The owner fell on hard times. They need to sell everything."

"But is the horse theirs or hers?"

He shrugged again. "I thought it was hers. She said she needs to sell it quick. Maybe I'm already too late." But when they stepped inside the barn, a horse nickered and swung her head over the door of her stall. While this ranch wasn't well cared for, it was obvious that the horse was. Its black coat gleamed like velvet and it appeared well fed.

"She is beautiful," Melanie said with admiration.

He nodded. "I know. Hopefully, she doesn't sell before I can convince Jake to let me buy her and bring her to the ranch."

"He's against it?" she asked with surprise.

"He wasn't thrilled about Midnight," he reminded her.

"But I thought he'd begun to accept him."

Dusty shrugged. "I didn't give him much choice. Once I won him, I didn't know what else to do with him," he admitted.

"Is that what happened with us?" she questioned, not daring to meet his eyes. "Once you convinced me to marry you, you didn't know what else to do with me?"

He slid his arm around her and turned her away from the horse, toward him. And his hazel eyes gleamed like the horse's coat, but with longing.

He sighed. "That was the problem. We didn't do enough talking." He shook his head. "No,

I didn't do enough talking. I should have told you everything. But the longer I took to open up, the harder it got." He frowned.

"Maybe that's why your mom isn't here," she pointed out. "Why she hadn't talked to your brothers."

He nodded. "What's your excuse?"

"What?"

"I've opened up to you, Melanie," he said. "But you haven't opened up to me."

She jerked back. "I don't have any secrets."

He snorted. "I have no idea how you feel about me or what you want me to do."

"What do you want to do?" she asked. "Can you give up the rodeo? Can you stay at the ranch?"

He tensed now like she had earlier. And she knew.

"I could do that," he rasped, but he sounded as if he was trying to convince himself more than he was her. "If that's what you want. If that's what would make you happy."

"But would you be happy?" she asked.

He looked from her to that mare. "Maybe… if I could breed stock for rodeos."

Then he wouldn't be entirely giving it up. Was that what he thought?

"It's not the same," she warned him. "Even

for Shep with announcing, it was never the same for him as being a rider." Even as a little girl, she'd understood that, and that understanding had forged her career path.

Dusty emitted a wistful-sounding sigh. "I always told Shep that I was coming for his job someday. That when I was ready to stop riding, I'd become an announcer."

Because he'd wanted to keep traveling with the rodeo.

Because he hadn't wanted to give it up.

She was right. The rodeo would always be his first love. But she had a horrible feeling that he was going to try to give it up to take on responsibility for her and their babies. And if he wasn't happy doing that, if he resented her for it…none of them would be happy.

CHAPTER SIXTEEN

USUALLY WHEN DUSTY entered the ring and approached the chute, he had to tune out the noise of the crowd. He had to concentrate on his tasks, attaching the rope rein to the halter, connecting the cinch to the bucking saddle...but this riding arena didn't have much of a crowd.

Just his family...

Only a few of them had seen him ride before. Dale and Jenny had brought the boys a few times. But the boys had been so young that they probably didn't remember.

Baker had come once, with some guys from his unit, after boot camp. Baker stood near the fence now, the brim of his hat shading his face from the rays of the sun as it sank lower in the Wyoming sky. He'd skipped dinner, but he'd showed up afterward when everyone had headed out to the ring to watch him ride. "I'm here now, and I brought my bag. I should be able to set whatever bones this beast breaks when he tosses you off and stomps all over you."

Dusty chuckled. He wasn't worried about Midnight being as hard on him as he'd been during their first encounter. There was no chute in the ring, but the horse was staying perfectly still, as if he was waiting for Dusty to slide on the halter and cinch up the saddle. But as still as the horse was, his eyes were a little wild and there was a nervous energy radiating from him. Or maybe that energy was radiating from Dusty.

Or his nephews…

The little boys were excited, even Miller, who stood at the fence with Ian and Caleb. The seven-year-old glared at Baker and said, "You don't have to be here. Aunt Melanie can fix up Uncle Dusty just like she did before, like she fixed me."

Baker flinched but otherwise didn't react to their nephew's comment. There was definitely an issue between the two of them. Good thing that psychologist was coming to dinner soon.

"Uncle Dusty won't need anybody fixing him," Caleb said, coming to his defense. "Me and Mommy watched him riding on TV, and he never falls off."

"Not never," Dusty corrected him. But he

was better than when he'd started out eleven years ago as a green eighteen-year-old with no practical knowledge of how to ride. Fortunately, some of the older riders had taken pity on him.

"And even if he does fall off," Caleb continued, "Midnight won't stomp on him. He didn't stomp me and Ian and Daddy Jake when I opened his stall that time..." He glanced to Ian, who nodded in agreement.

The little boy remembered that, but then he peered around the fence where the rest of the family was leaning and asked, "Where's Mommy and Daddy?"

Miller groaned and jerked his head toward Baker. "Ask him!" Then he turned and limped off to where Melanie and her mother stood farther down the fence, next to Sadie and Lem.

Baker released a low groan too, and it reminded Dusty of the noises he'd heard that night outside the foreman's cottage when he'd thought an animal had been wounded. Dusty wanted to reach over the fence and comfort his younger brother, but Midnight shifted and pushed against him, anxious to start.

So were Caleb and Ian, who had maybe forgotten the question he'd just asked, because he asked another instead.

"What's that weird rope?"

Dusty paused while looping the riding rein through the halter. He took the time to show all of his equipment to the boys and answer their many questions. Then he demonstrated how he slid the halter over Midnight's nose and behind his mane. "To keep the halter secure, most riders tie sections of the mane across this strap…" Dusty did, too, because he knew it made it easier for the crew to grab the halter and lead the horse out of the arena.

"You're tying knots in his hair?" Caleb asked with alarm, very protective of the horse that he probably considered his now.

Dusty smiled. "It doesn't hurt him." It was actually harder on Dusty, who had to fumble with the silky strands until they knotted.

"What's taking so long?" Jake called out from farther down the fence. "Some of us were up early today."

Dusty flinched now at his older brother's remark. Just because he'd taken the day off to go to town with Melanie didn't mean that he hadn't been up early. He had gotten up and tended to Midnight before he and Melanie had left for town. He'd spent most of the day with her, shopping, and stopping to check out the mare. When they'd left, he'd noticed a shadow at one of the windows in the house. Maybe he should have knocked, but he wanted his mother to come to him now—to come to them.

Like he wanted Melanie to come to him…

To tell him what she really wanted from him, if she wanted him at all anymore. He wanted her. She was so beautiful in that new maternity dress she'd worn since she tried it on earlier today, the loose sunny yellow one that complimented her dark hair and glowing skin.

"Don't mind Big Jake," Ben advised as he approached the fence. He must have just come from town because he'd missed dinner. "He's just worried that he's going to be replaced in this one's eyes." He settled a hand on Caleb's shoulder.

Caleb peered up at him and smiled. "Hey, Uncle Ben…"

"And I already did," Ben continued with a grin.

Dusty snorted. "Hey, Caleb, what do you want to be when you grow up?" he asked. "A boring old politician or a rodeo rider?"

"A rodeo rider!" Caleb exclaimed.

Jake mumbled something that sounded suspiciously like a curse. Dusty was unabashed. Served his big brother right for being so judgy.

"Boring politician?" Ben shook his head.

"How about boss of a whole city?" he asked Caleb.

The little boy shook his head. "No."

"How about you, Ian?" Ben asked. "You want to be boss of the whole city?"

"I wouldn't take it that far..." Emily said as she approached. Little Jake rode on her hip, his fingers clutching strands of her blond hair.

Ben slung his arm around them both. He assured her, "Well, you're the boss of the boss of the whole city."

And she chuckled. But then she asked, "Ian, what do you want to be?"

Ian's face flushed, and he looked embarrassed before peering shyly up at Baker. "I wanna be a fireman...like Uncle Baker."

And Dusty heard the soft catch of Baker's breath. His heart warmed that the little boy was being so sweet to his uncle, who was obviously hurting.

Then Little Jake held out his arms to Baker. But Baker hesitated then shook his head. "I should go get my bag from my truck..."

Dusty narrowed his eyes in suspicion. Baker had said just moments ago that he'd brought it, so it probably was in the barn—not his truck.

"You're not going to need it," Caleb called out after him.

"Are you ready yet?" Jake asked, his voice gruff with impatience and maybe some jealousy. "Didn't realize it would take you an hour to get ready for a second-long ride…"

"It's eight seconds, Daddy," Caleb called back to his stepfather.

Jake snorted, and Midnight echoed the sound.

Dusty looked at the horse and grinned. That was definitely wildness in Midnight's eyes. He was restless and ready for a rematch. Dusty had been feeling restless himself earlier, with being back at the ranch, with being auditioned for the role of ranch foreman.

Instead of a job, it did feel like a part that he was trying to play. Like he was pretending to be someone he was not, like when they were kids and he and his twin had tried to switch places.

But here…about to ride a bronco, he felt like himself. While the horse was restless, Dusty was perfectly calm. Settled. He knew what he had to do; he had to put on that show he'd promised Jake.

"You ready, Midnight?" he asked the bronco as he slid the riding saddle onto his back. Then he grabbed the end of the cinch, pulling it tight enough for him to climb on without it sliding off. He would pull it tighter once he was on. Since there was no chute, and the stirrups on the saddle were too high for him to reach from the ground, he had to use the fence to mount the bronco. Once he wrapped the rein around his glove and slid his leg across the saddle, Midnight was off as if he'd been waiting for this.

Dusty closed his eyes against the setting sun and gave himself up to the ride. Flying up and down in the air as Midnight bucked high and hard…

He worked to absorb the bucks, worked to grip with his thighs while lightly prodding Midnight with the worn heels of his old riding boots. Midnight jumped higher and harder, and Dusty felt as though he was flying…and then he made sure that he was as he subtly loosened his grip on the rein rope.

He forced his body to go limp as he flew through the air, so that it wouldn't hurt when he hit the ground. And he hoped that Caleb was right, that Midnight wouldn't stomp on him. He must have let go when Midnight had been jumping high because it seemed like forever before he came back to earth and struck the ground, so hard that the air left his lungs and he went numb with shock from the impact.

A SCREAM SLIPPED out of Melanie's lips when Dusty hit the ground with such force. One minute he'd been riding, almost with ease, a grin of delight playing across his lips, and the next it was almost as if he'd purposely let go...

Then she remembered his conversation with his oldest brother on the patio, the one on which she'd blatantly eavesdropped. And she knew he had purposely let go.

Her mother wrapped her arm around Melanie. "He's fine. He's fine..."

He was lying so still on the ground that she wasn't sure he was physically okay, and she pulled away from her mom to walk toward the gate where Jake was standing. But before Jake could open it, Baker leaped over the fence and rushed to his brother's side.

"Are you okay?" Baker asked as he leaned over Dusty's prone body.

Dusty groaned. "Yeah, yeah... I'm good..."

Caleb climbed over the fence and dropped into the ring with his uncles. "Uncle Dusty, you don't gotta give him back. You made it eight seconds." He held up a small pocket watch. "You made it ten..."

And what ten seconds they were...

Tingling spread throughout Melanie's body as she remembered those long seconds. With the sun shining brightly on him, Dusty had looked like a star performing on a stage with all the spotlights trained solely on him. The horse had been in shadow, just the conduit on which Dusty had electrified his audience. Had electrified her...

Even more so than he used to. She'd watched him compete so many times during all the years that they'd both traveled with the circuit. She knew how good he was, almost effortlessly so. But she'd been attracted to more than his talent; she'd been attracted to his energy. He loved what he did so much that he radiated that love.

If his plan had been, like he'd told Jake, to turn Caleb off rodeo riding, it hadn't worked. He'd made it look too easy, and he'd clearly been loving it.

"He's really good," Melanie's mother said, appearing beside her. "Better than your father ever was..."

Melanie glanced at Juliet then, worried that she was thinking about Shep, that she was missing him. And she felt compelled to admit to all the calls she'd missed today while she'd had her cell turned off during the doctor's appointment and her subsequent shopping trip with Dusty.

"Dad's been calling all day," she warned her mother.

Juliet nodded. "I know. He's been calling me too."

"What do you want me to tell him?" Melanie asked. Her mother had hidden her whereabouts from Dusty when she'd left, so she would have to do the same if Juliet asked. She owed her mother her loyalty, but she loved her father, too, despite all his faults.

"I'll talk to him," Juliet said. "I don't want you in the middle anymore." Her mother squeezed her shoulder. "I'm sorry for all the times I've put you there in the past..."

"Mom..." She couldn't tell her that it was okay. Not when it had hurt so much to see her mother in pain and to know that her father had caused it. She'd never wanted to feel that way herself, and so she'd been so careful with her heart, with her trust...until that impulsive moment she'd gotten married on her first date with a rodeo rider. She didn't want to be in the middle either, but she had to ask, "What are you going to say to him?"

Was she going to go back to him like she had all those times before?

Her mother shrugged. "You know your father. I doubt he'll let me say much..."

302 THE BRONC RIDER'S TWIN SURPRISE

Shep had always been like that. He talked fast and constantly, as if his words would somehow protect him from the truth being discovered.

But Melanie knew that the truth always came out. Her truth was that she loved her husband. The last few days, watching him being so sweet and caring with his nephews and with her, she'd fallen even harder for him. And because she loved Dusty, she knew she might have to let him go back to his first love, to the rodeo.

"YOU MIGHT HAVE to let this go…" Lem murmured.

Sadie glanced down at the man who walked beside her as they headed away from the riding arena back toward the house. Feisty trotted on the other side of her. "I'm okay," she assured him. "I know Dusty isn't hurt."

But Melanie hadn't been the only one who'd screamed when Dusty had flown off that bronco. Sadie had just held hers back with a hand clamped over her mouth. She couldn't react and scare the others. She had to be strong.

"I'm talking about Jessup," Lem said.

She gasped and glanced around, making sure nobody was close enough to overhear them. Dusty and the little boys were still in the ring with the horse, who pranced around like he was taking a victory lap. He really was a magnificent animal.

But Taye and Ben and Emily were walking back toward the house too. Hopefully, they weren't within earshot yet.

"Wait until we're alone," she cautioned him. Then she scooped up Feisty, grabbed Lem's arm, and hauled them both toward the house so they could beat the others back.

Once she'd closed the door to her suite behind them, she let Feisty loose. Then she let loose on Lem. "Don't talk about him where the others might hear."

"You think Dusty already knows," he reminded her. "You don't think he told his brothers?"

She shook her head. He was giving her time, just like she'd given him time. He'd had his years of traveling with the rodeo, of winning championships and sponsorships. Surely, after going to the doctor with his wife today, he had to know it was time to give it up, but then he'd looked so happy on the back of that bronco... She sighed.

"So if he hasn't told them, there's no reason

to look into this," Lem said. "You should just let it go."

"What!" she exclaimed. "I've let this go for years…too many years…" But she really hadn't. She thought of Jessup every day, wondering where he was, what had happened to him, if he'd ever stopped hating her. "I need to know."

He sighed and nodded. "I warned you…"

Her stomach lurched with a rush of dread, and she reached out and grasped Lem's shoulder. "Oh, no. He is dead."

"No," Lem assured her then murmured, "Well, I don't know…"

"What do you know?" she asked. "Why'd you bring this up if you don't know what happened to him?"

"Because I know how you can find out," Lem told her.

Her pulse fluttered again. "What…how…?"

"I started checking around with people who were around the ranch when Jessup ran away."

She could easily remember some of the special ones. Michael had been here since he'd just turned thirteen when Jessup had run away at eighteen. Big Jake had been here, too. But they were both gone now. And all of the hands who'd worked the ranch then had probably re-tired long ago. Had Lem tracked them down?

"So I called Whitford…" Lem tensed as if he was dreading what he was about to tell her.

"Whitford? The accountant who embezzled from the ranch?" she asked. She snorted. "I wouldn't believe anything he told you." Dale and Jenny had discovered his deception before they'd died. It was one of the reasons Sadie had hired Katie on full-time to help with the books—along with bringing her and Jake back together.

Lem shrugged. "I don't see any reason for him to lie about this…"

"About what?"

"He said Big Jake knew where Jessup went…that he sent him money for years. And that when Darlene left, he sent her money too."

She shook her head, unable to believe what she'd just heard. Whitford couldn't be trusted. And Big Jake…he would have never kept something like from her. "That sleazy accoun-tant is just trying to cover up his crime. He was the one taking that money."

"He emailed me proof. Canceled checks with Big Jake's signature. Checks made out to Jessup and then to Darlene. Big Jake was sending the checks."

Her heart began to pound harder, faster. "Where? Where was he sending checks?"

Lem shook his head. "A P.O. box," he said. "I'm trying to track down who rented it back then."

She shook her head now. "No. Big Jake would have told me..." They'd had no secrets from each other. If he'd been sending Jessup money, he wouldn't have hidden it from her. He wouldn't have hidden her son from her. "You're lying!" she accused him. "You've always been jealous of Big Jake."

"Sadie..." Lem said, his voice soft with pity.

She bristled with indignation, with pride. And she shook her head again. "No! You're just making trouble. Trying to make me think less of the man who was twice the man you ever were. More than twice!"

"Sadie, I have no reason to lie..."

And she knew that; that was why it hurt so much. She knew he was telling the truth, that her husband had kept a secret from her. A big secret.

Her son...

"Get out!" she shouted as the pain ripped her heart in two. She sucked in a breath and bellowed again. "Get out and don't ever come back!"

Lem didn't argue with her. He just looked
like a dog that she'd kicked, hard, as he opened
the door and walked out. And she had a feeling that she hadn't had to tell him.

That he wasn't going to come back.

Ever.

CHAPTER SEVENTEEN

DESPITE SOME BUMPS and bruises, Dusty was fine. The impact of hitting the ground had just knocked the wind out of him for a bit. Midnight hadn't stomped on his body, just his ego, as he'd pranced around the ring, tossing his neck and nickering at Dusty.

"Yeah, you won," he assured the horse as he tucked him back into his stall a short while later.

"He kicked your butt," Baker taunted.

Ben grimaced and agreed, "It was brutal."

"Uncle Dusty made it ten seconds." Caleb defended him again. "The rule is you only gotta go eight."

Dusty smiled until he glanced up and found Jake glaring at him. He raised his hands. "Hey, I fell off, and it hurt."

Jake grunted and muttered something that sounded a lot like, "Good…"

"Yeah, how did you lose the rope like that?" Caleb asked curiously.

"What rope?" Ian asked.

Everybody else had headed back to the house to set up for Midnight's victory party. He was surprised that Caleb and Ian hadn't rushed off for the cookies that were seemingly a part of every celebration at the ranch.

"Tell us about all the stuff again," Caleb begged him. "Show me—"

"Hey, guys," Jake interrupted. "We all need to head up to the house now, or there might not be any dessert left."

Caleb nipped his bottom lip with his teeth and nodded. Then he grabbed Ian's hand and they ran out of the barn.

Dusty braced himself for the lecture that was sure to come from his big brother now. But before Jake could launch into the evils of rodeo riding—and how it would be wrong for his son—Old Man Lemmon rushed into the barn nearly as fast as the little boys had just run out.

"Thank goodness, you're still here," he said to Baker. "You need to go up and check on your grandmother."

Dusty's heart skipped a beat. "What happened? Is she all right?"

Lem met his gaze with a very pointed look;

a look that let Dusty know this was his fault. He swallowed a groan of self-disgust.

"She's really upset," Lem said. "She threw me out of the house, and she…" He trailed off, as if choking on emotion, but he cleared his throat and added, "She's just really upset."

"Lem?" Ben asked so much with just his old friend's name.

Mr. Lemmon shook his head. "We're done. She doesn't want me to ever come back to the ranch."

"Lem…" Ben intoned, his voice gruff with sympathy and regret.

Dusty knew that Ben had set up his deputy mayor with their grandmother to give her a dose of her own matchmaking medicine. Given how cantankerous the old couple had been with each other over the years, Dusty was surprised they hadn't killed one another before now.

"Lem," Ben called out again.

But the old man had already turned and started walking away, his shoulders stooped. He'd always looked older than he was, but now he looked positively ancient.

This was Dusty's fault.

"I better go check on her," Baker said.

"I'm going too," Dusty said as he hurried

off after the paramedic. Ben and Jake followed closely.

"You're screwed now," Ben warned Baker. "Without Lem to distract her, she's going to focus all her energy on getting you married off."

Baker shuddered.

Ben sighed. "They seemed to be getting along so well. Too well sometimes. I wonder what happened…"

"I don't think this has anything to do with Lem," Dusty told him.

"Did you cause this?" Ben asked, his brown eyes even darker with suspicion.

Dusty shrugged. He didn't know for certain, but there was only one way to find out. He dashed ahead of the others, into the house and down the hall to Grandma's private suite.

Without bothering to knock, he pushed open the door. His heart slammed against his chest when he found her crumpled over in one of her easy chairs, her face buried in her hands. Her broad shoulders heaved up and down as she sobbed. Feisty had pressed her small furry body up against her mistress's side, and she trembled like Sadie was trembling.

He dropped to his knees beside his grandmother and brushed his hand over her soft, white hair. "Grandma, what happened? What's wrong?"

She shook her head. "Go away."

"Grandma, it's Baker," the paramedic said as he walked into the room too. "I need to check you out. Make sure your blood pressure isn't too high…"

She sucked in a shaky breath and a lot of tears before lifting her face from her hands. Then she glared at her youngest grandson. "And so what if it is?" she asked. "I'm not going to the doctor or the hospital."

"You might have to," Baker said. "You might need medication to lower it. Machines to monitor it, so that you don't have a heart attack."

She snorted. "I'm not having a heart attack." She drew in another breath, this one deep and steady, and straightened her shoulders. "Like that old fool Lemmon would probably tell you, I don't have a heart to attack me."

"He's the one who came to get Baker to check you out," Ben said. He and Jake now stood behind their youngest brother. "He's worried about you."

She sniffled. "He should be…"

"What happened, Grandma?" Jake asked. "What did he do?"

She blew out her breath now in a ragged sigh. "He told me the truth."

"And that's a crime punishable by banishment?" Ben asked, his dark eyes softening with humor even as he stared at her with concern.

Dusty might have been the most like Sadie with his stubbornness, but Ben was the most like her with his wit.

She smiled. "You're right. If I really wanted to punish him, I should have made him stay." She brushed a hand over her face, rubbing away the last traces of her tears. "Oh heck, now I'm gonna owe him an apology."

Ben chuckled. "He'll love that."

She nodded. "Probably too much."

Baker had snuck his fingers onto her wrist, and his brow lined as if he was still concerned. "Your pulse is pretty fast…"

"That's good," Sadie said. "Means I'm still alive. Don't throw dirt on me yet." She turned toward Dusty then. "Speaking of which, how'd you check out after getting tossed in the dirt like that?"

He forced a smile for her. "I'm alive yet too. Not sure Midnight's ego is going to fit in his stall though…" He sniffed. "They're having a party for the horse in the kitchen."

She chuckled. "They going to bring him in the house as the guest of honor?"

Dusty shook his head. "I doubt that."

"Are you up to joining, Grandma?" Baker asked.

She nodded. "Just give me and Dusty a few minutes alone."

His heart sank in his chest. It *was* his fault. Whatever truth Lem had told her must have had to do with him or with what he'd learned.

"Go!" She waved one of her big hands at his brothers. "Get out of here."

"Let me check your blood pressure first, Grandma," Baker implored her.

She sighed and relented. "You can check it after I talk to Dusty. Now give us some privacy."

All three of Dusty's brothers gave him a warning glare before they finally backed out of the room.

"Close the door!" she yelled at them, like she had so many times when they'd been kids running out of the house with doors gaping open behind them.

Dusty smiled at the memory and turned to find her smiling at him as if the same memory had crossed her mind.

"Some things never change," she murmured.

"No, they don't," he agreed. His brothers never seemed to. Sure, Jake was happy again that he was back with Katie, and Ben had fallen in love as well. But they treated Dusty the same way they always had, like he was the black sheep. "And then some things change so much that you feel like you're getting tossed up in the air and you don't know where or how hard you're going to land."

That was exactly how he felt now. He had no idea what he was going to do, and he felt as if he had no control over it. He couldn't make Melanie trust him again. It was something she had to give him freely or it wouldn't really be his. And he wasn't sure he could trust her to not do what his mother seemed to keep doing, take off at the first sign of trouble.

He wasn't sure he would survive if his wife did that again and took their babies with her. While he was scared that he was going to fail as a dad as dismally as he had as a husband, he wanted to be in his children's lives; he wanted to be a father to them.

"Oh, Dusty," his grandmother sighed softly, and he wondered if that was another thought they'd shared. If she felt the same way he did. She reached for his hand, covering it with hers. Veins protruded across the back of it, and her fingers were a little bent now, her knuckles swollen. Her hands, even more than her face, showed her age, showed how hard she'd always worked. For her family. For the ranch...

"Are you really okay?" he asked.

She nodded. "My heart isn't attacking me," she insisted. "It's just hurting."

"I can understand that," he sympathized. She'd lost so much, even more than he'd known.

She squeezed his hand. "I'm sure you can understand. And now I know how it must feel to find out that someone you love, that you trusted, kept things from you."

His brow furrowed with confusion. "Are you talking about Lem or me? I know I should have told Melanie everything before we got married, about the ranch, about my family..." And he wasn't sure that he would ever be able to get her to truly forgive him for not being completely honest with her.

"I was talking about me," she said. "And your grandfather..." She sucked in a breath, as if she had to brace herself just to say it. "Apparently, he knew where Jessup was and was sending him money. And he never told me..."

Dusty blew out a soft whistle at the shock of that revelation. What was wrong with his family? Why couldn't they be open and honest with each other? "That's the truth that Lem told you," he surmised.

She nodded. "I didn't want to believe him. I didn't want to believe that your grandfather would keep anything from me. But..." She sighed. "Those dang cigars of his...and that wasn't a secret he'd kept well. Not like this..."

"So where is Uncle Jessup?" Dusty asked.

"I don't know," she admitted. "Lem offered to keep searching..."

"I think my mother knows," Dusty said.

Sadie's brow furrowed now. "How? I didn't even know that she knew about him until you..."

Until he'd taken his cheap shots at her. "I'm sorry," he said. "For not being more understanding about how difficult that must have been for you."

"To have a son run away..." She nodded. "It's one thing to lose them to an accident, like your father. But to have someone you love choose to leave you..."

Like his wife had run away from him...

He shuddered.

She squeezed his hand again. "I'm sorry. I'm sure you and Melanie will work everything out."

He wasn't sure. If she couldn't trust him… If he couldn't trust her… He shrugged. "We'll see."

"Will you talk to your mother?" she asked. "I don't see how she would know where he is, but I…"

He nodded. "You know she blames herself for Dad dying. She thinks she distracted him, that she caused him to fall."

Sadie gasped. "I didn't know…"

"So I think she went looking for Jessup to replace the son she thinks she took from you."

A look of understanding spread over Grandma's face. "That's so sweet. But Dusty, she never came back." A tear slipped down her cheek. "I don't think she found him…"

Alive.

More tears followed, and she was sobbing again.

Dusty wrapped his arms around her and held her, offering her what little comfort he could. And he wasn't sure—even if he could find her—that he should get his mother to talk to Sadie now.

He wasn't sure if it was better that Grandma was left wondering what had happened to her runaway son, or if she had confirmation that he was gone.

MELANIE AND THE other women had heard the shouting the minute they'd walked into the house. But in deference to Sadie's privacy, and probably because she intimidated all of them except Taye, everybody had rushed right into the kitchen, only peering out when they heard footsteps in the hall.

Mr. Lemmon had rushed out without a backward glance at them, or at Sadie, who'd slammed the door to her suite shut behind him. But they could hear her shout a repeat of what she'd already said to him, "And don't ever come back!"

They'd discussed that one of them—they'd chosen Taye—should go to her suite to talk to her, but before Taye had washed her hands and started down the hall, Caleb and Ian had come running into the kitchen looking for cookies, distracting them. And seconds later, Dusty, Baker, Ben and Jake had burst into the house.

Melanie, Katie and Emily had breathed a collective sigh of relief then. Sadie's grandsons were better equipped to deal with her, to comfort her...

Melanie's mother and Emily had whisked the boys upstairs to clean up while she, Katie and Taye had lingered in the kitchen. Taye, worried about Sadie, kept peering down the hall. "Jake, Ben and Baker stepped out of her suite," she reported. "But Dusty's still in there."

Why?

Was this about what Dusty had learned? About his mother…

Remembering how upset he'd been when he hadn't found her at the ranch, Melanie ached to comfort him, to hold him again. Was Darlene as much the reason that Dusty hadn't been honest with her as his family's opinion of him? Had he not wanted to open himself up to that kind of abandonment again? As if involuntarily, she started edging down the hall herself. She slipped around Taye in the kitchen entrance and was close enough that she could hear Dusty's brothers talking.

About him.

"I wonder why Grandma wanted to talk to him alone," Ben murmured.

"Because it's Dusty's fault that she got so worked up," Jake said, his deep voice gruff with anger.

And his anger had anger surging through Melanie. "No, it isn't!" she blurted out, surprising herself and Dusty's brothers, who jumped like she'd just jumped to the defense of her husband. That was what she should have done all these weeks she'd been living on the ranch, when she'd heard Jake and his brothers disparaging the man she loved. Then she'd thought they'd known him better than she had, but now she was beginning to see that it was the other way around. She might not have known his real name when she'd married him, or about his family, but she'd known his heart.

It was a good heart; filled with love for the people he loved. He wouldn't have purposely upset his grandmother.

His brothers stared at her in shock, Jake and Ben's dark eyes wide. Baker's eyes were a lighter color, more topaz than brown. He was the one who spoke to her, his deep voice gentle. "Melanie, Dusty admitted it."

Exasperated, she nodded. "Of course he did because he takes the blame for everything. It's not his fault that your mother went back to rodeo riding after your father died."

Jake furrowed his brow and stared down at her. "What are you talking about?"

"You act like he did something criminal because he joined the rodeo," she said. "But it was fine for Ben to stay in college and go into politics, and it was fine for Baker to join the army. Why wasn't it fine for Dusty to follow his dream of becoming a rodeo rider? Why did that make him irresponsible, or like his mother, just because he loves the rodeo? And clearly, after you saw him ride, you can see that?"

She'd seen it, how much he loved it, and because she loved him, she didn't think she could ask him to give it up. Because she knew he would, and then he'd be miserable.

"Wow…" Ben murmured. "When you put it like that…"

"That's what he meant the other night," Jake reflected. "I didn't understand what he was trying to tell me…"

"I never considered him irresponsible," Baker said. "He was just determined to become a championship rider, just as determined as Ben was to become mayor."

She shook her head, unwilling to let him off the hook. "I heard the things you said to him."

"After Dale died," Baker said. "We needed him here, with us, with the boys, but he took off right after Dale and Jenny's funeral, just like Mom took off after Dad's. That was when I got angry with him."

That was what she'd seen and heard since she'd arrived at the ranch, all that anger and resentment. "And that was my fault," she said earnestly. "Because I took off and I didn't let him know where I was. He left to look for me.

He's been looking for me all this time. That was my fault."

Heat rushed to her face as guilt overwhelmed her. She had acted more like an immature child than a married woman, a woman who was going to be a mother. She wished she could blame it all on the pregnancy hormones. Dusty must have felt exactly like he had when his mother had taken off—abandoned. Shame gripped her now, making her stomach cramp and her head lighten. Feeling dizzy, she reached out to touch the wall of the corridor, to steady herself.

"Are you okay?" Baker asked.

The door behind the brothers opened and Dusty stepped out. "What's wrong? What's going on?"

"Your wife is letting us have it for being jerks to you," Ben said, but he was smiling as he said it. Clearly, she hadn't offended him. Though, after how quiet she'd been around them since her arrival at the ranch, she had undoubtedly surprised them.

Having always struggled with shyness, Melanie had surprised herself. Maybe that was why she felt slightly unsteady now, in reaction to the confrontation with these three enormous cowboys.

Jake nodded and agreed. "She's fierce in her defense of you."

"Those babies are going to be lucky to have you as their mother," Baker said. He reached out to squeeze her shoulder and, as he did, he peered into her face with concern. "Are you okay?"

She nodded. "Yes, I'm fine. I probably just need something to eat."

"Everything's ready for Midnight's party," Taye called from the kitchen, where she must have been eavesdropping with Katie.

"Time to get the party started!" Caleb called out from beside her.

The guys all hesitated, until Sadie stepped out of her suite. "Let's go!" she told them.

"Grandma, I wanted to check your blood pressure," Baker said.

She shrugged. "I'm fine now. Thanks to Dusty."

He shook his head. "I didn't do anything."

"That's the point, dear," she murmured, and she patted his cheek before passing him in the hall. She continued past everyone until she reached Melanie. Then she stopped and smiled at her with approval. "See, you're stronger than you think you are."

Katie had said that to her once, when Melanie had been struggling with morning sickness and the fear of raising her babies alone, and she hadn't believed her. But those words, coming now from the fiercest person Melanie had ever met, touched her deeply and empowered her. Feeling the strength, she was no longer so intimidated by this woman, by this family, so she hugged her grandmother-in-law.

Sadie's tall body was stiff for a moment before her arms wrapped around Melanie and she hugged her and pressed a kiss to Melanie's cheek. "You're also very sweet." She pulled back then and continued down the hall toward the kitchen, Feisty nipping at her heels. Then her grandsons did as well, following behind her, badgering her with questions to make sure that she was all right.

But for Dusty...

He stayed behind in the hall, staring at Melanie. And that look on his face...

It made her stomach flip, made her feel dizzy all over again...with desire. "What?" she asked when he just continued to stare silently at her.

He shook his head. "You are so beautiful."

She touched the dress he'd bought her, the lovely sunny yellow dress that she loved so much. She'd been so dumbstruck that he was wearing her wedding ring on that chain that she hadn't thanked him. So she did now. "Thank you for the clothes."

"I don't think anybody's ever done that," he said.

"Done what?" she asked. "Thanked you?"

"Defended me," he said, and his hazel eyes gleamed with emotion.

"Not even Dale?" she asked. As twins, she'd figured they had had each other's back.

He shrugged. "I don't know. Maybe...when I wasn't around..." He stepped closer to her, and he dipped his head down to brush his lips across her cheek. "Thank you," he murmured. Then his gaze focused on her mouth.

And Melanie linked her arms around his neck and pulled his head down until her mouth reached his. She kissed him deeply, with all the love she felt for him.

And because she loved him so much, she hoped his grandmother was right that she was stronger than she thought she was. Because she'd have to be...if she was going to let him go...

CHAPTER EIGHTEEN

A FEW DAYS had passed since Dusty's fall from Midnight, but he still felt the aches and pains, especially after spending so much of his day in the saddle, trailing Jake around the ranch like he was now. His big brother had a little less attitude with him since Melanie had confronted him and Ben and Baker in the hallway outside Sadie's suite.

He smiled as he remembered how he and Grandma had listened at the door as she'd defended him. Warmth flooded his heart like the sun shining brightly down on them. He loved her. He loved her so much.

And she loved it here. Even her mother was thriving on the ranch, happily helping out with the boys and in the kitchen. He was happy she was here because he didn't worry as much about Melanie while he was out in the pastures. He knew his mother-in-law would make sure that Melanie didn't overdo it. But even though his wife should have been resting more, she still had those dark circles beneath her eyes. Maybe she wasn't sleeping any better than he was, because he couldn't sleep for thinking of her, for aching to hold her again.

He hadn't had the chance since that kiss in the hall. She'd kissed him so deeply and passionately, like she used to. But they'd been interrupted when Caleb had come looking for him and had loudly proclaimed, "Sheesh, everybody's always kissing in this house!"

He and Melanie had pulled apart and laughed together. Then Dusty had taken the opportunity to pump the boy for information. "Who's everybody? Grandma Sadie and Old Man Lemmon?"

"Ewww…" the little boy had replied at the thought.

"Uncle Baker and Taye?" Melanie had asked.

Caleb had shaken his head. "Nah, Uncle Baker is never around…"

"Sadie's going to have to work harder on that one," Dusty had remarked.

"Hey!" Jake called out, his voice sharp with impatience, as if he'd been trying to get Dusty's attention. "You daydreaming or working?"

He definitely hadn't been doing as much

working as daydreaming, but the ranch was in good repair, everything running smoothly. Baker might not have been coming around the ranch house much, but he'd been at the ranch whenever he didn't have a shift at the firehouse. He had even darker circles around his eyes than Melanie, and probably Dusty, had.

"There's not much to do," Dusty pointed out.

Jake nodded with satisfaction. "Things are going well with the ranch now," he said, but then he uttered a ragged sigh. "Just wish the boys were doing as well."

Dusty had been sleeping in Ian's room since Ian usually slept with Caleb. Little Jake had been quiet for a couple of nights but had awakened last night with a nightmare. And Ian...

Ian had acted all confused again. Miller had gotten irritated, and even Caleb, who was usually patient with the little boy, had gotten frustrated.

"Mrs. Lancaster is coming tonight," Dusty reminded Jake.

Jake nodded. "We should head back to the barn now, so we won't be later for dinner." He used his knee to prod Buck to move a little faster.

And Dusty prodded his Appaloosa to keep

pace. "Did you think about what I said about buying that mare to breed with Midnight?"

Jake shook his head. "No. I don't want to go into the rodeo business."

Dusty groaned. "You won't even think about it?"

"We have all we can handle right now," Jake said. "And it's enough. Why was the ranch never enough for you, Dusty?"

"Like it was for Dale?" he asked. "I'm not Dale."

Jake sighed. "I know…and I don't resent you for that. I don't think you're wrong for wanting to ride in the rodeo…"

"You just don't want any part of it," Dusty said. And he knew that he needed to get his mother—if he could find her again—out to the ranch to talk to Sadie and to his brothers. But he and Sadie had decided that day in her suite to wait until after the school psychologist had had a chance to talk to the boys. Making sure Little Jake and Ian and Miller were physically, emotionally, and mentally healthy had to be their priority.

But Dusty couldn't help but think of that mare…

He didn't want to lose it.

"Why don't you start your own ranch?" Jake

asked. "You could move Midnight there and buy that mare."

"What?" Dusty asked, nearly as stunned at the thought as he'd been by Melanie defending him the other night. He knew better than anyone how shy and guarded she was; it had taken him weeks—no, years—to get her to talk to him.

"It would have to be close, so Caleb could keep bringing him carrots," Jake said. "But with all those championships you won and those sponsorships you had, you should have some money to start the operation."

He had the money. That wasn't the issue. He'd just figured that if he ever left the rodeo, he would return to Ranch Haven, not start his own ranch. But that place coming up for sale, where the mare was and where his mother had been, wasn't far from the ranch. It needed a lot of work, though. And was it too far from this ranch for Melanie to be interested in it?

"So it sounds like I didn't pass your test to become the new ranch foreman," Dusty mused.

Jake chuckled. "I don't think it's a job you really want."

"No," Dusty admitted. "But I'm happy to help out until you can find someone else."

Jake sighed. "I found someone else."

"That's great," Dusty said. "Why aren't you happier about it?"

"Because he doesn't know he's perfect for the job," Jake said. "He doesn't know that he actually loves the ranch."

"Baker…" Dusty ventured. The thought had occurred to him too.

"I just don't know how I'm going to get him to realize it," Jake admitted.

"Think like Sadie," he encouraged. "Come up with a good scheme."

"Is she really okay?" Jake asked.

Dusty nodded. "Yeah…she just wants everyone focusing on the boys right now, on making sure they're going to be okay."

"Let's get back, then," Jake said as he prodded Buck into a gallop.

Dusty followed suit, and because of that competitive nature of being a twin, he made the Appaloosa go just a little faster so that he reached the barn first. Midnight greeted him with a nicker and a head toss, as if he was still mocking him for falling off, and challenging him to another rematch.

"Careful," Dusty cautioned the bronco, "or I won't play matchmaker for you."

"Matchmaker for a horse," Jake snorted as he came up behind Dusty, leading Buck by the halter. "I don't know if Grandma would even go that far."

"Grandma would do whatever she thought was necessary to make her family happy," Dusty said. So he couldn't imagine why his uncle, whom he'd never known about, had run away from home. He hadn't asked Sadie that yet; he hadn't wanted to put her through any more pain than she'd already endured.

"You think she's going to find Feisty a mate?" Jake asked.

Dusty scoffed. "I wouldn't put it past her."

"What about Lem? You think she's going to forgive him?"

"She was just mad that he told her the truth," Dusty shared. "It was hard for her to hear."

Jake nodded. "Yeah, sometimes it is hard, but it's necessary." He reached out then and grabbed Dusty's shoulder. "I'm sorry I've been so hard on you. I just didn't understand how you could love something that took our mom away…"

Dusty sighed. "The rodeo didn't take Mom away."

"No," Jake agreed. "Selfishness did."

"No," Dusty said, jumping to her defense like Melanie had jumped to his. "We had it wrong all these years."

Jake looked at him in shock. "You've talked to her?"

Dusty nodded. "And I want her to come here, to talk to all of us...herself."

Jake shook his head. "No. We need to focus on the boys now. *Just* the boys."

Dusty wished he could, but maybe he was as selfish as Jake had accused their mother of being, because he couldn't help but focus on his wife, on how much he loved and wanted to regain her trust. To raise those babies with her...if she would let him back into her life and her heart.

"Why do I have to look so nice?" Miller asked as Melanie brushed his overly long hair. He was overdue for a haircut. She'd intended to get him one in Sheridan when his cast had come off three weeks ago, but when she'd received the news that she was pregnant with twins, Melanie had wanted to return to the ranch right away. And to her support group of the amazing friends she'd made here.

Taye, Emily, Katie, and Sadie, too, had embraced her mother as lovingly as they had her. Her mother seemed happier now than Melanie ever remembered her being. Was that because she wasn't with Shep or because she wasn't traveling or both? Melanie couldn't imagine leaving the ranch and all the people she loved here. Yet now she couldn't imagine giving up Dusty either. But as much as she loved him, she didn't entirely trust him yet. Or herself. Was she right to fall for him again? Or was she making another mistake? And what about the rodeo? Could she even travel with as easily as she got tired? Even now, she had to lean against the edge of the bathroom vanity while she brushed Miller's hair.

"Are we having another party?" he asked. Then he chuckled. "Is this one for Feisty? Did she feel left out?"

Melanie smiled at his joke, her heart warming with his improved mood. He had seemed happier lately, except when Baker was in the house. Fortunately, or maybe unfortunately, Baker was rarely in the house. And it wasn't that he wasn't at the ranch, because his truck was often in the driveway.

Whatever was between Baker and his oldest nephew needed to be resolved for both their sakes. Hopefully, the psychologist coming to dinner tonight would figure out a way to help them, or at least refer them to someone who could.

"Miss Emily is having a friend over to-night," Melanie said.

"Why? Are we throwing a party for her?"

Only if she helped them. Melanie shook her head. "No, we're just having dinner like usual."

Miller narrowed his eyes and studied her face as if he knew she was holding something back. "Who is it?" he asked. "Who's coming to dinner?"

"Just somebody Miss Emily works with."

His suspicion clearly grew. "She was acting weird today, saying that somebody was coming here tonight that wants to talk to us. Is it Mrs. Lancaster?"

"What if it is?" Melanie asked.

His little body stiffened with outrage. "Then I'm not gonna talk to her."

"Why not?"

"'Cause only the kids with problems talk to her," he said. "And I…" He trailed off as if he couldn't even say it, couldn't claim that he had no problems.

"Come on," she said. "We don't want to keep everyone else waiting."

Like she'd been waiting for her husband to kiss her again, like she'd kissed him that night in the hallway. Even as she'd done it, she'd known it was a bad idea; it was only going to make it harder for her to let him go. And she knew it would be better for both of them in the long run if she did.

She'd never seen her mother as happy as she was now. Juliet was standing in the hallway, waiting for them, when Melanie opened the bathroom door. She knew they'd have a guest, and she'd dressed up a little bit too. But it wasn't just the clothes that made her look so young and pretty; it was that she seemed so much more carefree.

"You go on down," Melanie told Miller. She wanted a moment to talk to her mother alone.

He glanced at her, with that suspicion still in his hazel eyes, before heading toward the stairwell.

"Is he okay?" Juliet asked with concern.

Melanie sighed. "Hopefully, we're about to find out," she said. She hadn't heard the doorbell yet so she hoped the guest of honor hadn't arrived. Because once Miller saw that his suspicion was right...

She sighed again and squared her shoulders. "How are you?" she asked her mother. "Are you okay?"

She knew her mom had talked to her father a couple of days ago because he'd stopped calling Melanie, stopped demanding that she tell him where his wife was.

"Never better," her mother assured her. She reached out and touched Melanie's cheek. "You look so tired, though, dear. Maybe you should skip dinner and lie down."

She was tempted, but she was too worried about Miller. "I'm fine."

"Are you?" Juliet asked. "I see how you look at your husband, how worried you are about your future and your babies' futures."

She was worried. "I just don't want to make the mistakes…"

"That I made," her mother finished for her. "I don't regret falling for your father, because I wouldn't have you if I hadn't. But I do regret fighting so hard to try to make our relationship work. If it takes that much effort, it's not meant to be."

Was that the case for her and Dusty? Would it take too much effort for them to figure out how they could both be happy when they wanted such different things now?

"Did Dad accept that?" Melanie asked.

Juliet sighed. "You know your father never listens to anyone but himself. He thinks if he makes a grand gesture I'll give him another chance."

"Grand gesture?" she asked. "Like what?"

"Like giving his job to Dusty," her mother replied.

"What?"

"He thinks Dusty was hurt and that's why he hasn't been on the circuit this season," she explained. "So he wants to offer Dusty his job. He thinks that if he retires, I'll take him back."

Melanie tensed. "Would you?" And, more importantly, would Dusty be interested in the announcer position now? He'd had an ongoing joke for years with Shep that he was going to take his job someday. Every time her father had interviewed him over the years, Dusty had warned him that he was coming for him, that being an announcer was the only way he could stay involved in the rodeo when he was too old to ride. So even when he was too old to ride, he wasn't willing to give it up.

He wasn't able to see his life without it. Her mother was right; if a relationship took too much effort or too much sacrifice, it wasn't meant to be.

Juliet was shaking her head. "We both know how miserable your father would be without the rodeo. I'd rather not have a husband at all than have one who resents me for making him give up what he loves."

And Melanie flinched as a sudden pain gripped her.

"Are you all right?" Juliet asked with alarm.

Melanie nodded. "Yes, I'm fine." And the pain passed quickly. Physically. Emotionally, she knew it would take longer for the pain to pass once she did what she needed to do. Once she gave up her husband.

Her mother opened her mouth to talk, but the doorbell chimed then, saving Melanie from any more questions. She hurried toward the stairs, anxious to be present so that she could temper Miller's reaction to Mrs. Lancaster's arrival.

But when she reached the last step, it wasn't Miller that she sought out. It was Dusty. He was standing by the hearth with his brothers, deep in conversation. But somehow he must have sensed her presence because he glanced up and met her gaze...with one of those looks...

Her pulse quickened with attraction and nerves. Then she remembered why she'd rushed downstairs, and she tore her eyes from Dusty's to look for his oldest nephew.

Miller was in the kitchen, helping Taye set the table. He hadn't gone to answer the door. So Melanie breathed a slight sigh of relief...

until she saw who walked into the kitchen with Sadie.

The man was nearly as short as Mr. Lemmon, but instead of white hair, his was dark. Probably dyed since the stubble on his face was gray. He wore boots with shiny silver toe plates and a bolero tie with his Western shirt and jeans.

"Shep Shepard!" Caleb exclaimed, his voice cracking with excitement.

"Is this your dinner guest, Miss Emily?" Miller asked with surprise.

Everybody was surprised, except for her mother...who stepped out behind Melanie to confront her husband, her face flushed with embarrassment. "Shep, your coming here isn't going to make a difference to me. It's just a disruption."

One they didn't need right now as the doorbell rang again. While Emily rushed off down the hall, everybody else continued to stare at Shep, but for Dusty, who'd come up to Melanie and was watching her with concern. "What do you want me to do?" he asked quietly. "Do you want me to throw him out? Or do you want to talk to him?" He directed his last question to his mother-in-law, who shook her head.

"I said everything I had to say to Shep," she replied. "I can't make him listen."

"I can," Dusty offered, and he turned around and started toward the other man just as Emily walked back into the kitchen with an older woman. Her hair was gray, and there were fine lines in her smiling face.

Emily had said that Mrs. Lancaster had been at the school a long time, probably so long ago that Emily had talked to her about her problems.

Miller sucked in a breath. "I knew it!" He whirled on Melanie, his face flushed, like her mother's was. But he wasn't embarrassed; he was furious. "You lied to me! I knew Miss Emily was bringing the school shrink to dinner! I don't wanna talk to anyone. I don't have anything wrong with me."

"Miller!" she called out.

But the little boy whirled back around to the French doors, pushed one open and ran out onto the patio. Melanie started after him, but her legs felt a little shaky.

Dusty grasped her shoulder. "I'll go after him," he said. "You stay here and talk to your father."

"But I came here to talk to you," Shep protested.

Dusty shook his head. "Family comes first," he told his father-in-law as he rushed out the patio door that Miller had left open.

"I'm sorry," Juliet murmured as she stepped closer to Melanie. "I shouldn't have come here. I shouldn't have caused more chaos in this house, for you and for the boys."

"Chaos is what we seem to do best around here," Sadie mumbled.

Melanie hadn't noticed that the older woman had, after escorting Shep into the kitchen, moved over to where she and her mother stood near the stairs. She had aligned herself with them, just like Dusty had, as if they needed protecting. Her compassion, beneath all that strength, touched Melanie's heart.

"I'm sorry," Melanie said.

Sadie shook her head. "No. Like your husband said, family comes first."

CHAPTER NINETEEN

DUSTY'S HEART WAS breaking as he caught up with his nephew. Despite all the progress Miller had made with Melanie as his physical therapist, he wasn't as fast a runner as he'd once been. The limp slowed him down, as did the pain he was clearly suffering.

But was that pain physical or emotional?

Or both?

"Hey, hey," Dusty called out. "You need to slow down. I'm old and injured back here." But he'd easily caught up to the boy.

Miller stopped just outside the barn and whirled back toward Dusty, as if surprised that he was the one who'd chased after him.

"Yeah, it's me," Dusty told him. "You're probably disappointed it's not Aunt Mel—"

"No!" Miller interjected. "She lied to me. I don't wanna talk to liars!"

Dusty narrowed his eyes as he looked at his angry nephew. "I don't believe Aunt Melanie would lie to you—"

"I asked her if it was Mrs. Lancaster coming to dinner and she didn't say anything…that's the same as lying, not telling something…" He looked so upset, he was shaking.

Dusty sighed. "True. That's a lesson I recently learned myself." He still regretted that he'd done that to his wife when he'd kept so much from her.

"That's why I know you won't lie to me," Miller replied. "You said you wouldn't."

"I won't," Dusty said.

"Then why is Mrs. Lancaster here? Is it for me?"

He nodded.

"But I'm not screwed up like Ian and Little Jake. I don't forget things, and I don't wake up screaming."

"Mrs. Lancaster is here for them too," Dusty said. "But we think it would be a good idea for you to talk to her as well."

"Why?" he asked.

Dusty reached out and gently cupped the boy's tense shoulders. "You know why."

Miller shook his head. "No, I'm fine. Aunt Melanie has been fixing me like she fixed you."

Dusty's heart ached for the little boy. "She's

fixing your physical injury, but you're hurting other places."

Tears pooled in Miller's eyes, eyes that reminded Dusty so much of Dale's.

"I miss him too," Dusty said. "I miss him so much."

The tears spilled over, and Miller threw his arms around Dusty, clinging to him. "It hurts so much," he sobbed into Dusty's shirt. "It hurts so much…"

"I'm so sorry," Dusty said, and now he was shaking like his nephew, hurting for him and with him. "I'm so sorry."

Miller sucked in a breath. "But I don't wanna talk to Mrs. Lancaster," he said.

Dusty's heart sank. He didn't know how to deal with this, how to reach his nephew.

"I wanna talk to *you*," the little boy said.

"So talk to me," Dusty said. "I do understand. My dad died when I wasn't much older than you are now. And I've lost some friends as well."

"What about your mom?" Miller asked.

He'd lost her, too, but the seven-year-old wouldn't understand how. So Dusty replied, "She's alive. Hopefully, she'll come to the ranch soon. Do you want to talk to me now?"

Miller shook his head. "No. Not yet. I'm not ready."

Dusty worried that the little boy might never be ready for that talk. And if he kept all those feelings bottled up inside him…

"Hey, Uncle Dusty!" Caleb shouted as he trotted toward the barn with Shep Shepard following close behind him. "Mr. Shep wants to talk to you."

Dusty didn't want to talk to him, and he'd already told him as much in the house. "I don't have time for this right now," he told his father-in-law.

"Seems like a lot's going on around here," Shep said.

"Yeah, it's a bad time to visit," Dusty told him.

"I came here to do more than visit," Shep said.

He could imagine that he wanted his devoted wife back at his side. But only Caleb stood beside him now, and Dusty suspected he hadn't been as successful talking her into another chance as he'd been in the past.

"Juliet wouldn't talk to you?" he asked.

Shep shrugged, seeming more irritated than despondent over his wife leaving him. "She talked. She just won't listen."

Not to lies…

According to Melanie, he'd told enough of those over the years and had accompanied them with empty promises.

"I came here to talk to you," Shep said. He glanced at the boys who stood between them then grinned. "You two know that your uncle, here, is one of the best rodeo riders of all time? Well, except for me… I was the best."

He hadn't even been close to winning the championships that Dusty already had. But then, he'd been sidelined with that injury early in his career. Dusty had sometimes wondered if that injury had really been enough to sideline him. Shep didn't limp like Dusty did. Like Miller did.

"You're Shorty?" Caleb asked.

Dusty laughed while Shep's face flushed a bright red. "No, he's not Shorty," he answered for his father-in-law. Shorty held more titles than Dusty did.

"Hey, boys, you should head back to the house," Shep said. "I gotta ask your uncle Dusty about some things."

Dusty shook his head. "Now is not a good time." And he focused on Miller again.

The little boy sucked in a breath and straightened his shoulders. "I'm okay, Uncle Dusty."

He appeared more composed than earlier, and Dusty knew that prodding his proud nephew in front of the others might just make things worse. He hesitated a moment, studying the boy's face before asking, "You can go back to the house?"

"I'll go back," Miller said. "But I still don't want to talk to Mrs. Lancaster."

"I'm sure you won't," Dusty said with a weary sigh. The kid was more like him than his late father: stubborn. "But you boys should head up before Miss Taye's cooking gets cold."

They scampered off then, Caleb obviously purposely slowing his usual pace so that Miller could keep up with him.

"Man, that older one looks like yours," Shep remarked.

"His dad was my identical twin," Dusty replied.

Shep whistled. "Nobody even knew you had a family," he said. "And to find out you're a Haven. I had no idea. Sheesh, you even once asked me for your mother's number, but I didn't put it together." He shrugged before continuing. "She was a great barrel racer, better than Juliet ever was. She had the talent and the drive. Could have been great if she hadn't had a family."

She'd given up that family to go back to it. Dusty understood why, even though she'd been wrong. "She went back for a while after my dad died," Dusty reminded him.

"Then left it for the other Haven brother," Shep said. "Helped him raise his kids."

Dusty felt like he'd been kicked. "What?" he said, reeling from the newest revelation.

Shep chuckled. "You didn't know? Guess I'm not the only one with family he didn't know about."

"So the rumors about you are true," Dusty said, pushing aside his own family's secrets. "That's why Juliet left you for good."

The older man squared his shoulders. "I think she'd take me back if you'd take my job."

"What?"

"I told her I'd give it all up for another chance." He shuddered, though, at the thought.

And Dusty knew he had no intention of following through. "Not going to happen," Dusty stated.

"She says no, but…"

She hadn't done that before. She was stronger now, like her daughter. Fierce.

Dusty smiled with pride in the women he cared about so much. "Just leave her alone," Dusty advised. "Let her be."

"I don't even understand why she's so mad. That kid was born before I ever met her. And there's no real proof that there are other ones. I think she'd give me another chance. You could just take my job for the rest of the season, finish recovering from that injury Melanie worked with you on…"

Dusty shook his head. "I'm not going back now." If ever. "Melanie's pregnant."

Shep shrugged. "I know. It's probably why her mama insists on staying here, to take care of her. But Melanie's a tough girl. She can take care of herself and the baby."

"Babies," Dusty said. "She's pregnant with twins."

Shep blew out another whistle between his teeth and Midnight stuck his head over the stall door before rearing up at the sight of the rodeo announcer. It was almost as if the horse recognized the older man. He was so dang smart that he probably did.

"So it's true. You did win him?"

Dusty nodded.

"You really are one of the best," Shep told him. "And you've got a lot of years of riding left in you. If you give it up too soon, you're going to regret it and you're going to resent my daughter."

"Do you resent Juliet?" Dusty challenged, wondering. "Is that why you cheat?"

"I cheat because it's easy," Shep admitted with another shrug. "Because it makes me feel like I did when I was riding. But I don't resent her. She resents me. As much as I love her, I can't make her happy. I think it might be the same for you and my daughter. Come back with me, Dusty."

Dusty shook his head. "No," he huffed with disgust. It was guys like Shep that gave rodeo riders a bad reputation for being the "love 'em and leave 'em" sort. But he doubted Shep had ever really loved anyone but himself. "I need to make sure the boys headed up to the house," he said. And weren't eavesdropping in the shadows where he'd just noticed a movement.

"They did," a soft voice assured him, and Melanie stepped into the light. "Why don't you head up, too, and I'll say goodbye to my dad."

She was strong. Strong enough to take care of herself. But Dusty wanted to be there for her. He walked toward those open barn doors but stopped when he was next to her. "I can stay…" He wanted to support her, especially because she looked so vulnerable and tired.

She shook her head and offered him a faint smile. "I'll be fine."

Would *they*? She had such a strange look on her beautiful face, like one of resignation.

Was she resigned over her father? Or over them?

WHEN DUSTY FINALLY left the barn, Melanie released the breath she'd been holding. "Daddy..." she murmured as her stomach lurched with nausea over what she'd overheard.

Emily had recently commented on how she'd overheard things she'd wished she could unhear. That was how Melanie felt about this entire conversation.

"I'm sorry if you heard any of that." At least her father had the decency to apologize. "But you know it's true, sweetheart. Dusty Chaps is one of the greats. And he doesn't do it just for the fame and the money."

Not like her dad had.

"He does it because he loves it," Shep continued passionately.

And she wondered if her father had ever loved anyone but himself. But as wrong as he'd been about the things he'd done, he wasn't wrong about Dusty. She couldn't argue that her husband loved being a rodeo rider.

"I know," she murmured.

"You got your mama now," he said. "She insists on staying here, with you. She can help you with the kids, and you can send Dusty back with me."

She sighed. If only it were that easy...

"You saw how upset his nephew is," she said. Or maybe he hadn't noticed. Her father rarely noticed anything if it wasn't about him. "He can't leave them right now."

He shook his head as if confused. And he probably was. Melanie was realizing more and more that he hadn't ever really put anyone before himself. Ever...

She'd kept making excuses for his behavior over the years, blaming it on what he'd had to give up. But now she realized there was no excuse for his behavior but selfishness.

"Well, that's too bad," he grumbled, and he shifted uncomfortably.

"No," she said, and her heart ached with all the hopeless love she held inside it. "What's too bad is that those little boys' parents died in a car crash. And what else is too bad is that as much as I love you, Daddy, I don't like you."

He jerked up his chin as if offended. "You let your mother poison you against me."

She shook her head. "No, Mom tried all these years to keep our relationship going. I don't like you because I don't like the way you've treated Mom. She deserved better."

Her dad's eyes got bright for a moment, as if tears were pooling there. And, for once, he didn't bluster with pride. He just nodded in agreement. Then he closed the distance between them, the distance that had always been between them even when they'd lived together, and he hugged her. "You deserve better, too, baby. But we wind up living familiar patterns to our parents."

She shook her head. "No." Dusty was not her father, no matter how much Shep might want to believe he was like the younger man. The true champion.

Shep had joined the rodeo for fame and fortune, and probably even all his empty affairs. Dusty did what he did because he loved it.

But did he love his family more, like he'd told Shep before running out of the kitchen after Miller?

She pressed her lips to his cheek. "Goodbye, Daddy."

He pulled back from her with a sigh. "You'll keep in touch?" he asked. "You'll check on the old man from time to time?"

She smiled faintly and nodded.

He glanced back at Midnight, who was peering over the door of his stall, and muttered, "Really was one of the greats…"

And she wondered if he was talking about the horse, Dusty, or himself.

He walked away then, his shiny toeplates kicking up dust from the barn floor. And suddenly she felt woozy. It had been a while since she'd eaten, and instead of sitting down to dinner, she'd wound up rushing out here.

Her legs felt too weak to carry her back to the house, so she walked toward the stall instead, toward the horse that meant so much to Dusty.

"So you're Moby Dick…" she murmured.

The horse nickered at her. But Dusty had conquered his white whale, had even partially domesticated him. She reached up to rub her hand along the horse's head. Midnight's coat was so soft, so velvety.

She'd grown up around animals, had even tried riding herself for a while. But morning sickness had kept her away from them since coming to the ranch. She couldn't deny the appeal of a fine animal, like the mare Dusty wanted to buy. "She'd like you," Melanie murmured. "You are handsome."

Just like her husband…

Dusty would have made a great announcer,

would have been even more famous than her father. But he'd turned down the job. Why? For the boys?

For her?

She didn't want him to make sacrifices for her or for the babies. Her stomach contracted then with an intense cramp, and she cried out in pain.

Alarmed, Midnight reared up in his stall, knocking her hand from his head. Her legs folded beneath her, and she reached out to catch herself, pulling open the door to his stall on her way to the ground.

She didn't hit it hard, yet pain radiated throughout her body before everything went black.

CHAPTER TWENTY

MILLER WAS TRUE to his word. He didn't talk to Mrs. Lancaster, despite her best efforts to engage the boy. The other kids had no problem chattering away to her, even Little Jake had prattled something incomprehensible. But Dusty was barely paying attention to the conversations or lack thereof, or to the food, which was probably as delicious as it usually was. He kept glancing from doorway to doorway, looking for Melanie to return.

Juliet, who sat beside him on the long bench, clasped his arm. "You know Shep," she said. "He likes to hear himself talk, and Melanie is too sweet to interrupt him like I did." She grinned as if really pleased with herself.

"You really didn't let him talk," he mused.

"Nope," she said with a chuckle. "I've heard everything he had to say too many times before."

"You're doing really well," he said, praising her strength.

"I feel two hundred pounds lighter." She smiled. "I'm going to be fine."

And he believed it.

"I'm more worried about you and Melanie," she said.

She wasn't the only one. "I'm glad you're not giving Shep another shot, but I sure wish Melanie would give me one," he admitted.

"Did you ask for one?"

He tensed, realizing that he really hadn't, that he hadn't laid his feelings out for her like he should have. "I've been afraid to push her," he said. "I don't want her to run away again."

"She won't," Juliet said. "She loves your family."

He glanced around the table at all their faces. "Yes, she does."

"And she loves you," she said. Then she sighed. "And that's too bad."

"I won't hurt her again," Dusty vowed.

Juliet nodded. "That's not what I meant. She loves you so much that she's going to send you back."

"What do you mean?"

"She knows how much you love the rodeo, and she doesn't want to take that away from you."

Dusty's heart swelled, filling with all the

love he felt for his wife. "That's what's been holding her back?" he asked. "I thought she just couldn't bring herself to trust me again."

Juliet shook her head. "No. After you talked to her, she understood, and she forgave you. She hadn't told me about her pregnancy or who she was really married to, so I think she realized she couldn't stay mad at you for not being completely honest with her."

"I should have been," he said.

"Then make sure that you are from now on," she advised. "Make sure you tell her exactly how you feel and what you want from your relationship."

"Her," he said. "She's all I want." As he said it, he realized it was true. He didn't need the money or the fame like Shep craved. He didn't even need the thrill that he'd gotten every time he got in the saddle any longer; he could get that raising rodeo livestock. Even if his idea for a ranch didn't come to fruition, it didn't matter as long as he had his wife. He glanced around again. "She really shouldn't be waiting this long to eat."

"She was shaky earlier," Juliet said, her brow lined with concern.

Dusty jumped up from the table then. "I'm going to go check on her."

Juliet started to rise up, too, but he gently pushed her back down with his hand on her shoulder. "Just in case Shep is still talking her ear off, spare yourself," he said. "I'll get rid of him."

But when he stepped out the front door moments later, he found that Shep's airport rental vehicle was gone. Only his truck and Baker's and Ben's SUVs were parked in the driveway. Shep had left.

So where was Melanie?

Had she needed some time to compose herself? To deal with what she might have overheard?

She had a sibling. At least one. She had heard those rumors already, so she couldn't have been too surprised. But hearing the rest her father had said, about Dusty coming to resent her if she forced him to give up the rodeo...

No wonder she'd been prepared to send him back. The last thing she'd ever wanted was a relationship like the one her parents had had.

And he would make certain she knew he was never going to become Shep. He would never betray her or keep anything from her again. He hurried toward the barn then, craning his neck to peer around the yard in case she'd walked off anywhere else.

But he caught no glimpse of her; just some chickens and a couple of barn cats sauntering around the yard. And Midnight...

Midnight met him at the open doors to the barn. Had Shep let the bronco out of his stall before he'd left? Or had Melanie?

"What are you doing, buddy?" Dusty asked him.

The horse reared up, agitated, and now so was Dusty. Where was his wife?

He edged around the bronco and into the shadows of the barn. And he saw her lying on the ground in front of the open door of Midnight's stall, her skin deathly pale. Fear gripped him, squeezing his heart.

"No!" he yelled as he ran to her. "No!" He dropped to his knees beside her and reached for her face, cupping her cheeks in his palms. "Melanie? Sweetheart?" he called out to her.

She didn't move, just lay so very still on the floor. What had happened? Had his horse trampled her?

"COME ON, COME ON. I can't lose any more family," a deep voice murmured. Then that voice rose as the man shouted, "Go faster!"

This wasn't her husband's voice, with his slight twang, but Melanie opened her eyes to look for him. "Where am I?" she rasped as she stared up at a white ceiling. Or a roof... She was in the back of some kind of van. She glanced around her, at the gurney on which she lay, at the front seats where a woman sat behind the steering wheel, and at the man leaning over her.

Her brother-in-law exhaled in relief. "You're conscious...thank God..." Baker sighed.

"What...what happened?"

"You tell me," he said. "Dusty found you lying in front of Midnight's open stall. I didn't detect any broken bones. But did he kick you? Step on you? Hit your head?"

A light shone in her eyes, and she flinched and closed them. "I don't know," she murmured. She was just so very tired, and it was too much effort to keep her eyes open.

"Melanie," Baker said. "Come on, stay with me..."

"I'm not leaving the ranch," she said, as if she was assuring Miller.

Oh, no, Miller. He would be so worried. She opened her eyes and meant to ask about him, but she asked instead, "Where's my husband?"

He was who she needed most. Whom she needed always…

"He's driving Miller and your mom. Miller was…" Baker shuddered.

And she knew it was bad. If only she could have woken up sooner…

But she hadn't just fallen asleep. She'd fallen. Then she remembered the pain. And she touched her stomach. "The babies…" she choked out. "I was in pain…"

But the pain was gone now.

"What was it?" Baker asked. "A sharp pain? A contraction? What did you feel?"

"I d-don't know…" she stammered. "It just hurt…"

"Are you in pain now?" he asked.

She shook her head. She didn't feel anything now. Did that mean that the babies were gone?

CHAPTER TWENTY-ONE

DUSTY PRESSED HARD on the accelerator, trying to catch the ambulance as it raced ahead of them, lights flashing. Had she regained consciousness? Would she be all right? And if she was, would she think that he wasn't with her because he didn't care?

He should have ridden with her. But Miller had become unglued, like a wild animal in pain. He'd launched himself at Baker, screaming at him. Dusty had had to restrain him while Baker got into the ambulance with Melanie and rode away.

Miller lay limply against Dusty's side, squeezed into that small space on the bench seat between the driver's seat and passenger's seat where Juliet sat. He'd flipped up the center console, so there was room since Dusty's truck didn't have a back seat. He'd never needed one before, but now that he was going to have a family, he would need to buy a bigger vehicle.

Wouldn't he? Or had he lost his wife and

his babies? He hadn't realized how much he'd wanted them until he'd seen them on the screen of that ultrasound machine. Now he couldn't imagine his life without them, and especially without his wife.

It had taken him too long to find her. He'd missed out on so much already. He should have been there in those first several weeks of her pregnancy when she'd been so sick. He should have been taking care of her.

Would he get that chance now? He pressed harder on the accelerator, and Juliet braced her hands against the dash. "Slow down, Dusty," she said. "We can take longer than eight seconds to get there. She's going to be fine."

Tears stung Dusty's eyes, but he blinked them away to focus on the road. They were coming into town now. They were close to the hospital. It was a small one, though. Would it be equipped to take care of her? Should they have taken her to Sheridan? No. That was too far.

"How do you know?" Miller asked, his voice raspy. His throat was probably raw from all his screaming.

"Because she has to be all right," Juliet said, and tears rolled down her face.

"My mom and dad weren't all right," Miller

said. "Uncle Baker said they would be, but he was lying."

Dusty took one hand from the wheel to wrap his arm around Miller's trembling body. "I'm sorry."

"It wasn't you," Miller said. "You would have saved them."

Dusty shook his head. "I wish I could have, but I don't know what Uncle Baker knows. If anyone could have saved them, it would have been him. It was just too late…"

Dusty could only hope that they weren't too late when they pulled into the hospital parking lot. His wife had to be all right.

MELANIE'S SKIN TINGLED, and she shivered at the sensation, shifting against the bed on which she lay. Then she opened her eyes and peered up at the man leaning over her. It wasn't her brother-in-law staring down at her this time. This was the man she'd looked for when she'd awakened last.

Tears trailed down his handsome face from where they'd pooled in his beautiful hazel eyes. Her heart ached at the look on his face. It was the look he usually gave her; that look of love and something else…

Something that had panic pressing hard

on her lungs, stealing away her breath. She reached for her stomach, pressing her palms over it. "Are they gone?" she gasped, her throat choking with sobs. "Did I lose the babies?"

"No," he said. And he pushed her hair from her cheek like he'd done so many times before. Then he leaned back and pointed to the screen of an ultrasound machine. The same image was frozen on it that they'd seen in the obstetrician's office a few days ago. Two little peas sharing one pod.

She sighed as relief filled her. "They're okay."

"Yes," he assured her. "They're fine. You're fine." But still those tears streaked down his face.

So she reached up and slid her fingers along his jaw. "Then what's wrong?"

"I…" He cleared his throat. "I just love you so much. I can't lose you again, Melanie. And I can't leave you."

Now tears pooled in her eyes. "Dusty… I can't ask you to sacrifice your dream for me."

"You don't have to," he said.

And she guessed at what he meant. "I can't live like my mom and I did with my dad, following him from rodeo stop to rodeo stop…

not with two babies. And I can't leave the boys. Miller…"

"Miller is waiting to see you," he said. "He doesn't quite believe that you're all right. Neither did I until you opened your eyes."

"What happened?" she asked. "I remember this pain…and falling…"

"You must have pulled open Midnight's door on your way down," Dusty said. "Because he was loose. It doesn't appear that he stepped on you, though…"

She smiled. "So your wild horse isn't as wild as he's rumored to be."

He shook his head. "I think he realizes that this family can't lose anyone else."

Her breath hitched, and she nodded in agreement. "No, you can't."

"*We* can't," Dusty corrected her. "We're family. And like I told your father, family comes first."

"But the rodeo is your first love."

"Yes," he replied. "But you're my last love. I want to be with you and with our children. I don't want to miss out on another minute with you, Melanie." He leaned over her again and pressed his mouth to hers, kissing her gently.

She clasped the nape of his neck in her hand and kissed him deeply. Then something tightened around her arm, and she gasped and opened her eyes.

Dusty chuckled. "Well, your blood pressure is going up. Maybe that's the trick. I need to keep kissing you to keep you from fainting."

"I feel like fainting now," she admitted.

He jumped up from where he'd been sitting on the edge of her bed. "I better get the doctor."

She reached out and grabbed his arm, pulling him to a stop. "No. I feel fine." She felt better than fine, happier than she ever had, even on their wedding day. Then, she'd been taking a leap of faith that everything would work out with them. Now, she knew it would. "I'm just shocked that you would willingly give up the rodeo and stay at the ranch."

He tensed then.

And she pulled her hand from his arm, a sudden uneasiness sweeping through her. "Oh, no, did I misunderstand?"

"I can't take the job working with Jake," he said.

"I understand that," she said. He and his older brother weren't the type of personalities that would work well together, not like Jake had worked with Dale. As Dusty had tried telling his brother over and over again, he was not Dale. "So what will you do?" But she already had an inkling. "You'll buy that beautiful mare," she answered before he could. "And that's not all you'll buy…"

He sucked in a shaky breath. "Not me," he said. "Us. I will only do this if you'll do it with me." He reached beneath his shirt and pulled out the chain and the ring that dangled from it. His fingers shook as he unclasped the chain and slipped the band off it. Then he held it out to her. "Can I put this back on your finger, Melanie? Will you be my wife in every way?"

Tears rushed to her eyes, but she blinked them back to focus on his handsome face, to hold his gaze as she nodded and said, "Yes, please. I will be your wife and your partner and your fellow parent."

He slid the ring onto her finger and leaned down and kissed her again. And tears dripped from his face onto hers. "I love you so much."

"I love you so much that I want you to be sure of what you want," she said.

"I'm sure," he said. "You and our babies and that dilapidated ranch…" He chuckled at that.

"Buying that ranch is a great idea," she said but, still worried about his nephews, she asked, "How will the boys handle that?"

"We'll stay living in the house at the ranch with them and everybody else," he said. "If you're comfortable with that, I can drive back and forth from that other ranch. It isn't far."

She clapped her hands together. "That's a great idea."

"I'd like to take credit for it," he said. "But Jake was the one who suggested it."

"He doesn't want to work with you either," she teased.

He shook his head. "He wants to work with Baker. I'm just not sure he's going to get his way. Baker is pretty determined to stay a firefighter."

She wondered, though, after how upset he'd been in the ambulance with her. He couldn't lose anyone else either, and she suspected he blamed himself for the ones that were lost.

"Put Sadie on it," she suggested. "She'll figure out how to make it happen."

He sighed. "Sadie has a lot of things to figure out right now."

"But not us," she said.

He leaned over her again and kissed her lips softly, gently. "No, not us. When we talk to each other openly and honestly, we can handle anything. I love you."

"And I love you…" she said. "I love you so much that I would be fine if you go back to the rodeo from time to time to ride."

He grinned and kissed her again. "I'm not leaving you or the babies any time soon. But if I ever did go back for an exhibition ride or something, I'd come back to you as soon as I could."

"I know," she said. And then she made her promise. "And I will always be there for you. I will never leave you."

He released a shaky breath then drew in a deep one and nodded. "I know. I trust you."

And she knew how hard that was for him, as hard as it had been for her. But she had no doubts that they'd done the right thing, that they were right for each other.

"GRANDMA, YOU CAN SIT DOWN," Baker said. "She's going to be okay."

But Sadie continued to pace the waiting room of the hospital. She believed her youngest grandson.

But he repeated what he'd told them all just a short time ago. "Her blood sugar and blood pressure had dropped again," he said. "And she had some Braxton-Hicks contractions. She's going to be fine. They're just going to monitor her blood pressure for a little while longer and make sure she's fully rehydrated before they release her. You all can go home now."

Sadie wasn't waiting for Melanie to be able to leave. She was waiting for—

The lobby doors whooshed open, and Lem Lemmon rushed through them and ran to her side. "Is she okay? Are you okay?" he asked.

Sadie closed her arms around him and hugged him tightly. "I am now."

He'd come when she'd called him.

"What happened?" he asked as he pulled back from her embrace. "Is everybody okay?"

She nodded. "Yes."

"Just a little scare with Melanie," Jake said. "But she's fine now. In fact, I think it's safe for the rest of us to go back to the ranch. Dusty will drive Melanie home when they release her."

Dusty was not going to leave his wife's side again; Sadie was sure of that. They were solid, and today had been a good first step toward making progress with the boys. While Miller hadn't opened up with the school psychologist, the other boys had. And Miller had opened up with Dusty in front of everyone when Baker had taken Melanie away in the ambulance.

The little boys would need more therapy and more time to heal from their tragic loss. But they were going to be all right. She was sure of it.

She needed to be sure that she was going to be all right too. So she waited until her family walked out those lobby doors to the sidewalk before she hugged Lem again. "I'm sorry," she said. "I'm sorry I was mean to you."

"You've always been mean to me, Sadie March Haven," Lem said. "It's part of your attraction for me."

She smirked. "You find that attractive?"

"You find me attractive," he said with a smug grin.

And she giggled like a girl instead of the eighty-year-old woman she was. "You are an old fool," she said.

He sighed and nodded. "Yeah, I am. But I'm your old fool." He chuckled and corrected himself. "I mean friend."

He was her friend for now. Her very best friend.

"Good," she said. "Because we have work to do…"

Her great-grandsons still needed more help and healing. But her grandsons were doing better now—all but one. And now she had a lead on the daughter-in-law who'd disappeared, along with the son who'd run away. Dusty had stepped outside Melanie's room long enough to share with Sadie what Shep Shepard had told him. That Darlene had helped raise her brother-in-law's kids…

That meant Sadie had more grandchildren.

"We're going to be very busy," she warned him.

He smiled. "Good. Busy is good. Keeps us going, keeps us alive."

She hugged him again, just because he was so dang cute and sweet, and she was so happy that he'd forgiven her. "Yeah," she said. "You can't leave me." She'd already lost too many people she loved.

It was about time she found some of them…

* * * * *

Get 4 FREE REWARDS!

We'll send you 2 FREE Books plus 2 FREE Mystery Gifts.

FREE Value Over **$20**

Both the **Love Inspired**® and **Love Inspired**® Suspense series feature compelling novels filled with inspirational romance, faith, forgiveness, and hope.

YES! Please send me 2 FREE novels from the Love Inspired or Love Inspired Suspense series and my 2 FREE gifts (gifts are worth about $10 retail). After receiving them, if I don't wish to receive any more books, I can return the shipping statement marked "cancel." If I don't cancel, I will receive 6 brand-new Love Inspired Larger-Print books or Love Inspired Suspense Larger-Print books every month and be billed just $5.99 each in the U.S. or $6.24 each in Canada. That is a savings of at least 17% off the cover price. It's quite a bargain! Shipping and handling is just 50¢ per book in the U.S. and $1.25 per book in Canada.* I understand that accepting the 2 free books and gifts places me under no obligation to buy anything. I can always return a shipment and cancel at any time. The free books and gifts are mine to keep no matter what I decide.

Choose one: ☐ **Love Inspired**
Larger-Print
(122/322 IDN GNWC)

☐ **Love Inspired Suspense**
Larger-Print
(107/307 IDN GNWN)

Name (please print)

Address   Apt. #

City   State/Province   Zip/Postal Code

Email: Please check this box ☐ if you would like to receive newsletters and promotional emails from Harlequin Enterprises ULC and its affiliates. You can unsubscribe anytime.

Mail to the Harlequin Reader Service:
IN U.S.A.: P.O. Box 1341, Buffalo, NY 14240-8531
IN CANADA: P.O. Box 603, Fort Erie, Ontario L2A 5X3

Want to try 2 free books from another series! Call 1-800-873-8635 or visit www.ReaderService.com.

---

*Terms and prices subject to change without notice. Prices do not include sales taxes, which will be charged (if applicable) based on your state or country of residence. Canadian residents will be charged applicable taxes. Offer not valid in Quebec. This offer is limited to one order per household. Books received may not be as shown. Not valid for current subscribers to the Love Inspired or Love Inspired Suspense series. All orders subject to approval. Credit or debit balances in a customer's account(s) may be offset by any other outstanding balance owed by or to the customer. Please allow 4 to 6 weeks for delivery. Offer available while quantities last.

Your Privacy—Your information is being collected by Harlequin Enterprises ULC, operating as Harlequin Reader Service. For a complete summary of the information we collect, how we use this information and to whom it is disclosed, please visit our privacy notice located at corporate.harlequin.com/privacy-notice. From time to time we may also exchange your personal information with reputable third parties. If you wish to opt out of this sharing of your personal information, please visit readerservice.com/consumerschoice or call 1-800-873-8635. **Notice to California Residents**—Under California law, you have specific rights to control and access your data. For more information on these rights and how to exercise them, visit corporate.harlequin.com/california-privacy.

LIRLIS22

Get 4 FREE REWARDS!

We'll send you 2 FREE Books plus 2 FREE Mystery Gifts.

FREE
Value Over
$20

Both the **Harlequin® Special Edition** and **Harlequin® Heartwarming™** series feature compelling novels filled with stories of love and strength where the bonds of friendship, family and community unite.

YES! Please send me 2 FREE novels from the Harlequin Special Edition or Harlequin Heartwarming series and my 2 FREE gifts (gifts are worth about $10 retail). After receiving them, if I don't wish to receive any more books, I can return the shipping statement marked "cancel." If I don't cancel, I will receive 6 brand-new Harlequin Special Edition books every month and be billed just $4.99 each in the U.S or $5.74 each in Canada, a savings of at least 17% off the cover price or 4 brand-new Harlequin Heartwarming Larger-Print books every month and be billed just $5.74 each in the U.S. or $6.24 each in Canada, a savings of at least 21% off the cover price. It's quite a bargain! Shipping and handling is just 50¢ per book in the U.S. and $1.25 per book in Canada.* I understand that accepting the 2 free books and gifts places me under no obligation to buy anything. I can always return a shipment and cancel at any time. The free books and gifts are mine to keep no matter what I decide.

Choose one: ☐ **Harlequin Special Edition**   ☐ **Harlequin Heartwarming**
   (235/335 HDN GNMP)   **Larger-Print**
                              (161/361 HDN GNPZ)

Name (please print)

Address   Apt. #

City   State/Province   Zip/Postal Code

Email: Please check this box ☐ if you would like to receive newsletters and promotional emails from Harlequin Enterprises ULC and its affiliates. You can unsubscribe anytime.

Mail to the Harlequin Reader Service:
IN U.S.A.: P.O. Box 1341, Buffalo, NY 14240-8531
IN CANADA: P.O. Box 603, Fort Erie, Ontario L2A 5X3

Want to try 2 free books from another series! Call 1-800-873-8635 or visit www.ReaderService.com.

*Terms and prices subject to change without notice. Prices do not include sales taxes, which will be charged (if applicable) based on your state or country of residence. Canadian residents will be charged applicable taxes. Offer not valid in Quebec. This offer is limited to one order per household. Books received may not be as shown. Not valid for current subscribers to the Harlequin Special Edition or Harlequin Heartwarming series. All orders subject to approval. Credit or debit balances in a customer's account(s) may be offset by any other outstanding balance owed by or to the customer. Please allow 4 to 6 weeks for delivery. Offer available while quantities last.

Your Privacy—Your information is being collected by Harlequin Enterprises ULC, operating as Harlequin Reader Service. For a complete summary of the information we collect, how we use this information and to whom it is disclosed, please visit our privacy notice located at corporate.harlequin.com/privacy-notice. From time to time we may also exchange your personal information with reputable third parties. If you wish to opt out of this sharing of your personal information, please visit readerservice.com/consumerschoice or call 1-800-873-8635. **Notice to California Residents**—Under California law, you have specific rights to control and access your data. For more information on these rights and how to exercise them, visit corporate.harlequin.com/california-privacy.

HSEHW22

COUNTRY LEGACY COLLECTION

19 FREE BOOKS IN ALL!

Cowboys, adventure and romance await you in this new collection! Enjoy superb reading all year long with books by bestselling authors like Diana Palmer, Sasha Summers and Marie Ferrarella!

YES! Please send me the **Country Legacy Collection!** This collection begins with 3 FREE books and 2 FREE gifts in the first shipment. Along with my 3 free books, I'll also get 3 more books from the **Country Legacy Collection**, which I may either return and owe nothing or keep for the low price of $24.60 U.S./$28.12 CDN each plus $2.99 U.S./$7.49 CDN for shipping and handling per shipment*. If I decide to continue, about once a month for 8 months, I will get 6 or 7 more books but will only pay for 4. That means 2 or 3 books in every shipment will be FREE! If I decide to keep the entire collection, I'll have paid for only 32 books because 19 are FREE! I understand that accepting the 3 free books and gifts places me under no obligation to buy anything. I can always return a shipment and cancel at any time. My free books and gifts are mine to keep no matter what I decide.

☐ 275 HCK 1939   ☐ 475 HCK 1939

Name (please print)

Address   Apt. #

City   State/Province   Zip/Postal Code

Mail to the Harlequin Reader Service:
IN U.S.A.: P.O. Box 1341, Buffalo, NY 14240-8571
IN CANADA: P.O. Box 603, Fort Erie, Ontario L2A 5X3

*Terms and prices subject to change without notice. Prices do not include sales taxes, which will be charged (if applicable) based on your state or country of residence. Canadian residents will be charged applicable taxes. Offer not valid in Quebec. All orders subject to approval. Credit or debit balances in a customer's account(s) may be offset by any other outstanding balance owed by or to the customer. Please allow 3 to 4 weeks for delivery. Offer available while quantities last. © 2021 Harlequin Enterprises ULC. ® and ™ are trademarks owned by Harlequin Enterprises ULC.

Your Privacy—Your information is being collected by Harlequin Enterprises ULC, operating as Harlequin Reader Service. To see how we collect and use this information visit https://corporate.harlequin.com/privacy-notice. From time to time we may also exchange your personal information with reputable third parties. If you wish to opt out of this sharing of your personal information, please visit www.readerservice.com/consumerschoice or call 1-800-873-8635. Notice to California Residents—Under California law, you have specific rights to control and access your data. For more information visit https://corporate.harlequin.com/california-privacy.

50BOOKCL22

Get 4 FREE REWARDS!

We'll send you 2 FREE Books plus 2 FREE Mystery Gifts.

FREE Value Over **$20**

Both the **Romance** and **Suspense** collections feature compelling novels written by many of today's bestselling authors.

YES! Please send me 2 FREE novels from the Essential Romance or Essential Suspense Collection and my 2 FREE gifts (gifts are worth about $10 retail). After receiving them, if I don't wish to receive any more books, I can return the shipping statement marked "cancel." If I don't cancel, I will receive 4 brand-new novels every month and be billed just $7.24 each in the U.S. or $7.49 each in Canada. That's a savings of up to 28% off the cover price. It's quite a bargain! Shipping and handling is just 50¢ per book in the U.S. and $1.25 per book in Canada.* I understand that accepting the 2 free books and gifts places me under no obligation to buy anything. I can always return a shipment and cancel at any time. The free books and gifts are mine to keep no matter what I decide.

Choose one: ☐ **Essential Romance**   ☐ **Essential Suspense**
             (194/394 MDN GQ6M)   (191/391 MDN GQ6M)

Name (please print)

Address   Apt. #

City   State/Province   Zip/Postal Code

Email: Please check this box ☐ if you would like to receive newsletters and promotional emails from Harlequin Enterprises ULC and its affiliates. You can unsubscribe anytime.

Mail to the **Harlequin Reader Service:**
IN U.S.A.: P.O. Box 1341, Buffalo, NY 14240-8531
IN CANADA: P.O. Box 603, Fort Erie, Ontario L2A 5X3

Want to try 2 free books from another series! Call 1-800-873-8635 or visit www.ReaderService.com.

---

*Terms and prices subject to change without notice. Prices do not include sales taxes, which will be charged (if applicable) based on your state or country of residence. Canadian residents will be charged applicable taxes. Offer not valid in Quebec. This offer is limited to one order per household. Books received may not be as shown. Not valid for current subscribers to the Essential Romance or Essential Suspense Collection. All orders subject to approval. Credit or debit balances in a customer's account(s) may be offset by any other outstanding balance owed by or to the customer. Please allow 4 to 6 weeks for delivery. Offer available while quantities last.

Your Privacy—Your information is being collected by Harlequin Enterprises ULC, operating as Harlequin Reader Service. For a complete summary of the information we collect, how we use this information and to whom it is disclosed, please visit our privacy notice located at corporate.harlequin.com/privacy-notice. From time to time we may also exchange your personal information with reputable third parties. If you wish to opt out of this sharing of your personal information, please visit readerservice.com/consumerschoice or call 1-800-873-8635. **Notice to California Residents**—Under California law, you have specific rights to control and access your data. For more information on these rights and how to exercise them, visit corporate.harlequin.com/california-privacy.

STRS22

COMING NEXT MONTH FROM

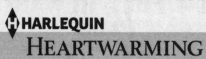

#431 WYOMING PROMISE
The Blackwells of Eagle Springs
by Anna J. Stewart

Horse trainer Corliss Blackwell needs a loan to save her grandmother's ranch. Firefighter Ryder Talbot can help. He's back in Wyoming with his young daughter and is shifting Corliss's focus from the Flying Spur to thoughts of a forever family—with him!

#432 A COWBOY IN AMISH COUNTRY
Amish Country Haven • by Patricia Johns

Wilder Westhouse needs a ranch hand—and Sue Schmidt is the best person for the job. The only problem? His ranch neighbors the farm of Sue's family—the Amish family she ran away from years ago.

#433 THE BULL RIDER'S SECRET SON
by Susan Breeden

When bull rider Cody Sayers attempts to surprise a young fan, the surprise is on him! The boy's mother is Cody's ex-wife. He still loves Becca Haring, but she has a secret that could tear them apart...or bring them together.

#434 WINNING THE VETERAN'S HEART
Veterans' Road • by Cheryl Harper

Peter Kim needs the best attorney in Florida for his nephew's case—that's Lauren Duncan, his college rival. But she's tired of the grind. He'll help show her work-life balance...and that old rivals can be so much more.

YOU CAN FIND MORE INFORMATION ON UPCOMING HARLEQUIN TITLES, FREE EXCERPTS AND MORE AT HARLEQUIN.COM.

HWCNM0622

Visit
ReaderService.com
Today!

As a valued member of the Harlequin Reader Service, you'll find these benefits and more at ReaderService.com:

- Try 2 free books from any series
- Access risk-free special offers
- View your account history & manage payments
- Browse the latest Bonus Bucks catalog

Don't miss out!

If you want to stay up-to-date on the latest at the Harlequin Reader Service and enjoy more content, make sure you've signed up for our monthly News & Notes email newsletter. Sign up online at ReaderService.com or by calling Customer Service at 1-800-873-8635.